September 18th 09

Hope you enjoy

my Book

Ken Crowther has always loved writing and from an early age at school, wrote in the back of exercise-books, some of which he still has. After his apprenticeship in London Parks, he ran his own gardening company, designing, building and maintaining gardens. During this time he wrote articles for local newspapers as well as monthly gardening magazines.

He joined BBC Essex as a presenter over twenty years ago and now has a three-hour morning programme each Saturday. During this time, he was a guest presenter on the television programme 'Gardeners Diary' for three years.

In 2004 Ken saw the successful publication of his first book 'Jack the Gardener' a tale of two young men growing up in the sixties as gardener apprentices in London Parks. His new book 'Two Weeks in Nice' follows these boys on their holiday in France.

TWO WEEKS IN NICE
COTE D'AZUR

Ken Crowther

TWO WEEKS IN NICE, COTE D'AZUR

Jack goes on holiday to France

Vanguard Press

VANGUARD PAPERBACK

© Copyright 2009
Ken Crowther

The right of Ken Crowther to be identified as author of
this work has been asserted by him in accordance with the
Copyright, Designs and Patents Act 1988.

A CIP catalogue record for this title is
available from the British Library.

ISBN 978 184386 528 5

*Vanguard Press is an imprint of
Pegasus Elliot MacKenzie Publishers Ltd.*
www.pegasuspublishers.com

First Published in 2009

**Vanguard Press
Sheraton House Castle Park
Cambridge England**

Printed & Bound in Great Britain

Dedication

To my dear friend, Allen.
For his ideas and inspiration over the years.

Acknowledgements

To my father for encouraging me to take holidays in the South of France as a young man.

To Vivienne, my wife, for her patience and tolerance in producing a manuscript from a series of rough pads written in pen and pencil to crafted text.

Chapter I

Victoria Station

Jack was all ready for his holiday in France, what an adventure; he had never been abroad before. Even though it was September, he looked forward to the warmth in the South of France. Dad had sorted his passport and bought some French francs and travellers' cheques, Jack would be paying those off for ages. His mum and dad had treated him to his fares and the cost of the hotel or pension as it was called in France. Would he remember any French from his couple of years learning it at school he wondered because his friend, Nick, had not got much idea either! What would the food be like? And more importantly what would the girls be like!

Jack's dad took him to meet his friend Nick up at Victoria in the car. It was Saturday morning and although he had tried to eat breakfast, he couldn't. Mum gave him a really big hug before he went and gave Jack yet another bag for him to carry with sandwiches and an apple for the journey. She always thought everyone would die without plenty of food, he thought. Anyway they met up with Nick and his dad, and they all went in search of the boat train to Dover. Both fathers fussed over the boys checking whether they had their money, tickets, passports and more importantly, all their luggage.

"Don't our fathers fuss, have we got this and that and your mum giving you a bag of food. She must think there's a war on," Nick said indignantly.

"Yes but this is my first holiday abroad and without them…" Jack replied.

"But Jack, I'm twenty one, already a man and you're only a couple of years younger," Nick retorted.

"Yes I suppose and as we're both still apprentice gardeners, they probably still think we're very young," Jack replied trying to smooth Nick's feathers.

"Yeah, you're right Jack."

At last they were on their own and Nick straight away got out his scruffy tin of tobacco and rolled a couple of cigarettes for them from Golden Virginia. The train rattled its way down the tracks stopping every now and then, although the boys hardly noticed, they were deep in conversation about their holiday discussing where and what they would be doing. The train began to slow down and grind as they do when turning on a bend. Jack was surprised, as they seemed to be over water, they must be in Dover. The boys dragged their bags out, Jack had a heavy old leather case and a zipper style bag made of canvas in a khaki colour. Actually he always thought it looked like an army bag. Jack seemed to have always fancied something about the armed forces, though it was not as if he could have even coped with the authority and discipline of it all. They moved along a long corridor and a large hall where they queued at the other end. In front of them were wooden type sentry boxes with windows in and men in blue uniforms and peak caps were waiting for the crowd to move forward. They shuffled towards these gateways and after having their passports checked, they moved past long tables. Some people were being asked to take their luggage out to be inspected, Jack and Nick were glad it wasn't them. They moved outside under a covered area and then onto the ferry for France!

The ferry was a big ship, but then as Jack thought to himself anything was big after the Woolwich Ferry that he had crossed with his dad. Wide steel gangways with men in navy uniforms were checking their tickets again on the way on. Nick suggested moving right to the back of the ferry as there was a bar. The weather was dry with the sun trying to peep through the clouds, for which Jack was thankful as he had been worrying about seasickness. Varnished seats and benches were all across the rear deck of the boat, they found a bench and dumped their luggage in a heap.

"Stay here Jack while I fetch the beers," said Nick. Jack, overwhelmed, sat there like a zombie. More and more people came along and sat around the area that led into a large lounge and bar. Families with very young children, couples, interesting-looking old men possibly French and some groups of girls. Nick soon appeared complaining that they wouldn't open the bar until the ferry set sail. They chatted about the girls around them discussing which they fancied and which they didn't.

"Let's have a shared 'kitty' for the money Jack," Nick suggested, "that way we won't have any problems. Let us put ten pounds each in now and then change to francs when we get to France." Jack was impressed at how well organised Nick was. Nick got out his wallet showing he had quite a few francs in it but pulled a ten pound note out from behind and folded his and Jack's, putting them into a separate section.

"There you go, I will move the loose change over to my left pocket as well. So how long to sailing and that first pint?" asked Nick. They settled down putting their cases and bags up in front of them with their feet on top.

Eventually smoke and fumes came from the funnel, a couple of toots and they moved away from the dockside. Nick was away like a bullet out of a gun; Jack stayed exactly where he was extracting the bag with his mum's sandwiches in. Jack as always inspected them, cheese with Branston pickle and corned beef with Branston's. Nick soon returned with the pints and they both sat with their feet up and enjoyed the sandwiches and beer.

"How does your mum know I don't like corned beef?" Nick asked.

"Just knows," Jack replied, he didn't let on that they were really all for him! Nick's mum obviously didn't reckon he would starve and he definitely would not. Outside the harbour walls the sea had a reasonable swell and as the cliffs of Dover faded into the distance, it was soon possible to see the coast of France. They were now on their second pint as the French coastline came into view and Jack left Nick and went over to the other side of the ship to get a better view. Soon you could see the houses, a road along the coast with beaches and wooden groins just like England. In fact it looked just like England except the houses looked more like chalet bungalows.

As the ship sailed inside the harbour, everyone started going inside and descending down the stairs past the bar. Nick suggested waiting, we have half an hour before the train leaves anyway. They eventually docked and Jack could now work out why they were going down inside the ship. It was high tide and the doors opened up onto the dock. There were restaurants and rooms for tea and coffee down here, next time Jack would check all this out, perhaps on the way back.

'You could have been in Dover, looked the same except all the notices were now in French,' thought Jack. They passed through the channels for their passports and baggage to be checked, and luckily walked through the Customs Hall without being stopped by men who looked like policemen in dark blue uniforms. The men were standing in rows and some behind long tables removing people's belongings from their cases. 'What a terrible thing to have done to your belongings, your Y fronts, shirts, socks, everything turned out,' thought Jack. It wasn't just men with big cases who were being checked either, one lady seemed to have filled half her case with small boxes. Jack noticed them being removed, Nick nudged him as he was wondering what was in them too. Nick thought it was drugs but he would think that, he thought all shady people were drug dealers. He knew people were caught for smuggling in cigarettes and cigars. Then they followed another alleyway, upstairs and across some rail lines in the docks, all marked with white lines to keep you in the right place, through some gates and onto a platform. Jack reckoned about half the ship's passengers were here but Nick just thought it was crowded. They had booked a couchette and seat, which became a couchette or bed after Paris. They eventually found it about halfway along the train. The doors had steps up into the train, the boys moved along the corridor until they found their compartment. It was difficult to get the luggage up onto the top rack, they struggled and eventually squeezed it all in with what was already there, which must have belonged to the middle-aged couple who were sitting in the seats opposite them. The couple were French as when they sat down, the man greeted them in French much to Jack's surprise. Eventually a young Englishman and another French lady joined them. The single lady said she was only going to Paris, and the young man was travelling to Nice, where Jack and Nick were going. They chatted across to him, he seemed quite nervous and within an hour Nick and Jack knew his life history.

He lived in Royal Berkshire near Windsor and he was going to stay with a French girl. She was a family friend who had visited them in England quite a lot.

They were soon underway and the electric locomotive pulled the train smoothly through the French countryside. Nick was soon on the wander to find the restaurant car and see whether there was a bar! He was soon back explaining it was just down the train three coaches away, and a buffet car. There would also be a man coming along selling beers and coffees. The train hurtled along and Jack thought of being in the South of France tomorrow. Much to Nick's disgust Jack bought Nick a cup of coffee who really wanted a beer. The coffee was strong and needed some sugar to make it more palatable. Jack and Nick moved to the corridor for a bit of peace, the young man they discovered was called Colin, and he did not stop talking. Nick and Jack were mates; they wanted time to chat, look at the girls and work out which were French, English or another nationality, and which they might fancy.

In the next compartment there was a tasty looking blonde girl, hair to her shoulders, full lips and dark eyes. Jack was more attracted to her, Nick was convinced she was English. She sat chatting to an older lady, very well dressed in a heavy sort of brown material dress with a fox-type fur around her neck. Nick nudged Jack and told him off for staring. The train was now well on its way and they had passed lots of crops growing different vegetables. Some of them looked like sugar beet and then fields of maize. At the edge of the fields were strange looking cages, very long, some nearly ten yards and over six feet high, legs to keep them off the ground and the wooden frame was covered with chicken wire. Jack wondered what they could be used for, funny people these French. Funny shaped cars that seemed to bounce up and down, then every now and then a 'Maigret' car with sleek running boards and the distinctive grill all shiny and black. Jack liked cars, perhaps he would have a 'Maigret' car one day and keep it polished like his dad's Vauxhall. He wondered what they would be doing now. Was dad in the garden or sitting in front of the television watching the sport? Nick had wandered off and returned with two beers and saying he had booked dinner, but it was after they had left Paris, wherever that was.

Chapter II

Jack was tired so he took his beer to the compartment. Nick wandered along the carriage to where there were some young people. Colin was now reading a book by Ian Fleming, one of his James Bond stories, Doctor No. Jack got out his newspaper and started to read but soon fell asleep dreaming that he had a blonde girl next to him. She was kissing him on the lips and caressing him, perhaps it was the girl in the next compartment. He woke with a jolt, Nick was standing in the corridor still chatting to a young guy with long hair tied back, both with beers in their hands. The single French lady was trying to get her bag down from the rack, Colin the chatterbox Englishman was helping her. When she stood up she didn't look at all bad, smart tailored dress with a long jacket type coat, shapely too. Maybe too old for Jack but then he had been through all that with Penny, his last love, perhaps older women twice his age were best left alone. Jack tried his French by bidding her farewell and hoped she had a good evening. "Au revoir Madame," Jack said, but he couldn't think of anymore.

Nick came back in and slumped in the corner and Colin started talking again, this time about sports cars. Jack had absolutely no interest in sports cars and Nick was more into trucks and lorries, so it fell on 'stoney' ground but Colin continued with the two boys nodding and grunting as he continued to chat about engines, top speeds, synchromeshed gearboxes. The French couple by the window excused themselves and passed them, Jack reckoned Colin had bored them silly as well, so they all moved out into the corridor by the window as the train pulled into Paris at Gare du Nord. The couple smiled at Jack and the boys decided to wander onto the platform with them to stretch their legs. There were vendors with trolleys full of long sandwiches made out of French loaves, stuffed full of cheese that looked like Kraft slices soft, white squidgy cheese that is called Camembert, salami and lots more. It all looked very tasty and was served on a paper plate slightly folded with lots of salad covered in an oily mixed dressing. Beers, coffees, pastries some with icing, a sort of cream and yellow with sultanas, and others which looked as if they had chocolate chips in. People were munching away, smoking cigarettes, drinking coffees and beers. All very casual Jack and Nick thought but Jack was beginning to worry that the train would leave without them. He noticed there were no engines on the front so he assumed it could not go anywhere.

All of a sudden the whistles blew and people disappeared from the platform and the guard went along the train closing all the doors. This time the train reversed out of the station and trundled along slowly for about an hour then still going backwards, pushed into another Paris station called Gare de Lyon. The boys knew that the train stopped twice in Paris but had no idea that this was the way it achieved it. Everyone got out again with the same routine of eating and drinking from the vendors.

"Are you sure you have booked dinner this evening Nick?" asked Jack.

"Of course I have but not until half-past seven," Nick replied.

They watched with interest as the train was transformed into a sleeper. Each compartment had couchettes each side of the panels, like bunk beds, that folded down and a conductor checked that it was set up correctly and that they were in the correct section. Jack went in to get the tickets out to show that they were in the right place, they were of course and whilst out on the platform another electric locomotive backed on to the train so two locomotives would pull them through the night. Back on the train the French couple were sorting out their luggage, stowing some underneath the bottom bunk. Jack and Nick's bunks were engine side top and middle, the couple had the bottom and their new friend, Colin, had the other top one. A Frenchman, about mid forties, who had joined them, very smartly dressed in a blazer was on the middle bunk, or couchette, as the French say. He had a funny twisty moustache, which amused both Jack and Nick. It twitched as he spoke to the other couple. Nick tried greeting the new additional Frenchman, who was called Maurice, then the couple who were called Jean and Renee joined in. Everyone was very friendly which was just as well in such a small space.

As the train sped up through the busy suburbs of Paris, eventually a few fields appeared and the train passed through the countryside. As half-past seven approached, another porter came through to say dinner was served. Jack and Nick found that Maurice had also booked and they wandered up the train together. It was absolutely fascinating seeing the mix of people in each compartment. There were people having huge picnics, setting up with tablecloths, glasses, plates and cutlery, the complete business. Jack couldn't believe it, imagine this on an English train, it just wouldn't happen. They were soon down at the restaurant car and they had walked the length of one whole carriage in a corridor along the side of the kitchens. The smells were fantastic and you could see through half doors, which were

22

serving hatches with chefs busy at work. Through into the dining room and the Maitre d'Hote checked their names and ushered them to a table for two at the other end of the carriage. Maurice, they noticed later, was put on a table for four at the opposite corner to a French looking lady. Jack couldn't help noticing how elegant she was, these French ladies knew how to dress. Now settled in with a breadbasket placed in the middle with the menu and wine list, Jack chose what he thought were prawns followed by pork. Nick chose onion soup and steak, which he had to try and explain he liked quite well cooked, the French obviously did not. Nick ordered a bottle of Beaujolais red wine because he knew his dad had bought that before and he did not recognise any other names on the list.

Jack could not believe it, his prawns were massive, they were actually crevettes and cooked in some sort of strong smelling sauce, which he was told was garlic. He tucked in chewing every little bit of the fishy meat he could find, then dipped bread into the delicious sauce just like he did in the café to soak up his fried breakfast. The wine went down well, it was not one Jack had drunk before, he thought it was a bit dry but when he went onto the second glass, he started to enjoy it. The meat course turned up after about ten minutes, they chatted about the fact that they were together on a train speeding across France. 'What an adventure,' Jack thought. The houses that they saw in villages and towns were different from those in England, with darkly tiled roofs and a lot of stone farm-houses and farm buildings. More cows around in this area and huge fields of ripening corn and wheat. Nick's steak arrived still with some blood coming out of it and as for Jack's pork, it was about one and a half inches thick cut circular with a sauce over it. Just meat on a plate, more bread was served and after they started eating, a big bowl of chips arrived and later a dish of mixed vegetables, some of which even as gardeners, the boys had no idea what they all were. The boys looked around them and noticed that generally everyone was eating one thing at a time. What a meal and they hadn't finished yet! Crème caramel sounded nice they thought but when it turned up on a dish with a rich dark treacle looking liquid around it, they were not so sure. One teaspoonful and they were delightfully surprised.

"You can give me this sort of food any day," Nick remarked as they then decided to have a coffee. This arrived in tiny cups, very strong black coffee, with sugar added. They really enjoyed it.

The light was now fading fast as the train rattled its way through France moving south mile after mile. After more talk of girls, sun and beaches they made their way back along the corridors to their compartment and couchettes. The French couple were already in their bunks reading, the blinds to the big window were down as were the ones to the corridor. The boys got themselves ready so they could crawl into their beds without disturbing anybody. Maurice who had eaten at the same time as them, returned greeting them and asked them whether they enjoyed the meal. At least that is what Jack and Nick thought he said. So they did their best to reply and answered yes and thanked him very much. The two boys stood in the corridor chatting before climbing into bed. Maurice appeared with a sponge-bag and wandered down the train to the toilet obviously to get ready for his night's sleep. The toilets were larger than those pokey ones on British trains with hot and cold water, good size basin, toilet, towels and very clean much to Jack's surprise. He had always been told that the French were not as fussy as the English, so far he would not agree. The corridor became quieter as time went on and it was now getting late. The lights of the stations and towns flashed by in the dark night. Nick decided to call it a day, as his beer and wine he had drunk earlier had caught up with him. Jack joined him and they took off their shoes, jumpers and jeans and crawled under the sheets and blankets.

Jack laid there for a long time, the train swaying and he thought sleep would come easily as he was so shattered. The others in the compartment were snoring and after what seemed like an age, he got up pulled his jeans and top on, then his shoes and went back into the corridor. He found Colin leaning on the rail, they chatted more about Nice and the family he was staying with and what a great time he was going to have. Then they drifted on to girls and films at the cinema, eventually Colin had tired and decided to call it a day. Jack let him go in first and he was just about to turn in himself when from the next compartment appeared the girl with the long blonde hair and legs to match. She smiled and leant against the rail by the window. She was lovely in a beige woollen top and beige cotton skirt with a blanket-type shawl around her shoulders. Jack tried not to stare as she pulled a packet of Gitanes cigarettes from her bag slung casually over her shoulder and her lighter followed. The cigarette leapt into life within those full red lips, dark brown eyes that seemed to smile at him as they made eye contact.

"Bonsoir Mademoiselle," Jack said in his best school French. She smiled replying in equally bad English that she had obviously learnt at school. With the greetings over, Jack could feel himself getting redder by the minute at his inability to speak in French and at chatting up young ladies. Sylvie, as he was soon to find out, offered him one of her cigarettes. Now Jack had tried smoking, had rolled a few Golden Virginia roll-ups but had not ever seriously smoked or ever smoked a French cigarette. He had a shock and struggled not to choke and cough, although it was a filter cigarette, the black tobacco hacked at his throat and lungs as he inhaled. They chatted some more with lots of graphic hand movements. Sylvie was at college studying art in Paris and was returning home to her parents for the summer. He hoped she would travel all the way to Nice, that way he would be able to see her again. Jack explained he was a 'paysagiste' or that is what the translation of a landscape gardener was, he thought. She was lovely and they decided to go to the restaurant car where the bar was serving all night. They had those funny little cups of coffee again and he smoked yet another Gitanes cigarette. After another coffee Jack tried again to find out where she lived, sadly it turned out to be Avignon and not Nice. He tried hard to work out how to ask her for her address but to no avail.

Back along the corridor they stood for a while outside her compartment. Sylvie explained that she would be getting off the train at about quarter-past one in the morning so must get some sleep. Her eyes smiled and those lovely red lips pursed a kiss as she left him standing alone again in the corridor. Time for bed he thought and after a trip to the toilet at the end of the carriage, he crept into his couchette.

Colin whispered, "You have been chatting up that girl haven't you?" Jack just smiled and soon drifted off to sleep. He awoke suddenly as the train was slowing down, was it Avignon where Sylvie got off, no it was only half-past twelve. He dozed off again thinking of her and what they could get up to in a couchette. 'Dream on' Jack thought to himself as the other five in his compartment were all sound asleep and snoring. The train slowed again and this time it was gone one o'clock in the morning. Again Jack was up with his shoes pushed on and slid out of the compartment and there she was waiting with her very large leather suitcase. After greeting her, he passed her a piece of paper with his name and address on, so perhaps she might write or come to England one day. Sadly there was no response of a return address, out came the Gitanes cigarettes again and Jack was beginning to enjoy these. The train then slowly drew to a halt. She opened the door and Jack helped her down with her case, he was amused looking along the train at how many people were getting off. As soon as he had got down onto the platform, the guard blew his whistle and waved his baton. Jack climbed back on board wishing Sylvie goodbye or 'au revoir'. With the door shut he watched her walk away but turning and pursing her lips towards him again. 'What a flirt,' he thought sadly because she was a beautiful one as well. He hoped that all French girls looked as gorgeous.

The next thing he knew was that the train was stopping and the carriages were jolting heavily. They had arrived in a station but it was still dark, 'surely we haven't got there already' mused Jack, then he dozed off again. Nick suddenly got up but he was soon back in his bunk snoring. Suddenly it was all action. The French couple had arisen and had obviously been down to the toilets for a wash and teeth clean as they returned with their spongebags and small towels. They looked at Jack as they left the compartment and said, "Le petit dejeuner?" He turned to Nick and asked him what they had said, "Breakfast Jack," he replied. The three boys, Jack, Nick and Colin quickly tidied themselves and scrambled down the train to the restaurant car. They had to wait about ten minutes and this was at 6.15 in the morning. They stood by the bar and were offered coffees while they waited. These turned out to be big white coffees in a bowl, delicious. The train was somehow different, not quite as smooth and they realised that the carriages were being pulled along by a steam train, as every now and then billows of smoke would pass the window. They were soon seated at a table, Colin and Jack sat against the window.

The countryside had really changed. The houses had pale terracotta peg tile roofs and were mainly white, many had shutters painted mostly greyish blue and a few green. The fields were different as well, many full of sunflowers and others with ripe corn maize blowing in the wind. The sky was bright blue and the sun was already up over the horizon. Jack couldn't believe what he saw. Breakfast was served, fruit juice, funny sticks of bread cut into little rounds, pots of red fruit jam and apricot then the croissants followed. Those with apricot jam were delicious, more bowls of coffee were served by the waiter. What a wonderful breakfast. The boys tucked in eating everything served, after a while they began chatting feeling a bit more human. Especially Colin, he wasn't boasting about his French friends so much or talking about cars. They talked about all the things they wanted to do when they arrived in Nice. Jack and Nick suggested Colin took their pension telephone number where they would be staying. Colin didn't seem very enthusiastic but he took their number down. Colin was telling Nick about how Jack was in and out all night chatting up the French girl in the next compartment.

"Oh no leave it alone!" Jack exclaimed, the boys did not, of course.

"I could have sworn she was English, she kept on smiling as I walked past," Nick replied. "So you were in and out all night, seriously or metaphorically? Her lips looked tasty, were they?" asked Nick. The questions kept on coming with Jack turning quite red, in fact nearly as red as the wine some passengers were drinking on the table opposite Jack pointed out, trying to change the subject. Red wine with breakfast, how could anyone drink that? They must be alcoholics thought Jack, but the boys would not leave him alone. So to keep them quiet, he eventually told them the whole story, the lips, her body, her perfume, their trip to the bar and her leaving at Avignon. They could not believe that he had got off with Sylvie in the corridor of a train! Well he hadn't, but then they didn't know and would never know, so he went quiet and they both thought he was love struck! As if he would be, she was nice and if France was full of girls like Sylvie, he would be back again.

The train pulled along the coast now, the sky was so blue, the sun had arisen, the sea was incredibly blue; they all thought it was surreal. How was the sea so blue and not at home in England, was there a secret ingredient? They just did not know. They wandered back down the corridors and the train slowed down, 'was it Nice station' they wondered but it was not the arrival time yet. It was St. Raphael, quite a few people got off including the French couple from the compartment. Jack helped them down with their cases, the steps down from the train were quite steep and difficult to manage with a large bag. The train was now full of people using it as a local train, students and old ladies, mainly dressed in black, which Jack found surprising. 'Why black they must have felt so hot,' thought Jack. The train passed coves and beaches with a few people already swimming, yachts were out sailing with mainly white sails but one had a huge billowing red one out the front of the boat.

"Talking of red sails," Nick suddenly said, "look at the rocks, they are all red as well, do you think the sand is red on the beach as well?" Jack had no idea yet.

Chapter III

The train plodded on past Antibes and along a very straight piece of the coast where they were very close to the sea. The airport was across the bay and there were planes coming in over the sea to land. Jack was getting quite excited with Nick telling him that once they saw the airport and the racecourse, they were nearly there. The train slowly entered Nice station, a high Victorian-style building with big wrought-iron arches and filled-in with glass and wood. The sun streamed in through the gaps in the sides, it really looked very majestic. There were announcements on the speakers, which none of them understood. Everyone poured out of the train, clambering down the steps with their luggage, down the platform and much to the boys' amazement; people were walking across the tracks.

"Shall we do the same?" Nick said to Jack.

"No, come on, the stairs for the subway are here," as they emerged on the platform by the entrance. At the barriers Colin was greeted by an attractive girl, who was quite short, she had a slight build with brown hair to her shoulders and big brown eyes. He kissed her on both cheeks and she gave him a big hug. Nick nudged Jack and whispered, "He wasn't lying was he?" Colin introduced them to Jacqueline, who shook their hands and welcomed them to Nice. Her English was good and she spoke with a sexy and slightly American accent. She asked whether they needed a hand finding their pension.

"No problem I've been here before with my parents," Nick said thanking her for her concern. After parting their separate ways, the boys went off to get a taxi.

"Hotel Les Cigalles," Nick said with confidence, the driver placed their luggage in the boot of the Citroen car. He drove out of the station, down across a complicated roundabout type junction and then up a slight hill, the road then suddenly widened and where there was a bus stop and a small park, the driver shot off right up the hill. It was a one-way street and then he entered a small driveway next to a very high brick wall. The boys jumped out of the taxi, Nick passed the driver a note and got some change. The path to the hotel was made of a sort of marble material, creamy white colour, hoses were hidden along the path.

"It's like being at work eh?" Jack commented. They walked under orange trees with real oranges growing on them and the occasional lemon tree, Jack followed Nick up a flight of steps to a terrace of gravel, which had tables and chairs set out. The path lead through the middle to two large high wooden doors. They entered to find an old lady in a room just off to the right. She chatted away in French to Nick, he gave her his name and she chatted on again, neither could understand what she was saying. After ringing a bell, a younger man came through and greeted them in English saying he was Monsieur Christophe and the proprietor. He handed Nick and Jack forms to fill in for the police check giving their passport details and the dates of their stay at the Hotel. Having completed these, he led them into a grand room on the ground floor with two single beds in it. After being shown the bathroom and how the shutters work, Monsieur Christophe warned them of the strength of the sun from midday.

At last they were here, Jack flopped on the bed exhausted.
"Come on let's go out and explore," Nick started to say.
"No, let's just stop for a while," Jack exclaimed. They were

booked in at Les Cigalles on half-board and their breakfast at 6 o'clock this morning seemed a long time ago and it was only mid-morning. It was hot, the windows were open and the shutters were shut, the floor was tiled and after Jack had taken his shoes off, the floor was lovely to put his feet onto. He pulled out some lightweight trousers and a short sleeved shirt from his case.

There was a gentle knock at the door and a French voice spoke. Jack opened the door to find a delightful old lady holding a tray for them.

"Bonjour Messieurs, j'amene des boissons pour vous," she said. It had glasses of freshly squeezed orange juice, cut French bread, butter and jam, Jack's favourite apricot jam. Nick swung his legs round off the bed and Jack popped the tray on the small table between the beds. They were soon tucking into the bread, delicious with jam on and washed down with the orange juice. Nick propped up the pillows saying he now wanted to sleep!

"Not me," said Jack. "I am off out to have a look round!"

"Okay," said Nick and was glad to go out really.

"Let's take our trunks in case we get to the beach," replied Jack.

"No chance," retorted Nick negatively.

They finished their snack and put the tray back out by the kitchen and wandered back out the front door through the garden.

"What time is dinner?" asked Jack.

"There was a card in the room," Nick explained but he had not read it through. Jack ran back into the room to check. It was from six o'clock so they had plenty of time.

Wandering back on to the main road where the taxi had taken them, they walked past shops and bars and eventually they came to Place Gambetta, where there must have been a market earlier. Some remains of fruit and vegetables were still laying about and some vans were taking fish from stalls and loading them into ice filled boxes.

"We will have to have a look at this another day," Nick commented. Over the other side was a station, not the one at which they had arrived, but a different one. The shops now were getting bigger, namely Prisunic and Galeries Lafayette, which looked like a John Lewis store back in London. After these larger bars and restaurants suddenly they could see the sea! The wide promenade had a two-lane dual carriageway running along it with beautiful palm trees and flowerbeds planted with Buzy Lizzies and grass borders that were bright green. The boys looked with amazement at this glorious strip of garden that was so well kept in the middle of such a busy road. There were people everywhere including some very well dressed women and girls. Crossing the road, the promenade up to the sea wall was wide enough for nearly three cars but it was for walking on not driving, although a few young people rode their bicycles along there.

"This is 'Promenade des Anglais' built during Victorian times," said Nick, his dad had told him that many English used to visit Nice in the winter and walk their ladies along the promenade.

"It's difficult to imagine so many people travelling all this way from England in such times, imagine the slow ship across the Channel and old steam trains travelling eight hundred miles across France. I bet they didn't have restaurant cars and couchettes in those days, but then just think of all those old cars running along the road here in front of those grand hotels. Do you think they went swimming? Didn't they use little cabins on wheels and wear bathing suits to their knees?"

"Yes probably but never mind the past, we should have brought our trunks and towels with us Nick," said Jack looking longingly at the sea. They sat on the low wall looking out at the incredibly blue sea, which matched the blue sky. The beach was full of pebbles, Jack was a little surprised but it did not seem to be putting off any of the people lying on them including a lot of very lovely girls.

"Nick look some of the girls are topless!" exclaimed Jack with his eyes nearly popping out of his head. "Let's go down and soak up the atmosphere," he suggested.

There was a large concrete looking breakwater with loads of rocks around it, which they headed for quickly stripping their shirts off exposing some fairly white skin, well that's the way it looked against the bronzed ladies on the beach. They sat and chatted about where to go tomorrow, deciding to set off early and catch a train down the coast to Cannes and have a look there. If they used the train to get them along the coast, it would make life easier. Having looked at the maps in the railway station the train ran out of Nice towards Italy along the coast through Menton to Monte Carlo and beyond.

"So there is somewhere to go," Jack said.

The line went up to Ventimiglia and after a little while on the coast, it turns inland into Italy. As for the other way, the line wanders along the coast to Antibes, Juan Les Pins and soon after St. Raphael then the line veers inland and takes the route through Les Arcs/Draguignan and onward off to Marseilles and the way they came. There were main line trains drawn by huge black steam locomotives and funny local diesel coach trains with big double doors that seemed to be left open with everyone hanging out. It looked fun and dangerous, perhaps they would find out tomorrow. These local trains stopped at every station, which meant they could possibly even go to a little beach or cove up the coast on another day.

After an hour or so, it was time to come off the beach and get something to eat. Putting their shirts back on, they wandered along from Place Massena into some of the back streets where there were lots of bars. Nick, after his holiday here with his parents, said that lunch was either best eaten on the beach as a picnic with what you have bought or in a bar where they normally served snacks. Two beers turned up and then Nick ordered two "Croque Monsieurs." Jack wondered what he was ordering. He needn't have worried; they were a bit like welsh rarebit or a toasted cheese sandwich. After eating two rounds and two more beers they were definitely feeling sleepy.

"How about trying to get a bus back?" suggested Nick. After the second attempt one of the buses took them to within a stone's throw of their hotel. Nick went straight in and collapsed on the bed, while Jack got into his shorts and went to the side area by the front door, where he had spotted some deckchairs. Laying back in the dappled shade with the sun warm enough for him to open his shirt up and his feet on another deckchair, he promptly fell asleep. As the sun moved around in the afternoon, Jack was in full sunlight and by the time he awoke he had burnt his chest and face! Monsieur Christophe Corbert, the hotelier, gave him a lecture on how the English always went out in the middle of the day and burnt themselves. Jack asked whether he could have an orange juice drink and was asked to follow him to the room off the kitchen. Monsieur Christophe soon appeared with a freshly squeezed orange drink with ice cubes in a tall glass on a glass saucer.

Jack went back to his deckchair where a really tasty girl had appeared with long brown hair, shoulder length, dark brown eyes, wearing a skimpy top that could only be described as covering a well-blessed bosom. She had a narrow waist and her skirt was hitched up showing a beautifully tanned pair of legs.

"Hello," said Jack on returning to his deckchair, "hot isn't it?" The reply was in English with a tantalising sexy accent. Her name was Anne, she and Jack chatted about Nice where she had been, which beaches were good, and the hotel she had stayed at last year and how she had enjoyed her holiday. Jack thought he was on to a winner, wouldn't Nick be kicking himself! They chatted for about half-hour when a stocky guy came out of the front door, he had dark hair and swarthy skin and greeted Anne and Jack in French. She then introduced her husband, called Serge, Jack nearly fell out of his deckchair as he thought he had already met the love of his life! They all sat chatting about life, they were both teachers from Paris that was why they spoke English so well. Jack hardly said anything, sitting dazed and then noticed the rings on her fingers on her left hand, he really must be more observant, he thought to himself.

Nick eventually appeared very bleary eyed with his shirt hanging out, Jack introduced him to his new acquaintances and then they soon went back to their room.

"What a little cracker she is," exclaimed Nick.

"Yes," Jack replied casually not letting on about his previous thoughts.

It was soon time for the evening meal, which started between half-past six and half-past seven. They were both hungry and after having a good wash in the basin, they changed into some slacks and short-sleeved shirts and they were ready. The dining area was at the back of the hotel on two levels with steps leading down to them. Despite having windows all along one side it was quite dark, due to plenty of plants that were overhanging the windows. These made it almost like a green wall of citrus plants, with oranges and lemons hanging from branches. The tables had tartan tablecloths and Monsieur Christophe showed them to their table that was adjacent to, would you believe, the lovely Anne and Serge. Jack and Nick politely greeted them in their best French and sat down, with Jack having his back to Anne. He was still embarrassed at his earlier exploits. Jack still wondered whether she had thought he had been trying his 'chat-up lines'.

The dinner was great, a sort of sausage pâté for the first course, then a meat dish with a big bowl of chips followed by salad and then a sweet of fresh fruit and cheese. All a bit strange serving it separately and the cheese did smell a lot! The pink wine or rosé as they called it, went down well. They were very full indeed so much so that they sat on the chairs outside with a coffee to settle down before going into Nice to see what was going on. Anne and her husband were the first to leave, then another couple plus a couple of German girls, which even Nick did not fancy. Everyone was friendly and it was fascinating to think that they all spoke different languages, although most were from the same continent. Nick had hoped there would be a tasty waitress but Monsieur Christophe's wife, Grace Corbert served and the old lady that had brought them their drinks and food to their room earlier, had worked for the family business for years.

"So come on, let's go for a stroll," said Jack.

They walked down the main boulevard Gambetta that passed the station for municipal trains. The wide pavements were full of people many drinking in the bars, smoking and chatting. It was a super atmosphere and they were soon sucked into the Mediterranean lifestyle. The bars on the main boulevard were expensive but walking around the corner to the side streets, they became smaller and more intimate. Choosing a bar full of young people, they tried out their poor French at the bar. They were soon joined by some people who tried their English out on the boys and soon a good crowd were sitting around a couple of tables, enjoying each other's company. As the evening went on Jack had switched to cognacs and smoking Gauloise cigarettes like a native. Nick needless to say was 'chatting up' a girl who was very tanned in white slacks, a tight black top with ample breasts, showing a slim waist, dark eyes and smooth skin and jet black shiny hair down to just below her shoulders. How does he do it, Jack thought, their heads were getting closer and closer, Nick was stroking her hair and kissing her gently on the neck and ear.

Eventually it was time to go, they scattered in all directions including Monique, Nick's new found lady friend, a quick kiss and she was gone.

"I thought you were in for the night," Jack said.

"No she has work tomorrow in some shop. I said we would meet again in this bar, is that okay?"

Jack was quite honestly beyond caring and the next clear thing he could remember was waking up in the morning with a knock on the door. Nick was snoring in the other bed. Jack felt rotten but crawled out of bed still in his trousers from last night and opened the door to the older lady, who had their breakfast on a tray. He pushed the pile of stuff aside on the bureau and the large tray was put there. Boy did Jack have a headache, so before anything he swallowed a couple of painkillers down with some water. Self-inflicted pain is always best kept to yourself, Nick too woke up with a thumping headache, and Jack said nothing except that breakfast was ready.

"We haven't got to go to the dining room have we?" asked Nick clutching his head.

"No, it is all here," replied Jack.

They had fresh squeezed orange juice, fresh baguette bread, apricot jam, croissants and fresh brewed coffee. The latter possibly was the most important in large bowls with hot milk to add, not that Jack needed milk, just sweet black coffee.

Chapter IV

Cannes

With a new day ahead they ventured down to the mainline station from where they could travel along the coast on the small diesel four-coach unit, to Cannes. They had heard it was full of the loveliest girls! After waiting some time, the train arrived and drifted along the coast, sometimes right on the sea and other times passing through tunnels and pine covered valleys, but villas and houses absolutely everywhere, some even right on the edge of the sea. How fantastic they both thought, not only to live here but we could even do gardening here.

"Now that's a thought for the future," Nick said.

With all their constant chatter, it felt they had arrived at Cannes quickly, even though it had taken them a long time. They came out of the station; it was quite a walk to the sea, in fact a couple of blocks. The beach was sandy but not that large, it was nearly eleven o'clock and already there were a lot of people. The private sections had deckchair loungers, lots of green and white and blue and white umbrellas everywhere and little tables with young men serving drinks. Well they cost money and what's wrong with lying on a beach towel anyway! They found themselves a spot about ten yards back from the water's edge where they quickly changed into their trunks and went into the sea. Oh! How fantastic and warm the water was in comparison to Britain, Jack couldn't believe it, you could just lie there and float in the water! They swam out to a raft that was about a couple of hundred yards out. It was a leisurely swim and on arrival they climbed up the ladders to lie on the deck. There was a real mixture of people and ages, Jack and Nick spent their time looking at the young ladies in their bikinis. The sun was very hot and so were the views to these virile young men.

After a while Jack and Nick dived in, well Jack's was more of a belly flop, trying to impress the girls, or not. Back on the sand, it was hot to the feet. Nick showered with fresh water at the showers situated at the top of the beach. Jack always believed that salt helped your skin to tan, so he laid down to let the sun do the drying. He slept for nearly an hour when he checked with his watch in the bag. Ouch, no tan but burnt, his back was fairly red. Nick was very amused and offered to rub some sun tan lotion on it. He had been rubbing oil on all that time and turning over slowly cooking his body like a hog roast! He was off to the bar to get a couple of beers and soon returned with chilled ones from the private beach bar and a carton of chips with loads of salt on, that's how the French ate them. "Any vinegar?" asked Jack hopefully.

"No that's not how they serve them," replied Nick.

The rest of the day was spent sunning themselves and swimming in between, reading paperbacks they had brought with them. Well reading wasn't quite true; both of them were lying there on their fronts looking over the tops of their books at all the girls and ladies! Jack had pointed out at an early stage, how lovely some of the mothers were with their young children.

Nick jibed Jack, "Well you've always fancied older women haven't you Jack?!"

They left the beach about five o'clock but could have stayed longer. However, by the time they had arrived at the station and waited for the train to Nice, walked up the Gambetta to the hotel, it was getting on towards dinner-time. Nick went off down to the shower room with his towels, he hoped he would be a winner with Monique tonight. He showered and popped on some aftershave called 'Old Spice' and Jack accused him of smelling 'poofy'. Nick's shower was painful and he was in serious need of some calamine lotion being rubbed on his very red back, as did Jack need too after his shower. They were very much the "Mad Englishmen being out in the midday sun!"

Dinner was very enjoyable again and the boys were being teased by Monsieur Christophe for burning themselves but the wine seemed to dull the pain somewhat. They were just enjoying their crème caramels and about to embark on the coffees, which perhaps they both could do with after the amount of alcohol they had been drinking, when Monsieur Christophe said there was a phone call for Jack! "Who?" he asked but Monsieur Christophe just said it was a man. It turned out to be Colin, the young Englishman they had met on the train. He was keen to meet them as he was finding life with the French family quite hard work. So they arranged to meet on the corner of Victor Hugo and Gambetta and go to a bar they had already agreed to go to.

"I'll meet you in about an hour's time half-past eight okay? See you there," Colin said.

They finished their dinner trying one of those little coffees that the French seem to drink. Jack thought it was horrible. Nick filled his with lots of sugar and enjoyed his small cup of very, very dark coffee.

They sat on the terrace for a while chatting to Anne and Serge. Jack drifted off into his dreams again of Anne as if no one else existed; he was abruptly interrupted by Nick, who suggested it was time to get off to the bar to meet Colin and Jacqueline. Jack hoped he would meet a French girl as tasty as Anne.

They had bought a 'carnet' of bus tickets as Monsieur Christophe at the hotel had suggested, which enabled them to use the tickets to hop on and off the buses as they pleased. Tonight they were tired so for the five-minute bus journey down Gambetta, they took a ride. At the bar the same crowd were already there and Nick was pleased because Monique was there too. Sitting down, Nick moved straight around to Monique, Jack sat with the boys. A waiter arrived to take their order for the draught lager, which Jack had learnt to order as "Pression s'il vous plaît." He did get a kick out of trying a little bit of French. A mixed discussion of differences between France and England followed and they still found it difficult to believe that the boys were gardeners. It was not as if they were interested in gardens, but they did suggest that a visit to Eze to look at the cacti and the Mediterranean gardens as well as Monaco with its superb gardens in front of the Casino would be interesting. Perhaps a trip up there on the train would be a good idea.

About nine o'clock Jacqueline and Colin arrived. After introductions and lots of shaking of hands, it turned out that one of the boys knew Jacqueline from the beach, where they used to go with their families. Colin and Jacqueline sat next to Jack and they were soon chatting about England again. Jacqueline had stayed in England a couple of times as part of her English course and she knew quite a bit of the South East of England but not Woodmanstern! Her English was very good but the accent made it very sexy indeed, Jack was mesmerised. Jacqueline chatted about how Colin wasn't coping very well with just her for company, he continually wanted to be on the go but he seemed worried about venturing too far as his French was pretty bad. Jack said it couldn't be as bad as his French but he did try lengthy discussions about the French way of life, different cultures and not forgetting quite a few beers in between. Colin was talking to some of the boys in broken 'pigeon' English while Nick had his arm around Monique and was obviously getting on well.

The evening went very quickly and at about eleven o'clock Jacqueline suggested to Colin that they made a move to go home. He had drunk a fair amount by then and he did not really want to leave. Jack suggested that they leave as well to help the situation but Nick resisted. In the end Jack left Nick and escorted Colin back to Jacqueline's little Fiat. They dropped Jack off up at his hotel with a goodnight kiss on the cheek from Jacqueline, Colin was asleep in the back. She asked Jack if they would like to join them on a trip to St. Tropez tomorrow.

"We will have to start off early because of the traffic, on second thoughts, let's make it the day after, if not Colin will have a hangover," said Jacqueline and probably Nick would be suffering too.

Jack slept soundly until Nick fell over and woke him at about two o'clock in the morning. He was obviously drunk and spent the next ten minutes apologising. Eventually sleep returned and the next thing they knew it was morning and the sun was beaming through the shutters. Jack arose and to Nick's disgust, he opened the shutters allowing the sun to shine in. The sky was a bright blue that one never seems to see in England, where does it come from? With Nick grumbling and swearing at the bright sunlight, the boys never heard the quiet knock on the door as the maid brought the tray of breakfast into their room. It was a great idea as Nick had a hell of a head. So other than black coffee Nick didn't eat anything. Jack as always was hungry and ate all the French bread and jam as well as the croissants. Nick returned to sleep, so Jacqueline was wise to move the trip to the next day.

"Come on Nick, the day will be wasted, just throw on some clothes and we'll get a bus to the beach and you can sleep all day!" Jack exclaimed.

Nick grudgingly obeyed much to Jack's amusement and after nearly an hour with bags of swimming gear, towels and books, they went out of the hotel, only being spotted by M.

43

Christophe, who commented on what a great night they must have had. "Watch the sun," he called after them, as they walked through the orange trees in the garden.

They went down to the bus stop and handing their carnet tickets over to the driver, they were on their way down Gambetta and eventually around Place Massena and onto the seafront of Nice, where the bus did a sharp turn left towards the harbour. Jack hurriedly pushed the bell and the boys alighted into the sunshine. Nick wanted to go to a beach further along, towards the casino, why, Jack had no idea. The beach was all pebbles for the miles that made Baie des Anges, unless the sand had been imported. With no mood to argue, they wandered along Promenade Des Anglais admiring the scantily dressed girls and ladies either coming or going to the beach. Jack spotted an area on one beach with plenty of topless girls sunbathing,

"What about there?"

No, Nick was having none of it and continued to stride on, amusingly quickly, considering his hangover. Eventually they arrived at a public beach called 'Casino Beach', would you believe, it was opposite the casino!

Chapter V

"Helena"

The private beaches with their sun loungers, parasols and private bars and restaurants appealed to the boys but were horrendously expensive. Plenty of very fancy men and women lounged beneath the parasols but the boys looked on to a world that was not theirs. Down the steps and onto the beach not taking shoes off until settled due to the pebbly beach. Jack preferred to be closer to the water than Nick so they always ended up in the middle as a compromise. There were a couple of families, some couples and several groups of girls. Jack had already taken a fancy to a blonde girl in a green swim-suit laying in a line of five girls all looking about their age.

Settling down on a pile of towels they changed into their swimmers, Nick piling shoes, shorts and tops as a pillow was soon asleep.

Jack, concerned that Nick had not put sunscreen on himself, squirted some from a tube waking him with a start, Nick rubbed it in half-heartedly and Jack gave up walking down a few yards of the beach to the sea. Even in these temperatures it staggered him how cold it felt as he dived beneath the surface taking a couple of strokes before popping back up. Not a good swimmer and mainly being a breast stroke swimmer he gently swam out from the beach. Something he'd picked up by watching others was floating on his back, feet crossed, breathing gently, staring at that incredible blue sky, all he had to do was gently fan the water with an outstretched arm and there he was in heaven...

His peace was eventually disturbed by a group of girls splashing and swimming towards him, including the blonde in the green. As she started to pass by Jack he asked in French if she spoke English.

"Yes" she replied with a heavy accent, "I'm from the Netherlands. You're English. Where from?" The conversation continued whilst they both trod water.

Helena eventually re-joined her friends and they were laughing and joking. Jack swam back to the shore hoping the joking was not about him.

He struggled up the beach over the hot stones collapsing in a heap on his towel, wiping himself off and pushing back his hair. He was soon dry and rubbing on some sun cream when Helena and her mates came up the beach and to his amusement she broke off to come and chat.

 "Why not come and join us, your friend doesn't look very chatty." Nick was still in the same position, asleep – mouth open, making the most disgusting noises. Jack grabbed a towel and followed. 'What a lovely bum she has,' he thought as he went off up the beach.

He was introduced and offered a drink as these lovely girls poured themselves a combination – some drinking coke with others drinking wine and beer, whilst others ate chips or crisps. He couldn't believe it! Chatting to these really lovely girls as they dabbed the water from their tanned bodies and started removing straps from their shoulders and rubbing sun cream over their necks and shoulders. Helena, who was shapely, tucked her straps over the edges of her shoulder and her friend, which Jack thought she said was Veronica, rubbed oil to the bronzed shoulder. Wouldn't he have enjoyed doing just that but he had only met her half an hour before. Her green costume set against the tan of her body with the blonde hair falling on her neck with droplets of sweat was making Jack very interested. Helena was from Scheveningen, which was a seaside resort on the North Sea and had just finished college at Rotterdam. Her mates decided to come to the South of France for a real holiday before getting a proper job.

As they chatted some of the girls removed the tops of their bikinis and laid there bare topped sunning themselves. Jack's eyes must have wandered as Helena soon picked him up on it.

"Have you never seen girls' bodies before?" Jack went scarlet and she changed the subject realising the embarrassment she had caused.

Jack talked about his life as a gardener and the work he did in London. Helena couldn't believe Jack was a gardener and the other girls joined in accusing him of spinning them a line.

"You wait till Nick wakes and check it out with him." Helena laid back to enjoy the sun pushing the straps right down her arms with her bust easing itself nearly out of the costume.

"Ok if I stay?"

"Of course," she replied, "We'll get some food later and have a picnic so please stay."

Jack, having been slightly aroused by this bevy of beauties, decided to roll over onto his front to save any embarrassment. The hard pebbles that greeted his body soon put paid to that. Jack awoke to a gentle stroking on his back and shoulder. "We've a picnic – would you join us?"

Pulling himself together and wishing he had put sun cream on his back before going to sleep he sat up to find Nick sitting between the girls downing a beer.

"Hi stranger, you've been asleep for ages." Jack resisted commenting considering Nick had been out of it most of the morning. Helena sat closely to Jack cutting up baguettes with a knife and passing salads and meats from one to another. Jack sensed an interest in him; she gently touched his leg as if by accident so he now paid even more attention to her. She had a very full body and sparkling blue eyes and a beautiful tan to go with it. Jack continued telling her where they were staying and what they'd been up to and where they'd been drinking the night before. Jack thought it to be quite a dodgy area, but the girls' hotel was not far from the bar, Helena and some of her mates would try and meet tonight. 'That'll cramp Nick's style with his French girlfriend, Jack thought inwardly. Lunch continued as he appreciated the finer points of her face with its slightly freckled nose, long eyelashes, fine mouth but not full lips, definitely shapely from there downwards all in the right places.

Jack stroked her fingers and after lunch he suggested they walk along the beach together. This was something Jack often did so he could check out all the people especially the girls on the beach and in the water. This time with Helena it was different, they walked at the waters edge sometimes in the water, carrying their shoes as the pebbles were difficult to walk on. Jack linked hands and found a positive response from her, as they strolled along towards the airport end of Nice. Jack hadn't even noticed who was lying under the umbrellas on the private beaches.

Helena, who was keen on swimming and sports, suggested they cool off with a swim. Leaving their shoes on the edge of the beach they dived into the sea together, she was a much better swimmer, using crawl and soon was ahead of Jack. "Come on," she called, "let's swim out."

Jack, with his breaststroke was left behind. He turned over swimming on his back up and down over the soft swell and eventually passed most of the swimmers. Suddenly from behind there was a big splash, which made Jack cough and splutter, getting water up his nose. She apologised profusely and treading water beside him kissed Jack on the side of his face.

"I cannot swim as far as you but we could cross along to the floating platform?"

She continued alongside Jack all the way and they climbed onto the platform sitting facing out to sea, feet in the water.

"It's a great place to dream out here facing out to the horizon. The odd ship, sailing boat and cruiser going past. You could be anywhere possibly, except Britain, it would be too cold."

"And Holland," Helena chipped in. Jack put his arm around her now warm body as they had dried in the sun and wind. She leant towards Jack and they kissed deeply, turning slightly towards each other.

"You're lovely," he said.

"You're cute," she replied.

As they kissed again Jack was conscious of others sitting on the platform watching their behaviour, bit strange, he thought. Not only that, he was getting rather too interested and it could show.

Jack quickly said, "Join me," as he slid into the water.

After Jack arose out of the water again Helena was there. They kissed and swam off towards the beach. Jack with his leisurely strokes and Helena would swim on her back just in front of him getting closer and closer.

"You're a tease…"

"I know, but it's fun."

They were soon back on shore and had to walk quite a few yards to find their shoes. The conversation on the way back was about friends and what they did and what was happening tonight.

"Helena, I cannot see you tonight, Nick and I are seeing some old friends and tomorrow they are taking us out for lunch."

"Come on, I won't see you until tomorrow night – that's not good enough."

At that point a young Arab boy selling Banyans, a type of doughnut, came past. Jack had an inside pocket in his trunks with some coins in. Buying two Banyans, he suggested sitting by the sea and enjoying them. Helena went quiet, he put his arm round her – she shrugged him off.

"Come on, I've only just met you – you're lovely but I'd already arranged it and yes I do want to see you again."

She warmed a little smearing jam from the Banyan on his face. They walked back holding hands to the others and Nick, who was now bright red from sleeping in the sun, was busy chatting to Helena's two friends about water skis. Jack was sure that Nick had never been water skiing and as for being an expert, he did tell a good story; they were fascinated.

"Let's all go for a swim."

"Just been," Jack replied.

"So, where have you two been then?" Nick asked sarcastically.

"Swimming," Jack replied. They played ball with a small, coloured ball and rackets at the edge of the sea and with a larger one in the sea.

It was quite late by the time they decided to go, as the sun was quite low on the horizon.

"Let's go for a drink before we part."

The girls showered and changed. Nick couldn't take his eyes off them until Jack nudged him in the ribs. The boys rubbed off the salt and with the covering of their towels were soon in their shorts, sandals and shirts. Jack, holding Helena's hand, and Nick with a girl on both arms left the beach up the stairs. Crossing at the lights they headed for one of the bars just off the front up a side street.

Collapsing in the chairs outside, "Good Dutch girls drink beers," Nick said.

"Okay," they replied, "Get them in."

They were in the bar for a good hour when Nick realised the time and suggested they catch up later, Jack making discreet signs and kicking him under the table at last got his attention. Nick was a nightmare with a few drinks.

"Yes Jack, what are we doing?"

Jack then went through his story of family friends with Nick looking completely bemused. They eventually left, all of them kissing on the cheeks, one called Anne-Marie giving Nick a bit more than that and Jack was surprised at the fantastic kiss from Helena. They left promising to catch up on the beach the day after tomorrow.

Nick was a pain and trying to get him to hurry back to "Les Cigalles" was very difficult. In the end Jack opted to catch a bus which seemed to take ages to reach, as they had to cross Nice to get to the main street for the bus stop. Eventually, back at the hotel, Nick collapsed on the bed and was very soon asleep. Jack washed and changed and it was soon time for dinner. He left Nick and went out of the room.

"Where's your friend?" he was asked by Monsieur Christophe.

"Asleep," replied Jack.

"Did you not wake him?"

"He's drunk too much!! He can sleep!!" Monsieur Christophe left it at that as he served the first course of artichoke and a small bowl of brownish, oily looking liquid. After sitting staring at it for some time wondering how to attack it, he watched the French couple, that lovely one he fancied who just happened to be married, start to eat theirs. Anne pulled a couple of the outer leaves off and abandoned them; Jack watched curiously, what next? Well, eventually she pulled some more off, dunked them in the little dish, then up to the mouth and appeared to chew the end of what looked like a tough petal. Those lips - he watched her repeat this action several times. 'Concentrate on the meal Jack and stop staring,' he said to himself. It didn't really taste of much and the brown oily stuff had quite a peppery, vinegary taste. He plodded away at the artichoke, being conscious of not being beaten. Then suddenly, no more leaves or petals. As he looked back round at Anne and Serge, they smiled back at him, so what did he do now?

While he was still glazed with confusion, Monsieur Christophe returned to collect plates and dishes, passing Jack he said, "You've got the best bit now to eat, they are very good aren't they?"

Still confused, Jack cut it up, dunked it and ate it, he discovered that 'globe artichoke and vinaigrette' is quite a delicacy. The next course was easy; beef in a thick gravy with some pasta and salad. Jack did enjoy his food and the crème caramel that followed was delicious. Afterwards, Monsieur Christophe would offer some coffee but Jack couldn't quite get the hang of this strong black stuff, even with sugar in it. The French couple, Anne and Serge, came over and sat with Jack, checking out that Nick was okay. After hearing the problem was beer, they were less interested and instead, discussed their travels today into the hills behind Nice to a little old village called Eze. It had small streets, no cars and was also known for its cactus gardens. Perhaps Nick and Jack should go there, as they were gardeners, Anne suggested. Jack told them about the beach and meeting the Dutch girls and that they were off to St Tropez tomorrow with a girl who lived in Nice and tonight going for a drink with them.

"Perhaps I'd better wake Nick; he's going to be hungry. Hmmm that'll teach him!!"

Jack returned to the room to a snoring Nick. He felt like leaving him but he wouldn't be there if it were not for him. He shook him; Nick grunted. More grunting. After being really heavily shaken Nick jumped up shouting, "What's wrong?"

"Nothing, it's late, you've missed dinner and we're being picked up in about half an hour by Jacqueline and Colin."

"Oh hell, I'm starving and... oh, what a head!!"

Jack found the aspirin for the head, got him his clean shirt and slacks and suggested a good wash would help. Nick set to with pills, gargling, cleaning teeth and even washing. Splash of deodorant under the arms and dressed.

A knock at the door and Monsieur Christophe was there, with a big smile on his face. "You have a lovely French young lady waiting to take you out,"

Jack had really warmed to him; he was such a kindly man. Outside in the foyer area Jacqueline did look lovely, her lips with a touch of lipstick and those dark eyes and a pretty blue dress with a lighter blue edging and a blue band to match in the hair. Very nice, Jack thought.

"So, where are we off to?" Nick asked. Jacqueline asked if they had been round to Nice Harbour, they hadn't and she continued to suggest that they should not be too late as she wanted to pick them up at nine o'clock the next morning, to avoid the traffic. So, perhaps a drink followed by a walk up by the castle for a 'Crêpe & Coffee' tonight. 'Quite an organiser,' Jack thought. They climbed in the back of the little Fiat 500, a tiny little car but fun. Even though Nick's legs were curled up in the back he was amused especially when Colin opened the roof so they could see the stars. Jacqueline pointed out Place Massena, where all the festivals were held. Left past the flower market and up past the World Wars memorial. Very impressive, set into the rocks. They continued round there and down into the large harbour. They parked the car and walked to some large ships or ferries, which went to Corsica and along the side, where there were some great-looking fish restaurants.

Nick nudged Jack saying, "I could do with visiting one of those."

"Perhaps another day," Jacqueline dropped in, "but if you want fish restaurants you wait till tomorrow in St Tropez."

The boys were blown away by the size of the boats in the harbour, huge three masted schooner-type boats, which they thought must enter the 'Tall Ship Race' and cruisers, the size of car ferries with speed boats strapped to the back decks. Having had enough, they were back in the little car up the hill to a little restaurant. Just inside there was a hotplate on which the crêpes were cooked. Colin chose Brandy, Nick joined him and Jacqueline suggested that Jack try Grand Marnier, so he did, and delicious it was too. Then coffees, espressos, or black little ones again. No, Jack couldn't get the hang of them at all, when the bill came Nick went for it so they could split the cost as he held the kitty they had, but Jacqueline insisted on paying. Colin and Nick got on very well looking at all the different cars and bikes that were around, so Jacqueline, on returning to the car suggested Jack sat in the front.

"Watch her!!" Colin said, "She likes English boys."

Dropped off at the hotel at about eleven o'clock, they promised to be ready at nine o'clock the next day. Jack got another kiss on the cheek before leaving the car, and it wasn't from Colin!

The next day they woke early ready for breakfast in the dining room. The sun was already shining brightly and the sky was bright blue as it seemed to be every day they had been in France. Nick made up for the night before, asking for more bread and coffee. The coffee came in a big bowl-like cup and they thought sterilised milk was used but with sugar, they drank loads and considering they had always been 'tea boys' it came as a surprise to them both. To finish with croissants and apricot jam made it for them both.

Having thrown their swimmers in a bag, they were outside on the terrace at quarter to nine ready and waiting. "Toot toot" went the horn, familiar now as she had used it last night when picking them up and on leaving. They were soon down at the parking area and climbing in the back. Jacqueline drove the Fiat very nippily, in and out of lanes, down and across by the railway station, along by the railway,

"Bit grotty," Jack said to Nick.

"Not everywhere in Nice is beautiful!" Jacqueline dropped in.

Then up out to the airport, which they had seen at the end of the beach, then all of a sudden they were on a dual carriageway, a bit like a motorway with big signs saying 'Marseille'. Those roads had people dodging about from lane to lane when they suddenly came to a toll-booth with long queues. Quickly through and on their way again.

"Funny, paying for motorways," Nick said.

"However, they are better than the roads in England." Jacqueline agreed as she took her little car there last year and found it quite a challenge. Every now and then on the road you would see places called 'Aires'.

"What are they?" Nick again asked.

"I'll show you the next one." She nipped off at the next 'aire' through the trees to the parking area.

"There you are."

"So what's this for?" Nick asked.

"To save fatigue and in turn, to stop people having accidents." Jacqueline continued, "You stop here, use the toilet, walk amongst the trees, even stretch on the bars over there. If you're French and it's lunch time, you get your food out the car, with a tablecloth and plates, sit on the picnic benches, then have an hour for lunch before hurrying on your route"

Jack said, "Come on then, let's climb out and use the facilities." On returning he sat next to Jacqueline while the other two hadn't returned. "France is very different isn't it? You have different values than the English."

"Don't look so worried," as she gently stroked the side of his face with her petite hands. "I love England though."

55

Back in the car, Colin got in the rear with Nick and Jack stayed where he was. He chatted away even more about the family values of France with his new friend Jacqueline. Sunday they all went out for lunch. Grandparents, children, grandchildren, it was an important day of the week. Jack said that he did the same at home but as yet his sister was not yet married or had children that he knew of. Jack rambled on about sister Kate and her silly boyfriend Richard and how they often treated him like a twelve year old. She started asking about any girlfriends he had at home. He had none, which he hadn't. Jacqueline seemed sceptical but, at this, Nick chimed in, "He's a disaster with girls, always picks the wrong ones, not like me!" Nick being his usual modest self.

They came off a slip road and round to a small toll-booth at St. Maximim with signposts to Draguignan and St. Tropez, so at least it wasn't all the way to Aix-en-Provence, which is where the motorway carried on to. From here they joined another wiggly road running through a valley of pine trees. Jack chatted some more but soon nodded off to sleep, awakening at St. Maxime as they sharply turned onto the coast road again. They were back to the blue, blue sea and the scenery was again a little different. There were large houses and villas that dominated each side of the road draped with climbing plants, Bougainvillea with its rich purple flowers, others with their bright orange trumpet flowers called Campsis. Nick and Jack hadn't come across Campsis before and they also spotted Plumbago, with their pale blue flowers.

They discussed what it must be like to grow all these plants outside. Jack had only used them in the Royal Festival Hall when working on the indoor gardens. Palm trees and a Pittisporum with a larger leaf than they had ever seen before, all grew here by the sea. The plants were very different to those near Nice; there were more pines, not Scots but Corsican, with the slightly longer needles and larger cones on them.

"Private beaches, villas right on the beach. That must be great!" Colin said.

"Sea, wine and women all in one place!!" Jacqueline remarked, "Is that all you think about?!"

The boys all mumbled, Jack sitting next to her trying not to comment.

Next they went to a place called Cogolin, where there was a huge junction and Jacqueline swung the little car to the left and they were soon passing some even bigger villas and houses and eventually after about ten minutes they arrived at St. Tropez. Nick and Jack were very quiet as they took in the sights, delightful houses and villas, narrow streets and shops.

"Isn't this where Bridget Bardot lives?" Jack asked.

Jacqueline laughed saying, "I don't think you're likely to see her – the house is down towards the beach and has a fence all round in front, in fact, she's becoming quite a recluse after acting in a few films."

They continued driving through the small streets up to the top of what must have been a fort or defence in times gone by. She stopped the car by the roadside and all the boys clambered out.

"Have a look and we'll drive down to the port, park up and after a wander have some lunch," Jacqueline instructed.

The areas within the fortification were covered in long grass drying in the hot sun and with the odd wild purpley-blue Scabious showing colour. The view was mainly out to sea as they were now standing on the peninsula. They could see land on one side leading to the port of St. Tropez which was just out of sight, but a couple of large motor cruisers were approaching.

"It'll be great to see those boats, they're huge!" Nick commented.

In the other direction they could see a distant peninsula which had a long rugged end, with what looked like marshy land in between. Beyond the peninsula were more beaches and what looked like harbours with even more yachts. Taking advantage of the rough ground the boys relieved themselves; it would have made an amusing picture Jack thought, as they stood in a row on top of the fort. Jacqueline patiently waited. The car then took them back round some more tight corners, passing houses with balconies on the first floors that had bright oranges and reds of the Campsis and more Bougainvilleas. Suddenly, they arrived at the port with lines of yachts all moored stern in that were tied to huge rings set into the stone edges. It looked very impressive indeed, in fact the boys got out of the car in awed silence. Jacqueline had parked adjacent to the edge of the port in front of a very smart looking restaurant called La Provencal. Colin and Nick were off in a flash as they had seen a Ferrari parked up the other end. Jack waited for Jacqueline to park her car.

"Thanks for waiting," she said, and she held his hand briefly and squeezed it. They strolled along the row of yachts worth millions of pounds, to the corner where just outside the harbour huge boats were moored.

"Nearly the size of a ferry!" he remarked. "Well maybe not that huge."

"Those are owned by large companies," Jacqueline told him and she pointed at one with several boats looking like speedboats on a lower back deck.

"Just look at that," Jack said, "boats on boats, ridiculous!"

"That belongs to the President of Fiat, I think!"

"He didn't make all that money on my car did he!!" They laughed. What an amazing place, Jack had seen the wealth on the south coast near Nice, but this was unreal. The two of them sat on a large lump of stone on the far end of the harbour, continuing to watch the sailing boats and cruisers coming and going. The sun was strong and Jacqueline had a soft, blue linen hat to protect her head.

"You should watch the sun, it's dangerous," and she squeezed his hand again, but lingering a little longer. Jack turned to face her looking closely into her eyes, they didn't move for a while, until they heard Nick and Colin noisily approaching.

She nudged him in the ribs as Nick called out, "And what have you two been up to?"

"Nothing, why?" Jack smiled.

"Wow, what an amazing view of the boats," Nick shouted and Jack repeated the story of the President of Fiat's boat.

"Let's eat," said Colin and Nick in unison. "I'm starving."

Jacqueline walked along past the main restaurants to one in the middle of the line of them facing the boats. Being ushered to a front table by the waiter the boys all ordered beers and Jacqueline a Diablo-Menthe. The sun shone on them and they sat in front of the terrace with one of the boats facing them. Cars came to park next to the Fiat, not that the Fiat minded the odd Porsche or Ferrari by it. Colin asked Nick to take a picture of him next to the Ferrari with Jacqueline and Jack, beers in the air to give him a cheer.

"What a poser!" Jack remarked.

"So let's hear some more about you?" Jacqueline continued.

Jack told her of the good times that he and Nick had working in the gardens, their trips to the pub, up to the South Downs.

"Where I've been to stay near the Chilterns, they sound a little like that."

He described the back of Brighton with its rolling corn fields, leafy lanes and the odd nursery, missing out anything about Penny, his former lover and lady friend.

"You'll have to take me there when I next come to England to study."

The lunch was fantastic starting with a fish Hors-d'oeuvre or something Jack couldn't pronounce and followed by gambas, which were a cross between lobster and large prawns. The boys started by picking at them but Jacqueline showed them how to break open the shells and suck out every bit of meat. Jack watched her lips as she pursed them around some of the shell of the fish and then dabbed them with the bread. Nick nudged him with his foot under the table and then winked at him. Jack knew what he was implying, and yes, she did like Jack. They finished the fish with a salad and then desserts. Crème Caramel, Apple Tart and Ice cream for the lads, and an espresso, which was a small strong coffee, for Jacqueline. The waiter offered more wine so Jacqueline suggested they try some Muscat with their desserts. Jack thought it tasted like sugar water, but after drinking it and finding it strong, they sat in a warm stupor watching the lovely people of St. Tropez go past!

Jacqueline treated them all even though they complained, and suggested they walk outside the port on the other side where there was a beach. This was the side Bridget Bardot had her house, but they weren't to get excited, as they were unlikely to see her. In the heat of the afternoon it seemed a long walk but eventually they sat on the sand. Having taken their swimming bag, Nick was suddenly in his trunks then in the water. Colin was soon asleep and Jacqueline took her skirt off to reveal very nice thighs, set off in a black bikini bottom. Jack eventually took his shirt off and shoes and sat next to her as she lay quietly, close by. He stroked her arm and she smiled, "I'm pleased to have met you Jack."

He watched to check Colin was asleep, although his snoring indicated he was! Nick was still swimming so Jack carefully leant over and kissed her on the forehead. She smiled so he kissed her again and she got up onto her elbow and faced him.

"So, young man, tell me all about your girlfriends in England."

Jack reddened and moved further away. "I haven't got a girlfriend."

"Come on, that's what they all say." He didn't know what to reply, and eventually, "Well, I did have one but she got another boyfriend and since then I've been going out with my mates."

She pulled him to her and kissed him on the lips and he then discovered that they were as tasty as he'd thought watching her eat at lunchtime. She lay down again and Jack settled on his side next to her, stroking the side of her face and neck, running his finger across her lips and then moving to kiss her, as he did her arms went round him and he ended up half on top of her. He could feel her lips kissing his cheeks and then he was in heaven as their lips met and her tongue found its way into his mouth.

He could feel himself getting very interested then both their passion was stopped by Nick returning from the sea and shaking water over them both. "Sorry, am I disturbing you?"

Jack, again turned scarlet.

"Come on Jack what about a swim?"

"Go on," Jacqueline said.

He discreetly changed into his trunks covering himself with a towel. By this time his interest had definitely deflated but he turned to her blowing a kiss as they made their way to the sea.

"Jack, look at all these women on the beach, some must fancy two lovely men like us!"

There were a few that were topless but not usually the younger women, but still Jack could not keep his eyes off them. He seemed to find half-naked women fascinating and how their boobs were all different shapes and sizes. As his thoughts were of Jacqueline and what she would be like, they hit the water. It was initially cold but after dunking under and swimming for a couple of strokes underwater and emerging it was warm and comfortable. Jack turned over on his back and gazed at the sun, his booze at lunchtime still left him a little dazed but Nick swum out as he always did leaving Jack to float with his dreams. What to do tomorrow? He really quite liked Jacqueline but she'd be working tomorrow in the bookshop, then there was Helena, would she be at the beach tomorrow? A tasty Dutch girl she was but it was difficult to get her away from her friends for a good time. He was just contemplating who could be the best when Nick came thundering back to him.

"How are you getting on with Jacqueline? Are you in with her? Does she fancy you?" A few beers and Nick went on and on.

"If you didn't keep disturbing us I'd be able to tell you," retorted Jack.

They swam along the beach and then came out of the water allowing them to peruse the scene of girls and ladies along the beach on their way back to a sleeping Colin and Jacqueline. They sat chatting on the beach for some time with Colin snoring until Jacqueline suggested they should return to Nice. The long lunch had stretched into the afternoon and it was now gone five.

The boys would be late for their supper at Les Cigalles, although they still weren't hungry after their lunch. Could they meet up that night? They were wondering.

"Let's see what time we get back" Jacqueline suggested.

Jack sat in the front resting his hand across the rear of the driver's seat, the lads in the back were soon asleep and Jack gently caressed her neck as she drove. "You're quite a distraction Jack, if we hadn't any passengers I'd be tempted to stop the car…!"

The drive back seemed long and as they turned onto the coastal road, they joined a queue that slowly trickled along. Some amazing houses on the left, however, looked a little run down. Jack chatted away about imagining all those beautiful people that must have lived there before the turn of the century. The parties, the fun and sadly a property company will come along in the future and build blocks of apartments. They then passed a massive campsite on the right running down to the sea. What a fabulous place to stay! Jacqueline then asked whether Jack ever fancied camping, if so, when he came again, they could go off to the South West of France and up to the Black Mountains near Carcassone and Toulouse. 'When I come again…' thought Jack. He did not really fancy camping, the damp in the tent and sleeping on the ground, no he liked his luxuries!

The traffic was really slow and often stopped, and this time Jacqueline leaned across and kissed Jack firmly on the lips. He blushed as the car behind hooted as there was a gap in front. The boys slept on and Jack continued his caressing running his fingers just below the back of her neckline and to her shoulders. Jack realised this was a distraction and when they started back onto a twisty road through the pines, he stopped. Jacqueline complained but Jack just replied, "Later."

"Is that a promise?" she asked. Jack noticed the signs reminding drivers how long it would be to drive to different towns and then another with the same message.

"Do they think we're stupid or something?" Jack said.

"No," said Jacqueline, "it is to make you think!" The road continued to twist and eventually it rose up a straight stretch under the motorway and joined the Draguignan route just by the toll-gate. Jacqueline picked up a ticket on the way through the barrier and they were soon off down the motorway.

"I could get used to this life you know, France is a lovely place to live!" said Jack enthusiastically.

"You would have to learn the language better but I'll teach you," replied Jacqueline.

Jack soon joined the boys in sleep as the little car hurried along.

He woke when the car stopped – but that was the toll-gate down near Cannes, which is the last one on the way to Nice. They were past the new blocks of apartments built close to the road and then the racetrack, the airport and into Nice. They had all driven back for several hours and the traffic had been very heavy. The Fiat had plodded away down to the main road to Nice and even Jack, whose hand had caressed Jacqueline's neck, ears, legs and anywhere else he could decently caress without causing an accident, had himself fallen asleep too. When he awoke apologising, they were in the heart of Nice, just turning passed the station up to the hotel. When the car stopped and before the boys in the back awoke, Jack moved across and kissed Jacqueline on the lips. As their mouths met it was like magic and Jack was physically moved. She pulled away whispering in his ear, "We have an audience…" as Colin had opened his eyes. Jack shook Nick, who snorted and wiped his eyes.

"Are we home?" he asked yawning.

"Well yes," replied Jack.

"Okay, thanks Jacqueline it's been fantastic! Are we meeting for a few beers tonight then?"

Jack reminded him how tired he looked, Nick argued forgetting all about their arrangement they had made with the Dutch crowd! 'Oops' thought Jack this is getting tricky. He eventually gave up trying to follow Jack's thoughts and climbed out the car. Nick went off in a huff.

"You have upset poor Nick," Jacqueline said as Jack bent down and kissed her goodbye. "So when do I see you again Jack?" she asked.

"Tomorrow?"

"No, I have got to help my father at his work, okay. The day after, do you fancy going to Eze? I know you are after a free ride?" exclaimed Jacqueline laughing.

"I have never been there," chimed in Colin.

"Okay we'll make a day of it and I will arrange it," replied Jacqueline.

Jack wandered into the hotel to be greeted by Monsieur Christophe, "Nick tells me he is sorry but you have not eaten dinner, go sit down in the salle à manger and we will prepare something for you," said a concerned Monsieur Christophe.

Jack thanked him very much and dashed up to their room and splashed some water under his arms and changed his top and dragged Nick with him. It was not until they had eaten some delicious onion soup and a huge basket of bread that they started talking again.

"Well why couldn't we go out with them tonight?" asked Nick.

"Because you and I had arranged to go back to that bar where your friend Anne-Marie and that lovely Dutch girl, Helena are tonight!" exclaimed Jack getting very irritated.

A plate of cold meat arrived with Grace serving them. Her English was not quite so good but she asked if they had enjoyed their visit to St. Tropez and had been good boys and then she asked if they would like some coffee. The answers were all "Oui," except for the coffee. The meats were interesting, beef nearly raw, spiced sausage and some white looking meat, which could have been veal, they were not sure. The other meat was tough but tasty, may be it was horse Nick suggested as they tucked into it all. Madame very kindly left them a plate of fruit all prepared too.

Once they had eaten they were off back out to the main road and down to the café. It was nearly nine o'clock and the sun had set beyond the coast now. Tonight all their friends were outside, Nick soon joined up with a beer and his arm around Anne-Marie. Jack's friend Helena was not there but some of the others had come over. He moved around grabbing a chair and sat just behind them, he tried hard not to ask where she was but eventually curiosity got the better of him

"She will soon be here," said Hugo one of the Dutch boys. "Stunning isn't she?" he commented and Jack had to admit she was. He was really torn between a stunning blonde, tanned skin full bodied Dutch girl and a petite sexy French girl; it could get tricky, especially in the evenings. He hoped Jacqueline would not suddenly turn up as she now knew where Nick liked to drink. Tomorrow Nick had promised Colin that they would hit the Casino, Jack would try to get in but he was younger than Nick and Colin. While he was day dreaming about all these things, who should walk in but Helena as Hugo had said she would. Jack had forgotten how lovely she was with a toss of her long blonde hair and a wide smile; she walked across the bar with another friend towards Jack. He leapt to his feet and hugged her giving her a kiss on the cheek, not satisfied with that she kissed him fully on the lips! The friend she had come in with was also very pretty and amazingly tall, she was at least six feet high and Jack was not particularly short but she towered above him. They both wanted beers so Jack raised his hand for a waiter to take their order.

Sitting behind the big group, it gave Jack the opportunity to talk to Helena as he understood they would only be in France until the end of the week.

"So where shall we go tomorrow Helena?" asked Jack. He was wondering if they had been to St. Raphael.

"Yes but how will you get there?" she asked.

"Oh Nick and I will buzz down on the train," Jack replied.

"Oh we always take the bus everywhere."

"Trains are much more fun and generally not much more expensive."

"The buses stop at the station, so we could all meet there that would be great," said Helena.

"Okay but I will have to get Nick to agree and he's with Anna-Marie," replied Jack. They sat back enjoying the atmosphere, Helena put her arm around Jack pulling him closer.

"Are you coming to Holland to see me when we are home Jack or is it just a holiday hit?" she asked with her big blue eyes gazing at him. She told Jack that she lived out of Amsterdam near the coast at Schevingham. She described the wide sandy beaches and that her parent's house was just out of the town in rural surroundings. Her brother was older and had a job working with a fish company, something to do with processing and her father was a teacher. Jack seemed to be getting the whole family history, she seemed to be getting rather keen. He was getting anxious as to what to say, perhaps just play along and see where it goes.

"Okay Jack, we know you are a gardener but what about girlfriends, brothers, sisters and family and your life in London?"

He thought he had explained some of this on the beach, so why again Jack thought. So he went through his family information for Helena, with her taking an amazing amount of notice, squeezing his arm occasionally and even stroking his hair, which he really hated.

So, leaping up, he offered to get some beers and joined Nick, who was well ahead as normal on the beer front. The talk got sillier as the evening went on, the trouble with Nick was that with a few beers, he chatted away and of course Jack was busy trying to keep the Dutch and French link well apart.

Nick eventually agreed with going to Juan-Les-Pins and to meet at the station around ten o'clock , they paid the bar bill and left for a walk down to the beach. Hand in hand, Jack with Helena and Nick with Anna-Marie, walked down past more bars and restaurants and ended up emerging onto the Promenade Des Anglais by the Negresco Hotel. There is something about Nice, the palm trees, the warm smell of the air scented with lavender and pine wood, and as they crossed to the promenade, they could hear the gentle sound of the sea on the beach. As they walked along, Jack slid his arm around her waist and he could feel her flesh beneath her thin dress. Helena suddenly stopped, turning towards Jack, she put her arms around his neck and their lips met. Jack could now feel her whole body against his but just as he was enjoying the sensation, she pulled away.

"Let's walk some more," Jack suggested, keeping his arm around her and Helena now slid her arm under his shirt and caressed his back with her fingers. They were walking towards the harbour and soon came to a large covered area with seats facing the sea. Let's sit for a while, there were deck chairs in the front of the area, so Jack pulled them together and they sat close.

"I can think of more intimate places to be Jack," remarked Helena.

"Shsh... quiet," Jack whispered in her ear as they turned towards each other and kissed. The embraces became more intense and Jack moved his hand up towards her firm breasts. She moved his hand away. "Come on Jack, not here," murmured Helena.

Time just slipped by as eventually Helena said it was midnight and that they should be going. Her hotel was back up near the bar and Jack popped his head around the corner to see where Nick was. There was no sign of him, so they walked on up to the hotel.

"Shall I see you to your bedroom door Mademoiselle?" Jack said, tongue in cheek.

"I wouldn't, there are four of us in there!" said Helena.

They stood next to the plants by the door and again Jack felt her warm body against his. He pulled away due to his ardour becoming rather aroused. She was a little shocked he felt but he kissed her again saying he would be off and would see her tomorrow around ten o'clock at the main station. Jack now had the long walk back to his pension, he crept in through the front door and into their room to find Nick completely clothed and sound asleep on top of his bed. Jack was soon tucked up after a glass of water to wash down the beers.

Nick and Jack awoke to a commotion outside their door, Jack was the first to realise and poked his nose out of their door to see what was going on in the foyer of the hotel. A large family group was arguing with Monsieur Christophe and Madame Grace, it sounded very heated but as they were arguing in French, speaking quicker and quicker, he had no idea what it was about. So, back to waking up Nick and persuading him to not only wash, but to get changed too.

Eventually the noise from the foyer stopped and life seemed to have returned to normal. The boys ventured out for breakfast in the dining room. Monsieur Christophe explained that a family had arrived on the overnight sleeper from Paris and they had not confirmed their booking with Hotel Les Cigalles and fortunately Monsieur Christophe had kept their original paperwork to prove it. So after more shouting and arguing they all left to find another hotel.

The bread and croissants were ready on their table and were delicious. Nick drank several large bowls of coffee to help with his bad head.

"Not drinking like this tonight! And we will have to dress really smartly for the Casino," said Nick

"But first Nick, I have arranged to go to Juan-les-Pins with the Dutch crowd and you did agree."

"Well I know I agreed but I really can't remember much about last night," Nick sighed nursing his head.

"We did say we would meet them at about ten o'clock at the station so we really need to hurry Nick," said Jack getting irritable.

Chapter VI

Thieves at large

At the station there were at least nine in the group when they arrived, Jack and Nick led the way buying the tickets. Luckily most of the rush hour had finished and the queues had died down, there were about five booths open so they all went to different ones to see who could get served first. The people in the queues were buying simple tickets; others weekly even overnight trips up to other parts of Europe. Jack loved trains nearly as much as Nick. They checked the times and found that in five minutes one was due coming from Monte Carlo onto platform 1. They crowded onto the station like a school party and it wasn't until then that Helena came over to Jack.

"Aren't you talking to me today Jack?" asked Helena and gave him a huge kiss. The train soon arrived; it was a big heavy steam engine with a mainline train going up to Paris. They climbed aboard and settled in a couple of compartments. Jack sat next to Helena and began chatting to her.

"How do you get from Amsterdam to Nice by train?"

"I don't know, we travelled down by coach, which only took fifteen hours," replied Helena.

"What a hell of a long journey!" exclaimed Jack.

"It was only fifteen hours" said Helena.

"Well I suppose it took us nearly that long on the train all the way from Woodmanstern, in Surrey," said Jack.

"Where?" asked Helena.

"It is where I live," explained Jack. Then he went into details about it being a suburb of London and Surrey was a county in England. It sounded like a similar system in Holland.

It was hot on the train so they pulled a big window down. Nick now had his head out looking at the sea and the little marinas as they travelled along. The train's first stop was Juan-Les-Pins, now they all wanted to go on to Cannes – the following stop.

"No," said Nick, "Juan is much nicer!"

So as the train pulled in, Juan it was. Jack had not entered into this discussion as in the corner against the corridor, Helena had been laying against him, her warm flesh so close yet so far from him. He had stroked the top of her arms gently and up her neck and under her beautiful soft hair. These Dutch girls were tasty he thought. Nick had already started to acquaint himself with Diana, another of the girls in the group. She was really tall, blonde and good looking.

It is quite a walk to the beach as the railway at this section of the coast lays back a couple of blocks. They walked down the main street leading to a roundabout on the road running along the promenade.

"Which way Nick?" someone shouted.

"Turn right," he replied. So on the right it was, each section of beach had a small roundabout, cars and motorbikes and scooters were everywhere.

"Busy town, eh...?" said one of the boys. Nick suggested stopping for a beer but everyone wanted to get down to the beach.

"Come on Nick," Jack said, he walked next to him and pointed out that the bars will have beers and chips, a bit more expensive but not a disaster. With that Nick grabbed Diana saying

"Come on we will be first on the beach," The others followed. Not Jack, he held back hand in hand with Helena and walked slowly down the road looking at the shops and people.

Down on the beach, sand glorious sand, the girls were thrilled as they had been on Nice beach most of the time. Towels were laid out, tops off and there they were oiling their bodies to achieve a good tan before they returned to Holland. Jack changed discretely into his trunks, with Helena sat next to him teasing and trying to pull away the towel. Her yellow bikini that she had on today looked fantastic against her tan, not much of it either.

"New one?" Jack asked.

"No just a change," said Helena.

"You look fantastic," remarked Jack.

"Come on with you, swimming will you cool off...!" commented Helena and so it did as they waded out into the blue Mediterranean Sea.

All were in the sea, even Nick and Diana who seemed to be getting on very well with linked arms and treading water, what were they up to! Jack and Helena after spending a great deal of time on the float, returned to the beach. She started drying off herself, Jack offered to dry off her back. She undid her straps and Jack nearly fell over patting her gently.

"Come on, dry me!" demanded Helena laughing. He did just that and then put sun oil on her back and shoulders. What he could have done with her front! As Helena settled down, she went back to her bag for Nivea cream and looked for her purse to offer Jack a beer. She rummaged right through her bag, looking increasingly worried.

"Has anyone seen my purse at all?" called Helena. Nobody had. She started to panic, "It's got my driving licence and about six hundred francs in it for me to buy my gifts!" cried Helena. "Come on, has anyone been here all the time?" she shouted.

"Well we were all in the water together for quite a long time," said Jack trying to stay calm. Everyone searched their bags and one of the girls, Marianne, had also lost her purse and her camera.

"Someone has been here going through our things!" shouted Helena. Jack jumped up. "Marianne, how much did you have in yours?" she asked. Marianne had a similar amount too.

"We ought to report this. That is a lot of money and a camera being stolen too! Let's ask at the bar to see what we can do," Jack replied. The boys headed over to the bar and asked if anyone spoke English, fortunately the barman spoke a little and he kindly called the police for them. They all crowded together, there were nine of them and all checked their possessions. What had started out as a good day was turning horribly wrong.

Within minutes they could hear the police sirens and a police car arrived with two gendarmes jumping out on to the pavement. They were soon on the beach near the bar where Jack and Nick were. With the help of the barman, they explained that two of the Dutch girls had had their money, purses and camera taken. The police were totally dismissive of the boys and marched over to the Dutch girls across the sand. They tried to explain what they had lost but none of them could speak much French in the group. The policemen asked them for identification but that was stolen from their purses. The boys were amused as all the Dutch had identification cards like most Europeans, they hoped they were never stopped as they had no intention of carrying their passports around with them all day and everyday.

The interrogation went on, what colour were the purses, how much money was in them, was there anything else to help identify the contents. The questions went on and on, one could just imagine the amount of things the girls had in their bags and the challenge of explaining that to the policemen. It was just as well they were girls as the policemen were young and it made it all the more fun, well that is what Jack was thinking. As for the camera, they wanted to know the make, type, model and even the colour of the case and lens type. Now they wanted them to go to the police station to sign a statement and collect a crime number. The girls with Jack had the directions translated by the barman, who had been really helpful through all this drama. The police station was beyond the railway and was a brick built building with the obligatory French flag flying from the mast outside. With quite a struggle, they were eventually, after much discussion in 'pigeon' French, escorted to a small room and had to wait what seemed ages. The original policeman from the beach arrived with a report sheet, all typed out in French, they did not understand a word that was written but the two girls signed their names as requested and put their names below filling out their home addresses underneath. They all thought the matters were finished but they were asked to stay which scared them all a bit. Marianne and Helena looked at each other and did as asked and waited ages again. Jack was growing impatient and went out of the door to the desk where a policeman came over and spoke very quickly in French. Jack did not understand but recognised the word 'important' and went back again to the girls looking bemused.

"We are going to help them or something he said, what a way to spend a day of our holiday," Jack sighed. Just as they thought they had been completely forgotten an older man came in with several sheets of paper and a thick folder in his hand. He spoke very good English with a heavy accent and explained that he would like the girls and Jack to look at some photographs of some men that may help them find the culprit.

They all sat looking at pages of men's heads and shoulders. They turned about two thirds of the pages, when Marianne stopped them.

"This Moroccan-looking man offered cheap watches to us," Marianne said.

"Are you sure Mademoiselle Marianne?" asked the policeman. Jack agreed he had seen him too as he had shown an interest in the fake 'Rolex' watches for 20 francs. Well the police became very excited at this, not that the girls or Jack could understand them! Eventually the last policeman who had spoken to them struggled to explain this was not the first time that he had been picked out. However finding him and putting him in a parade and getting holidaymakers like themselves together and to be available for a court case, could prove quite difficult. Anyway the policemen were pleased and gathering their paperwork, the girls and Jack left the police station a little relieved and a bit bemused.

They walked slowly back to the beach to find their friends to find they had all dressed and were enjoying a few beers at the bar, ready to go back to Nice. The barman could not have been more helpful.

"Monsieur, mademoiselles, we are so sorry for your treatment here in our country and let me at least offer you all a drink," said the bar owner. They all accepted their drinks and then the chef brought out two big bowls of french fries sprinkled in salt… which they all enjoyed.

Jack was beginning to worry about the situation he was now getting into, he had not experienced becoming so involved with people. He felt mean that he could not offer to see Helena later as they had agreed to go to the Casino that night. It was now mid-afternoon and they all decided that they had had enough of Juan-Les-Pins. They walked back to the station to wait for their train, which this time was a diesel railcar unit with the doors left open as they travelled along. That seemed very casual to Nick and Jack. They arrived back in Nice and on to the station.

"Drinks are on me, let's go to our favourite bar," called Nick. They all agreed and the mood picked up except for Marianne, who was concerned about how she was going to get a new identification card.

"We'll phone the Dutch Embassy in Paris tomorrow, I am sure they will help," said Helena.

"Yes, they'll let you out of the country," joked Nick. Jack made a face at him and sitting next to Helena, he put his arm around her, kissing her gently on the cheek.

"Thank you," she said "for being with us."

"That's what friends are for," replied Jack

"Now I know you will keep in touch when we go home," smiled Helena.

Jack was really struggling with his emotions as she turned to him kissing him firmly on the lips. Nick started whistling at them from across the table.

"If it's a trip to the police station that achieves that, I am off, who's coming?" Nick shouted.

"You are cruel," said Helena, "Jack has been great to us, he is a lovely man. It was a long session hanging around in the police station."

Jack was getting worried about Nick, he had drunk quite a few beers and he would forget where they were going that evening. Jack excused himself as Nick walked to the bar.

"Hi Buddy, you're well in there aren't you?" jeered Nick.

"Yes may be but remember we are going to the Casino with Jacqueline and Colin this evening," said Jack.

"Oh bugger, I had forgotten," said Nick. "We had better cancel the beers and be off."

"Sorry guys, something has come up. Jack and I have to be going now." he said rather too casually. "Got things to do." He blurted this all out before Jack could reach Helena. So Jack asked innocently what he was talking about.

"We've that old friend that we told you about, he had asked us to join him tonight," Nick said.

"What tonight after all we have been through today, are you sure it is not that French friend of his that you are interested in Jack?" asked Helena.

"No of course not," retorted Jack a bit too quickly.

"Well cancel it then," she replied.

"We can't," replied Nick coming to his friend's aid. This did not please Helena and as Jack went to sit down with his arm to go around her, Helena got up and moved away.

"Can we see you tomorrow on the beach?" asked Jack.

"We'll see," replied Helena tossing her long hair, "and I thought you really had feelings for me, Jack."

Nick in the meantime still standing called to him, "Are you coming Jack?"

Reluctantly Jack left giving Helena a peck on the top of her forehead, which is all she would let him do.

"See you all soon," Nick shouted across the bar to them as he dragged Jack away. Reluctantly he caught up with Nick on the main drag to walk back to their hotel.

Late again and they had to look smart for their evening out.

Chapter VII

Casino

Back to the hotel, have a shower, eat dinner and go out to meet Jacqueline and Colin. Nick was keen to have a look at the Casino, so they dressed in their best trousers and short sleeved shirts.

When she walked in to collect them, Jaqueline smiled, saying, "You guys look handsome…!" to which they were both very pleased.

Colin was waiting in the car and they were soon on their way down to the Casino, which is situated on the Promenade des Anglais. They parked around the back and walked to the grand steps, which led up to the Casino. The foyer had huge chandeliers hanging on long gold chains and the ceilings were really high and very highly decorated. Men in dinner suits and bow ties were everywhere and as they walked towards the Casino entrance, two men politely asked them to register. At the desk they were all asked for identification, Jacqueline passed over her 'carte d'identite', Colin his passport, Nick forgot his but had his driving licence and Jack had his passport. There was a lot of reading and checking going on and then they approached Jack announcing that he was too young to enter!

Nick was amused, so Jack said, "Don't worry I will go to a bar and meet you afterwards."

Further discussions went on and they felt it was unfair on Jack, eventually Jacqueline decided it would be better to go to a bar with Jack and then pick up the boys around midnight. Having settled that, Jacqueline suggested taking Jack to a bar along from Nice at a village called Villefranche by the sea.

"Come on Jack, let's go!" Jacqueline walked with Jack back around the corner to the little Fiat and climbed in. "So where shall we go? Along to Villefranche, there is a great bar come restaurant there and we can watch the sea." Jacqueline commented smiling.

Into gear and off back onto the front past the palm trees and going towards Nice harbour.

"Do you want to stop in the Old town?" she asked.

"No, let's keep going and go on to this village you were telling me about."

So with that settled, they drove up out of the harbour climbing passed walls festooned with Campsis and Bougainvillea still in flower and passing magnificent villas and houses. Jack was thinking how at home Bougainvillea only flowers the once, when Jacqueline suddenly said how the Bougainvilleas seem to go on flowering all summer Jack could not believe they were thinking the same thoughts at the same time! Telepathy or was it a message, had he got something really going here.

"You are quiet Jack," Jacqueline commented.

"Just thinking," replied Jack. "You are lovely," he remarked as he stroked the back of her neck underneath her dark hair.

The road dropped slowly back towards the sea and Jacqueline suddenly swung the car off to the right down a fairly steep hill. The road was narrow but opened up to a car park in front of a harbour full of small fishing boats. Jack was really surprised not to see a load of expensive yachts moored here. How fantastic and they really were fishing boats with their numbers on the sides in black in a red coloured square. They parked by a large memorial to the dead during the Second World War and were happy to jump out of the car walking straight to the edge of the quay. From this area a narrow road led along the edge of the sea and against the cliff was an array of restaurants and a couple of bars then past more parking.

"Where does this lead to…? Oh a beach!" commented Jack.

"It is said to have one of the deepest natural harbours in the world. It was sheltered from the east where Monaco and Monte Carlo were by a piece of land sticking out called St. Jean-Cap-Ferrat, where some seriously wealthy people had their houses and villas right down to the water's edge."

Jacqueline grabbed his hand to pull him away from his dreams as he gazed across this bay of what now, as darkness fell, had become deep turquoise coloured water. They went to a bar with tables outside. The chairs were unusually comfortable, wood with cushioned seats.

Jacqueline ordered Kir Royale for them both before Jack could say a word. "Des oliviers Mademoiselle?"

Jack was having a lesson in French without realizing it. The drinks turned up in tall fluted glasses and a large bowl of mixed coloured olives.

She picked up her glass, "To us Jack, it is the first time I have had you all to myself for an evening," smiling at him. Jack felt a little worried at her positive attitude, but as he always told himself, 'I live in England, she lives in France and the same with Helena from Holland. Sit back and enjoy yourself' he told himself.

Jacqueline had moved her chair around slightly so they both faced the water. The sun had now gone long ago over the horizon and the night sky was clear with loads of sparkling stars in it. She stroked his arm gently, making him feel warm inside.

"So what is this fizzy drink Jacqueline?" asked Jack enjoying every sip.

"It is Cassis liqueur with Champagne mixed together, try some olives Jack, they are delicious."

He did but as hard as he tried, he really didn't like them and washed the bitter flavour away with another swig of his drink. Jacqueline ordered another two for them but she drank hers more slowly savouring the beautiful flavours. When the waiter brought them out, he ordered some cashew nuts, which he found much more to his liking. He put his hand on her soft skin just above her knee and slowly moved his fingers across her thigh, which resulted in Jacqueline leaning across and giving Jack a delicious kiss. She put her arm across his shoulder with her hand just below his shirt collar, her fingers were very tender with their touches.

They chatted about life in France and England, the differences and how life was supposed to be stricter in France. The importance of family life, meals together and particularly on Sunday, the whole family might go out for lunch including the grandparents and if there were any, the grandchildren too. Jack thought this was good and told her of how they all got together on Sundays for a roast dinner that his mother had cooked. She was a great cook, they often had roast lamb with mint sauce and roast potatoes, parsnips with cabbage and lovely thick gravy.

"People would travel continents for them," he joked.

"I will have to visit and try them then won't I?" Jacqueline remarked as she leaned towards him.

They kissed but with more meaning than before. He sat back and held her hand just looking at her beautiful black hair, few freckles and strong features showing her very French descent. She was wearing a light blue flowered cotton dress, which showed off her figure and Jack's mind drifted off. Back to the cashew nuts and drinks, which Jack had to admit to drinking half of Jacqueline's too as she was driving, he felt a little heady.

"Shall we go for a walk? Just excuse me for a moment," she said to Jack. Jack presumed she had to go to the toilet but when he tried to pay, it was already cleared. He got up thanking the waiter as she returned and she caught hold of his hand.

"Let's walk around past the boats Jack," so off they strolled.

They set off down to the harbour with his arm around her pulling her closer. When out of the bright lights and under the soft lantern-type lights of the port, he pulled her to him. Jack shocked himself but Jacqueline reacted straight away by putting her arms around his neck. He felt her very full bust pushing into his chest and in the hot evening, their bodies fused and her tongue searched his mouth and his lips pulling closely together. Jack was nearly suffocating, so this is what French girls are like he thought as he kissed her neck and she squirmed against him, running her hand inside his shirt on his hot flesh. Jack tried to slide his hand into her top to feel her breasts but trying this difficult exercise in a public place, he caught her nipple causing Jacqueline to pull away. They moved further down the quay-way, away from people to find others sitting on some of the flat rocks by the water mixing in with the local fishermen doing some night fishing. Jacqueline led him along a narrow path leading along the back of some old buildings very close to the water. They emerged into a small quay jutting out into the sea from one of the large villas, the owners had even imported a load of sand to create a small beach.

"Should we be here?"

"They won't know," she answered, kicking her shoes off. Jack took his off and they walked at the water's edge, it was warm on their feet and legs obviously after a hot day. She turned to him and now moved his hand up to her breast.

"Are you sure no-one will come out?" he said.

"Don't worry, the house is all in darkness."

He undid her top to find a very saucy, lacy black bra underneath with her nipples nearly trying to get out. Kissing each other now more urgently, she led Jack out of the water to the beach, she sat down patting the sand. He quickly joined her as she slipped off her top, Jack followed suit and they sat together, with him kissing her on the mouth and fumbling behind her to undo the lace that held her very full breasts. He wondered whether to bother as the breasts were nearly out of it, in the end the clasp popped and out they came. Jack moved slowly down her neck kissing her tenderly all the time and greeted the nipples, which were dark even against their tanned mounds. He gently kissed her and they became even harder to his tongue. Jacqueline pulled back and lay back in the sand, Jack resting on his left elbow caressed her gently with his fingers across her face. Her eyes searched his as his fingers crossed her lips, then again down to those gorgeous mounds tipped in brown.

Although they seemed alone, Jack was not relaxed, "I feel someone is watching" he said.

"Don't be silly" as she pulled him to her, flesh against flesh and again he started to lose himself in kissing her.

His hands moved down to the waistband of her skirt, it was tight but it was made of a soft silky material. So he was able to ease the fabric through his fingers until eventually he found himself caressing her warm crutch through lacy panties, that must have matched the bra he had just removed. He couldn't see as it was now quite dark. She had undone the top of his shorts, the belt and button and was caressing his now very interested penis. He suddenly spotted a light come on in the villa and then another, he went very cold with fright, Jacqueline seemed very relaxed but he rolled away from her.

"Jack, don't go away from me, what's wrong?" Jacqueline whispered.

"Somebody has come into the garden," said Jack with the whites of his eyes showing alarm. They had indeed and she quickly pulled Jack to her, "Do you want your clothes?" he whispered to her.

"No just lay quiet; it is most likely a security guy checking the house."

"Let's hope he hasn't a dog and comes down to the beach."

They lay very still and Jack's ardour died completely and as he accidentally rubbed his arm across her bust as they lay facing each other, her nipples and breasts had softened. She kissed him gently on the nose; it seemed like ages then more noise and not only did the door shut but all the lights went out in the house too. They even heard a heavy metal gate bang shut, which could have been the front gate.

"Let's go," Jack whispered "I have had enough...!"

"Calm down, they've gone now," said Jacqueline, a bit irritated by Jack's panic.

"But we're on a private beach. Come on Jacqueline."

She put her top back on but not her bra, which she stuffed into her bag. Jack tidied himself and he was persuaded again to walk along the small beach on the edge of the water with the fluorescence of the sea. He calmed down and from holding hands, they were soon back together in embraces. He could feel her nipples hardening through her thin top, this was just too much for Jack and he was becoming a little too excited. Jack tried to relax and was running his hand inside her top, as she moved her body slowly in between his legs. She pulled him again from the edge of the water and up the beach. Jacqueline pulled him to her and started hurriedly undoing his belt and shorts again.

"I can't," he said, "I have no protection with me..."

"Don't worry, it's ok," which he took to mean that she must have been on the pill. That surprised him. Jack had always heard how in these mainly Roman Catholic countries they didn't use the pill. Anyway he had gone beyond caring, Jacqueline slipped her top off and stepped out of her skirt and they lay on the now cooling sand. He could not wait any longer, taking her lace knickers off, running them down over her feet, he kissed the small mound between her legs, she was very moist and he quickly removed his pants and rolled onto her tanned body. Her hands went down to his erection.

"Quick," he said as she guided him to her. Jack unfortunately was so excited that the moment of ecstasy was short lived. They lay motionless together, the sweat between their bodies stuck them together like glue. She kissed him very gently with her soft lips and stroked his back. He pulled away lying naked next to her. 'What happened there?' he thought, looking up at the stars, which were so bright. Nothing was said for ages. She ran her hands with soft fingers across his chest and down his stomach and back.

"You're cheeky Jacqueline," Jack said.

"Takes two," she giggled but he thought she had led him on and wouldn't give up even though he would have done that.

"Let's go for a swim."

Jack thought about it, why not indeed. Jacqueline was first up standing above him with a beckoning hand. He felt shy at that moment in the darkness he felt very naked. He rose and their hands met, she got him running into the water, which was amazingly warm.

Jacqueline swam out away from him, the splashes of water shining in the moonlight. Jack turned over on his back and slowly swam, he was tired but felt better from having the opportunity of a rinse off. He was floating on his back when Jacqueline appeared below him. Jack spluttered in the water and choked.

"I am sorry," she said as she stood next to him with the water up to their chests. She kissed him and they moved closer, what a wonderful feeling it was as their bodies touched in the water. He ran his hands down her back to her bottom and it was the first time he had realised what a lovely shape it was! He pulled his two hands to each cheek and to his surprise, she suddenly jumped up putting her legs around his waist and arms around his neck. He nearly lost his balance but as he steadied his legs their mouths met. Even in the water he was again getting aroused, their chests together the sea rising and falling on their bodies.

"Don't drop me, you can hold me forever..." Jacqueline said. He lowered her slightly as her hands loosened around his neck. They were both feeling very passionate again and Jack could feel his erection suddenly move between her legs. Jack held her tight as she tried with one hand guiding him to her. They stood like one as she moved gently up and down him... he exploded and again nearly fell over, but clinging on to each-other, his legs gave way and they splashed into the water in a heap. Jack arose choking again and he couldn't see Jacqueline for a moment and then spotted her swimming further out, she was like a fish and loved swimming under the water.

Jack walked out to the beach wondering to himself what had just happened to him and then with a panic wondered how late they were for picking up the boys and how would they get dry... Jacqueline was all so casual, they stood together contemplating, she came over and stroked the water off his back and down across his buttocks and legs.

"Your turn," she said smiling up at him, he did the same but he was a bit rougher. "Gently" she hissed at him. The contours of her body were beautiful he thought to himself. "Front now," she flicked the water off his strong arms, then started on his chest, down his stomach, each leg, then gently touched him. "Behave you saucy scamp," just gently brushing the water off. Then down his legs, crouching in front of him, with her hair tickling in between his legs. "Now me," which was a lot trickier

86

trying to brush off water from two ample breasts with hands and fingers. He tried to gently work the water down around her tummy being careful not to go near her beautiful mound of hair.

"Come on," Jack said, "We can't be that wet other than dripping hair," and quickly dressed with their clothes sticking to them.

Jack eventually found his shoes and moved towards Jacqueline, with her silhouette and hair shining in the moonlight, then kissed her gently on the side of her wet neck. They set off carefully round back along the narrow path to the rocks and the quay into the lit area. Jack couldn't see his watch in the dark before and now to his surprise saw it was nearly half past twelve.

"Let's have a coffee or hot chocolate before we go," Jacqueline suggested.

So Jack had hot chocolate and Jacqueline had a café crème. The waiter chatted away to her and it turned out he was amused at their wet state and guessed they must have been swimming or 'skinny dipping'. Jacqueline and Jack sat together quietly musing and smiling possibly as the last few hours they had spent together was rather unexpected.

"What time will they be finished at the Casino?" Jack asked. "About one o'clock to half past, we will go soon…" said Jacqueline with froth on her lips.

They drank up and headed the Fiat back towards Nice, off up the hill from Villefranche known for being the deepest harbour but more importantly for Jack's night of love, to pick up Colin and Nick.

It was now nearly two in the morning, no sign of Nick and Colin.

"I'll go and have a look," Jack suggested.

"No good, they won't let you in, stay here and I'll go," said Jacqueline. She jumped out of the car and ran up the steps, showing her identity card to the security men. They started arguing with her, Jack wondered what about. Ten minutes past and Jacqueline emerged with a boy on each arm. Nick a little hung over as was Colin, was very delighted as he had had a good win and being Nick, had spent most of it at the bar and blamed Jack because he and Jacqueline did not pick them up earlier. However, he still ended up with more cash than he went in with. Colin had lost too much chatting and changing what to bet on Nick remarked. An argument broke out between the boys and Jack carried on stroking Jacqueline's nape of her neck. Nick suddenly noticed in the midst of it all and shouted, "So what have you two been up to?"

"We went on to Villefranche and had a few drinks," Jack said as casually as possible.

"What, until two in the morning!" remarked Nick "I don't believe a word."

"We had a lot to chat about," said Jack trying not to laugh, Jacqueline winked at him, but Nick would not give up and kept taunting them all the way back to the hotel. Jack tried to get him to change the subject and tell him about the Casino as he was not allowed in.

Nick explained how amazing the inside was of the Casino. There were beautiful chandeliers dripping with crystals, thick plush red carpet everywhere, grand flights of stairs, which led to private rooms. Nick was wondering what went on inside them. Colin had nudged him, as he was going around looking up at the ceiling with his mouth open. They were supposed to be looking cool and used to such places. They had several people looking at them, probably thinking they were far too young to be in such a place. Fortunately nobody questioned them again and they made their way to the gaming tables, 'wow what an experience' Nick was thinking, just like the James Bond film. All he needed was a beautiful lady on his arm and a martini, not that he saw anyone drinking that. They had obviously had a good time and Jack wished he could have joined them but his time on the beach with Jacqueline was unforgettable.

The journey to the hotel became a bit calmer and they arranged to meet up late morning the next day for a trip up to St. Paul de Vence, the area where the artists live.

"Where shall we meet, because we'll be down on the beach?" said Nick.

"I'll pick you up down by Casino Beach," replied Jacqueline.

They climbed out of the Fiat and Jack popped his head back in through the window to kiss Jacqueline goodnight.

Jack and Nick suddenly realised that they did not have a key and Monsieur Christophe locked the door around twelve thirty, oh dear. Fortunately their room was on the ground floor and they had left the shutters slightly open. Putting his hand through, Jack lifted the catch and eased the windows open and they managed to climb in.

"So come on Nick how much did you win?" asked Jack before Nick could start asking him questions.

"Loads of money Jack, about three hundred francs!" smiled Nick. "Don't let on to Colin, but I spent at least a hundred francs at the bar, the drinks were so expensive. Well, let's go to sleep now. Hey, didn't we arrange to meet the Dutch crowd on the beach at ten? We'll try, eh? At least we're both winning with girls."

"Yes, I feel bad having started a relationship with Helena, then going off with Jacqueline, and then at home there's Penny," said Jack thoughtfully.

"No there is not Jack, you're finished with that older woman, Penny. Get over it – that's why we came away on holiday. She dumped you Jack, she was a good experience. So come on, don't lay there wondering whether you are being loyal to her. Just think how lucky you are, all you need is a lovely girl in England, then you can visit one in Holland, crossing over on the ferry or pop down through France to here. Maybe the parents would let you stay with them, if they approve. Even though we are just gardeners." Nick was really into this deep conversation.

"Not just gardeners Nick, we are great gardeners," Jack shouted at the top of his voice.

"Shsh, you'll wake everyone up, shut up and go to sleep," said Nick, much to Jack's surprise. Then he suddenly remembered he still had not found out what Jack had got up to. So he spent the next half-hour trying to find out what Jack had been up to.

"Swimming…!" Jack said.

"Swimming!? I don't believe you…!" Nick retorted, and turned out the light.

Chapter VIII

Saint Paul-de-Vence

Next day on the beach, same place they had got used to, they were swimming and sleeping. Nick had been off to get Bounty Bars from the beach restaurant, when all of a sudden, they were surrounded by their Dutch friends including Helena, who came straight over to Jack sitting next to him kissing him on the cheek. This totally confused Jack, as she was angry with him the previous afternoon. He wondered what her friends had been saying to her for her to be so friendly again – women! Out came the rugs and towels, beers and boxes of previously packed salads and snacks. The Dutch were so prepared!

"Come on let's go swimming," Helena said. She quickly undressed into her bikini and they were out into the water swimming out to the float.

They sat on it for a long time chatting but eventually Helena said, "You're not the same Jack, what has happened?"

Jack of course denied it. He explained he was very tired having gone out with some friends until late the night before and hoped it wouldn't make any difference to his feelings for her.

On returning to the beach, they were all around Nick sipping beers and busily chatting. Lunch-time soon came and it was time to leave.

"We are going out with Colin, an English friend who is staying down here." Jack kissed Helena on the lips and said they would try and catch up tomorrow feeling a bit awkward. Luckily they had reached Promenade des Anglais as the little Fiat approached.

In the boys piled and set off out of Nice, climbing up the twisty hills. The little car struggled round some of the bends but eventually they were driving up through Cagnes-Vence and on to St. Paul. What amazing views thought Jack and nudged Nick to look across the valleys. St. Paul was a beautiful medieval fortified village and some of the ramparts are still there. Like so many old villages it was very busy with tourists but Nick, Colin and Jack were not bothered, there were many arty shops and art galleries. It had become popular as Marc Chagall, a Russian-born painter who painted in an impressionist style had lived there. His works were more of mermaids than anything and in the shops they were able to buy prints and posters, there were lots of plates on the walls in the shops, all brightly painted. Neither Jack or Nick had any idea nor knowledge of famous artists, Jack was anxious to learn more as his interest in France grew, it was a whole new world to him. Jacqueline suggested that they went into the museum and looked at some of the paintings. There was a collection of 20th century paintings, sculptures and ceramics, so much to see and take in.

Jacqueline put her arm around Jack and squeezed his waist as they strolled into the museum to queue to go round. Jack was spellbound, this was his first experience of looking at paintings and artefacts. They strolled outside amiably into a very peaceful area, very light with bright blue sky, running water coming down the mountains, and lots of indigenous trees. Someone had told Jack how the artists from Paris came south for the bright light.

Having had a good look around they decided to drive on to the next village of Vence. This was a beautiful village too but not nearly as busy. As they were all so hungry they drove on again to Tourrettes-sur-Loup, which was smaller so they hoped it would be less expensive. This too was quieter than St. Paul and had little arty shops, which were run by many artists themselves. Colin and Nick disappeared to find somewhere to buy cigarettes so Jack and Jacqueline went on ahead to eventually find a café and sat in the shade outside. Jack ordered a beer and Jacqueline ordered a diablo-menthe again, holding hands Jacqueline leaned forward and kissed him gently on the cheek. Jack was starting to get a bit worried about how keen she seemed to be on him but he thought to himself there was no need to worry as he was in England and she was in France!

Colin and Nick arrived and ordered more beers and then they all decided to have the "plat du jour", which Jacqueline explained to them, as most restaurants offer a set meal including a dessert or cheese and usually wine too at an amazingly fair price. The meal they thought they were having was not quite what they had expected except Jacqueline of course. It was a sort of rabbit stew, with little bones sticking up, poor Jack had not seen anything like it before but with grim determination not to look a fool, he started to eat it. He was amazed at how tasty it was and enjoyed it, this was followed by tarte aux pommes with a big spoonful of cream on top. He and Nick were really getting into the swing of things and washed it all down with the local rosé wine.

"So, what's up tonight?" Nick asked them all. "I think Colin and I should stay home tonight with my parents, Nick," Jacqueline answered.

"Oh," Colin responded. Nick and Jack looked at each other, there was no argument.

"How about us all going to the beach tomorrow at Juan-Les-Pins?" suggested Jacqueline. That settled, they finished their lunch and made their way back to the car and drove back to Nice.

Nick and Jack had been to Juan-Les-Pins before on the train but it would be handy to be driven there by car. Arriving back in Nice they left arranging to meet the following day. The boys went into the hotel to have a rest before dinner. Before they knew it, it was time to eat again and the dinner was superb, they spent all their time chatting about the different girls they had met so far.

"Bit tricky," said Nick, "I'm getting on fine with the Dutch girls and you have now got caught up with Jacqueline." Not easy they decided, although Jack still rather liked Helena, so a trip to Juan would be ideal. "Let's hit Nice tonight and find another bar," Nick suggested. Jack was all for that idea.

The boys set off and wandered down around the back of the station, occasionally turning left and in theory going towards the Promenade des Anglais. They suddenly came across a very brightly lit bar with three entrances and a black and white floor. The tables were marble-looking and most of the chairs metal. The long bar was again in marble and with a round shiny tube all along the front. Bar stools were along the bar and as they entered they became aware of how many young girls and women were in the bar, in fact more than men. There was a very old guy in blue trousers and shirt that shuffled across to them to take their orders. Beer was not difficult to order and they ordered "Pression" beers and went to sit down. A small alcove at the end of the bar had even more girls sitting. Jack was surprised that a couple would suddenly get up, freshen their make-up and leave. Then another one, then three more, very strange thought Jack.

After watching this go on for some time and enjoying their beers, the boys were fascinated as the women returned had a few more drinks and chatted to one and other. Nick suddenly realised that they must be in a bar full of prostitutes, which made them both feel a bit uncomfortable and yet they couldn't resist watching them. Some of the girls were really young and attractive, Nick was dying to ask them what they charged and what it would be like to go with one of them. He was so intrigued that he started daring Jack to ask one of them, but he was not really interested. After a while and a few more beers drunk, they decided to leave. As they left a dark-haired girl with slight features, slim, attractive and with chestnut brown eyes left. She was dressed in a red 'see-through' dress and the boys could see her red knickers and bra underneath. Nick walked slightly ahead of Jack and it looked as though he was stalking her. After a couple of streets, she suddenly stopped and turned to speak to him. Jack was embarrassed and was back too far to hear what was said, he half expected Nick to disappear with her into a doorway! After a brief discussion the girl walked away and Nick returned.

"Well, what did she say?" asked Jack full of curiosity.

Nick suggested they found another bar and on the way he explained that she first asked Nick something in French that he hadn't understood, then in English asking him if he wanted to go with her.

"So what did you say?" asked Jack impatiently.

"Well yes of course," said Nick.

"So then what?" asked Jack.

"She told me that for total sex, it would be a hundred French francs. I told her how beautiful she was and couldn't the price be less? She laughed giving me a list of other sexual delights!" Nick laughed and Jack was totally shocked. They wandered down the road reading and talking about the many options written like a restaurant menu. Jack asked Nick how the girls could do that every night of the week.

"Maybe they enjoy it," Nick suggested.

"No, it must be the money," Jack said.

They had wandered back onto one of the main boulevards and to a very lively bar with lots of young people in it.

"This is more like it," Jack said sounding quite relieved to be in a more comfortable atmosphere.

"I don't know, I could have gone with quite a few of those girls, except for the fact that I hadn't got enough money," said Nick, Jack was horrified at what he was saying.

The evening was a good one and they spent a great deal of it drinking and chatting to the many girls that could speak English.

After a sound sleep with the help of the alcohol, the next day, after a late breakfast, they got their beach things ready to be picked up about ten o'clock.

Chapter VIX

Juan-les-Pins

Sitting outside on the terrace chatting to each other, the boys discussed the oranges in the front of the hotel. Jack had only seen a couple in the conservatory at Kenwood House up at Hampstead but to see them growing naturally was fantastic. Amazing how they flower and fruit on the same plant in the same year. Here in Nice, the oranges and lemons had fruit ripening and the attractive white flowers smelt wonderful filling the morning air. It was glorious; Monsieur Christophe joined them bringing them both large cups of coffee, which he had learnt they liked.

"Jeunes hommes," he said smiling. Jack asked him about the varieties of the citrus fruits in the garden. "Un moment," Monsieur Christophe said disappearing into the hotel. He returned with a little notebook with all the varieties written down. Some of the plants were very old, in fact planted by his father-in-law when he ran the hotel. The trees took some time to mature to fruiting unless they were grafted he explained, or more to the point, actually showed them to the boys as he struggled to explain in English. Jack asked whether he could copy some of the names down as he could possibly use them for a project at college.

"You're on holiday Jack, what a boff you are," Nick jibed at Jack.

Jack ignored him and at that moment Jacqueline arrived giving Jack a kiss on each cheek on arrival. Monsieur Christophe stood watching them all smiling and wished them all a good day.

In the car and away to Juan-les-Pins, Jacqueline suggested they go on the coastal route, as this would give the boys a chance to see the coastline. It was very straight and flat after leaving Nice and passing the airport. This area seemed a bit desolate and not very attractive, camper vans and caravans were parked up on the ridge overlooking the sea, the other side of the road had scrubby pine trees and a few old abandoned industrial units. At last they came to an attractive coastline, the stone started to turn into red rock. The little Fiat hugged the twisty roads, there was very little between them and the sea, which had a bright blue sky above it giving it an incredible green blue crystal sheen. Fantastic, the three boys could not believe the beautiful view. The road went down to the sea level in places revealing attractive coves with small sandy beaches. Others had marinas absolutely crammed with yachts and boats. The railway ran along the coast and disappeared, occasionally into a tunnel and sometimes across a long viaduct across a valley. Several times a small diesel train of about six coaches trundled along in between a huge black steam locomotive dragging a line of coaches, just like Jack, Nick and Colin came down to Nice on and others with Italian writing on them.

The journey nearly took two hours as Jacqueline had driven around the main towns like Antibes to show the boys the sites. Eventually they arrived and after drifting along the beach road for a parking space, they decided to try further inland. Colin picked up a large picnic bag from the boot and they all got their things and strolled to the beach. Nick suggested stopping for a beer at the corner bar but was overruled! Once settled on the beach, towels laid out and the boys with trunks on and

Jacqueline in her bikini, dark blue against her tan, Nick could not take his eyes off her. Colin unpacked the picnic bag to reveal a fresh baguette, pâté, salad, sausage and cheeses, not forgetting a cool bottle of rosé wine. Everything for a proper picnic French style. Nick announced he was going to cool off before lunch in the sea, Jack thought he needed to, the way he had been eyeing Jacqueline up and down to cool his ardour! Colin joined him leaving them to put the lunch out under the large umbrella that had been pushed into the sand to give it shelter from the strong sun.

Colin and Nick were longer than they had anticipated, leaving Jack and Jacqueline alone for a while. They talked about the other evening Jacqueline had driven Jack to Villefranche, leaving Nick and Colin at the Casino. Jack could not help worrying how involved he had become.

"I'm very fond of you Jack, I don't just make love to anybody..." Jacqueline said. Jack was worrying even more, she was getting too attached to him. "You must both come over for dinner and meet my parents before you return to England, I've told them all about you."

"Okay," Jack said kissing her gently on the lips and hoping that Nick would help him out of that one. Colin noisily returned up the beach with Nick, all got on very well considering what a bore they thought Colin was on the train. Nick had spotted a lady, or girl, he said it was difficult to judge, but she had tussled blonde hair, blue eyes, heavy hips and a nicely tanned body.

"Perhaps after lunch, I'll try and chat her up or catch her swimming even," he smiled cheekily.

Lunch was a delight, they sat back on their towels and feasted on the picnic, breaking the baguette up. Jacqueline tried to persuade them to try the sausisson, which was a bit like salami. Jack did not like it but enjoyed the cheese called

Emmantal with bread and lettuce that they called "salade", the tomatoes were huge and Jacqueline had cut them into quarters to make it possible to eat them without them oozing all over the place. Occasionally a little wine would dribble down Jacqueline's chin, Jack watched her tongue lick it from her lips, Jack found it very sexy just watching her eat. So much so he had to move his position, as it could possibly have become obvious. The rosé wine made him feel very sleepy, it went well with the bread and cheese. Jacqueline had also packed a soft cheese called Camembert to eat on its own with grapes. The boys were not too keen on the flavour and could not believe that Jacqueline ate the skin as well. This was followed by a creamy sweet like yoghurt but sweeter and all that plus the largest peaches they had ever seen. With a knife Jacqueline cut them into quarters, the flesh falling off the stone, Jack was watching and picked up a slice. The softness of the skin reminded him of Jacqueline's back he caressed the other night. Jack leant across to her whispering just that into her ear. Nick, quick as a flash said, "Colin, perhaps we should leave the young lovers," to which Jacqueline reddened in the cheeks.

"Don't be silly, it's just that you want to get back to chatting up the lady in the bikini," she retorted.

"Well, yes," he remarked sheepishly.

"So what about Colin, who can we fix him up with?" Jacqueline continued how she had been trying to find one of her friends for him but he always turned shy! Poor Colin, it was his turn to go red so Jack took the lead and asked him what sort of girls he liked. He was not sure really but he could not cope with a French girl as most of them did not speak English with the exception of Jacqueline.

"I am waiting to meet a slim brunette with short hair that is English and likes racing cars with enough money to buy me one!" They all laughed and told him to keep dreaming.

"Perhaps we should go to Monte Carlo to meet a nice lady, have you been there yet?" asked Jacqueline.

"No," they all replied in unison.

"No, well what about tomorrow?" asked Jacqueline even though she would have to do all the driving again. Nick looked hurriedly at Jack who said they had arranged to see a crowd on the beach the next day, they both looked at each other quizzically. What were they both getting into? Jack was getting seriously worried.

They had all drunk a fair amount of wine and after packing up the remains of the picnic, they laid back on their towels to enjoy the sun. Jack found Jacqueline had moved closer to him lying at a slight angle to him, putting her head just below his ribs. Her soft hair tantalizingly touched his warm flesh and just as he was dozing, she turned her head and with her beautiful pursed lips kissed his chest. Jack returned it by caressing her side and shoulder, trying not to get too friendly. Colin was soon asleep snoring and Nick restless as always and craving for a Bounty bar, put on his sandals and muttered something about going wandering. Jack tried to pretend he was asleep but this French lady had really attached herself to him as she moved around laying tight in next to him. He could feel her breast pushing against his chest and she now ran her fingers up and down his neck and chest. Jack found it difficult firstly to resist her and secondly, far more importantly, his interest was starting to show.

"How about a swim to cool off?" Jack suddenly blurted out much to Jacqueline's surprise, she was just enjoying this surreal moment.

"Okay if that's what you want to do," she said in a rather irritated way. She was a lady who wanted to have her own way Jack was beginning to find out. They both ran into the sea across the hot sand, Jack's entry to the water was a little less graceful more like a belly-flop, while Jacqueline did a graceful dive. They swam out together; the water shimmered, the hot sun beating down on them. Jack liked lying on his back, just floating, something that was so much easier in the Mediterranean Sea. Was it the high amount of salt? Well that's what he had been told. Jacqueline soon swam back in from having swum a long way out. She was a much more proficient swimmer than he was but she did live by the sea didn't she, he was thinking. She was swimming under him and all around like a dolphin; Jack soon gave up trying to float on his back and trod water as she came close to him gently kissing him. They slowly swam in until Jack found he could stand with his shoulders just out of the water, soon they were embraced again with her legs encircling his waist. He held her delightfully shaped bottom as they kissed. Strange how nobody took much notice here in France, in England it would be very different he thought.

Back to the beach to soak up the sun and Colin was now awake with still no sign of Nick. "So where have you two been, looking so smiley?" Colin enquired.

"Just swimming…" replied Jack.

Lying back on their towels, Jacqueline was soon reading her book and Jack was trying to make out the French written in the Nice-Matin newspaper. From the pictures he understood there had been some dreadful fires and the firemen had been battling with them for two days. The fires Jack thought were nearer Marseilles than Nice. Colin was asleep again and Jack must have joined him as the next thing he was woken by a terrific roar of large red planes flying overhead. He understood these to be water planes from Canada, that fill up with water and shower the forests, then refill again from the sea, lakes or even people's swimming pools, wherever they could pick up water. It was an amazing sight to see and he hoped they were able to put the fires out soon as the devastation across the mountainsides was tremendous.

They all watched in amazement when Nick interrupted their thoughts to announce he had friends to meet that evening and needed to get going. This was news to Jack but he didn't disagree and went along with what Nick was saying, he had either met someone on the beach or he had had enough of Colin and Jacqueline. On the way back to Nice, Jacqueline asked about the next day but Nick reminded her they had promised to have a day with their foreign friends. She looked very put out but Jack asked her whether she was free the next night for him to take her out on her own.

"Of course," she replied, "but I had hoped you would both come to lunch to meet my parents." Nick said again he was sorry and Jack was relieved he had stuck to their plan, not knowing what that plan was. Through the traffic and into Nice they were soon back at their little hotel.

Once inside Nick started grumbling at Jack.

"It's alright for you Jack, Jacqueline is all over you like a rash and it makes it very difficult for me. Let's face it Jack, we did come on this holiday together." He had a point but as Nick always did, he went on and on about it... "If we hadn't met Colin on the train this wouldn't have happened!" Poor Nick was getting very upset.

"Calm down old chap, we can work this out. I have now only agreed to see her for one dinner on my own this week. We can do our own thing the rest of the time, now let's get changed and showered ready for dinner and we have even got time to sit out on the terrace with a beer beforehand."

Nick calmed down and they were both soon 'spruced' up and Nick continued to whinge a bit about how they had missed the opportunity with the Dutch girls because of Jacqueline. The truth was none of them fancied Nick, which was why they had not wanted to meet that day, but Jack could not bring himself to say that, he just told him not to be so silly. After all they had visited some beautiful places by car with Jacqueline that Nick seemed to have forgotten to mention.

Jack was beginning to feel niggled now and retorted. "Look leave it now, what is done, is done. And in any case, supposing you had hit it off with that French girl in the bar, what was her name?"

"That's different," retorted Nick.

"No it isn't, let's call it a truce and go out and enjoy ourselves tonight and where shall we go tomorrow" Jack asked.

"Monte Carlo on the train?" said Nick hopefully.

"Okay, seems like a great idea," Jack replied and they both settled down to an enjoyable evening. Anne and Serge joined them. It was nice to catch up with them, Jack still could not stop gazing at this pretty woman.

The beers appeared and M. Christophe brought out some nuts too. Dinner was excellent that evening, it was veal in large cutlets served with french beans in a separate dish and french fries. It was fascinating how we each eat so differently. The English pile it all on one plate Jack commented and plough through it all. The French were inclined to eat the meat first, pick at the chips and finish with the beans. They seem to treat each portion as a meal. Nick questioned whether the French eat less or more as they definitely drank more wine than the English, most English only had wine on birthdays and at Christmas.

The second course was cheese, which they found difficult to deal with and then the fruit or dessert last, which was usually chocolate mousse or crème caramel. That evening it was the chocolate, which they both loved and vowed to try to buy some to take home to England. They never refused the coffee, trying to take in the true flavour of France but those little cups of strong coffee were so small.

"Well give us a good cup of tea any day," said Nick and they both chuckled.

That evening they strolled back down to the seafront and as many people did, they walked along the Promenade des Anglais, taking in the other people, usually the girls. It was funny how few English girls there seemed to be in Nice. They had only met a couple of groups, one lot from Manchester and a giggling blonde and her friend from somewhere in Essex, which Nick pretended not to know. They walked past the flower market and up towards the harbour, stopping at a bar near the war memorial for a rest and of course a beer. They chatted again about Jacqueline, and Nick seemed more sensible now, he was worried as was Jack as to how keen she seemed, even trying to get him to meet the parents! Jack had already decided to try to leave it alone until after tomorrow night, then just write when he got home.

"She is tasty Nick, you have to agree though I saw you looking at her on the beach. You're jealous aren't you Nick?" asked Jack; they bitched a bit and then set off towards the harbour to visit more bars.

France Jack found a fascinating place, he even wondered if he could work there but the language was difficult. On the other hand he now knew a great teacher to help him. Jack and Nick wandered up the back area behind the old port, after having a quick drink at the café on the road by the corner of the war memorial. Nick could not resist having a drink but Jack was determined to have a look at some of the typical gardens of wealthy Nice. It was such a lovely balmy evening and still so light. Down the road and past the yachts, all lined up by the docks and off through the narrow streets full of antique shops and bric-a-brac. Many English dealers came to France to buy pieces of furniture, old lace fabrics and china. The craze that had started in England for old items had not come to France yet and seemingly with the exchange rate in England's favour, they were doing good business. Not for Jack though.

The streets were narrow and often only wide enough for one car as they walked further away from the port coming to smaller houses. Large doors at the bottom, which were either garages for those with cars or store rooms with wine, honey and stacks of chopped wood ready for the winter. Suddenly from beyond these charming houses to wider streets and lined with plane trees many of these houses had quite large gardens with railings across the front. Some even had gates and many traditional Cupressus hedges. Jack and Nick wandered up the roads, checking them out, remarking how a great deal of these gardens had a high amount of paving. Some, possibly the wealthier, had square cut marble and others had crazy paving of a natural stone. It was creamy buff and had darker brown marks within it, not pointed or laid like it was in England. The paving was rough-hewn and did not look as if it had been cut by a saw. As for the pointing, most of the paving did not have any and what did, had the cement smeared in between the joints. However, all the gardens were very tidy, which gave the impression that either they were keen gardeners, which the French were not noted for or they had gardeners. If they did have gardeners, when did they work, Jack and Nick had not noticed anyone during the day. Could it be possible for Jack to come and work here. Maybe not, his French was pretty awful, which brought his thoughts back to Jacqueline.

Nick nudged Jack and wondered what he had been thinking about, he had been so quiet. Jack told him what his thoughts were and explained how much he would like to work in that part of France.

"Do you know you have been a lucky bugger this week, having a girl like Jacqueline, who lives in a place like this and she is so keen on you. She'd take you anywhere you know if you asked her to," Nick said enviously.

They continued up the road admiring the different methods of gardening. Mimosa cut into unruly hedges and further up the road, Escalonia and Laurel hedges then Tamarix everywhere with its feathery leaves. The boys were taken aback with such beautiful plants everywhere. Feeling very weary they turned back towards the main road to look for a taxi and home to bed.

Chapter X

Monte Carlo, Monaco

Early next morning Jack and Nick got up and Monsieur Christophe had kindly prepared a picnic for them. So they had a quick breakfast in the dining room and were soon out on their way to catch a bus to get them half-way down Gambetta. That way they only had to cross one block and they would arrive at the station to catch the train to Monte Carlo. It took a long time to queue for a ticket so they were glad to arrive early. They had checked the time of the trains and one leaving Nice Central at ten o'clock would get them there between ten thirty and eleven o'clock. If they had missed that, there was another in half an hour then no more until mid-day. From what they could understand, on the platform were little cut-outs of the layouts of the train showing where each carriage would end up and that the train was a main line one from Marseilles to Ventimiglia in Italy. The plan showed the buffet and restaurant cars, just as they had in Calais, when they boarded the train at the beginning of the holiday. Nick was happy he had found a kiosk that sold Bounty Bars and he had bought a Mars Bar for Jack.

The train arrived with a rush of steam and clanking of steel, the French locomotives were huge. An inspector alighted with his rounded peeked cap, helping older people out of the train and checking tickets of people getting on. He checked the boys' tickets and pointed them to the next carriage, they had no idea what he was saying. Climbing up into the carriage, Jack and Nick noticed stickers on some of the compartments with just 'reserve' on them. They avoided them and went into one where settled on one side was an elderly French couple who greeted them, one older man by the window and three girls from Belgium who naturally spoke French too and they all struggled with their English. They were older than the boys, possibly in their late twenties, not very good looking except one, who had light brown, wavey hair. In fact Nick nudged Jack as they appeared stepping into the carriage. Jack hoped they didn't notice this. The usual pleasantries were exchanged and as they were all settling in, a young lady in a smart suit, white blouse and a very short skirt, rushed into the compartment as the whistle went off and the train pulled away.

The carriage was so warm the young lady soon took her jacket off and rested it on her knee. Nick could not keep his eyes off her. Eventually she asked him in 'pigeon' English if they were on holiday. Jack left Nick to respond in broken French and English with hand movements, which Jack thought was quite amusing. Her name was Annette and it turned out that she worked in an office in Monaco selling advertising for radio stations. Jack wondered where this conversation was going, as Nick sat there saying the odd "oui" and "non". Annette, who was possibly in her mid-twenties, leant towards Nick. As she did her cleavage increased as the blouse buttons were undone quite low. Jack watched Nick's eyes and wondered whether she had noticed their direction. She was a pretty girl with dark round eyes, an olive skin but not sun-tanned at all with short black hair. She lived in Nice and caught that train everyday starting work late. In advertising, starting around ten thirty meant being able to contact England and other parts of Europe more easily as they did not start very early either. It meant going home late but that did not matter too much except Fridays when Annette liked to go out dancing. She chatted on so much that Nick moved to sit next to her. She was either lonely, forward or could have just been friendly. Jack stayed in the corner and kept out of the conversation as Nick explained their life history to her, most likely speaking far too quickly for her to understand. The one thing she could not seem to understand was that they were gardeners, or 'jardiniers'. She kept on asking were they growing flowers or vegetables and getting more confused until Jack intervened because he had already looked up the word before he left England. They were paysagistes – "Ah," she said, then she understood.

The train slowed and they pulled into Monte Carlo station. This was a very smart and modern building with a huge mural on the wall and escalators to take you to the correct access point. The Palace and old town, the port or the Hotel de Paris, all led down different tunnels and stairways. Annette offered to show them around the radio offices, where several stations were based. Jack had no objection as the little principality had always interested him. Coming out suddenly from an exit and into the heat and sun, down three blocks of very smart offices, there were little exclusive shops underneath. These were mainly haute couture boutiques Christian Dior, Chanel and many others including exclusive estate agents. The pavements were curbed in a really attractive Portland coloured stone but shiny, Jack had never seen such care taken over a pavement. They walked down into a dipping road and to the left, a large four-storey building in a 'pinky red' colour appeared where Annette claimed to be aiming for. She greeted the doorman, who responded to her with "Bonjour Mademoiselle Boyer." So she was not married then, Jack nudged Nick to tell him but his eyes were wandering everywhere and so was his mind Jack reckoned. They took the lift to the third floor and turning left through some swing doors with stickers all over it, there was a smart sign saying Radio Monte Carlo.

Annette showed them the advertising office first, which had about six desks in it and there were piles of papers and telephones everywhere. A very bronzed young man greeted them and Annette asked whether she could show the boys around. Michel shook hands with them and greeted them in perfect English. He suggested that they also popped into the studio of Radio Riviera, as that station was English speaking. On the wall in this office, were big boards at the end with pictures and slogans written on paper all pinned randomly. It turned out that this was how they started putting advertising campaigns together. After explaining how they worked, they moved on to the 'News' room, which had two journalists, a television, a teleprinter and in the corner was a tiny box studio. From there the news and weather were broadcast for the Radio Monte Carlo programmes. They then moved on to a studio where a disc jockey called Johnny, was playing records and chatting in between. He had two record desks to his side, a big old reel to reel tape recorder and in front, about six sliding switches and an assortment of cassettes that he occasionally slotted into a machine. These were the jingles or introductions he played in between their programmes. A great deal of the music seemed to be American or English with only a little from France.

Nick and Jack were fascinated and seemed to be there ages and Annette suggested they went upstairs to Radio Riviera. Through another set of swinging doors, much more cramped, she took them first to an office and introduced them to the Station Manager, Ed. He had a Canadian accent and they found out later

111

used to work for Radio Luxembourg. Onto another studio, where they stood quietly, while Dave Fischer chatted about the weather and road conditions along the coast into a piece of music and Dave told Nick and Jack all about the station and how they used the BBC World Service news and many like Dave, were from the BBC anyway.

"Let's face it, where would you rather work and live, here or London?" asked Dave, he had a point thought Jack. He gave the boys car stickers and was back chatting to the listeners.

Annette ushered them out and down by lift to the ground floor. Nick was last to shake hands with her on departing and asked whether they could all meet up for a drink in Nice tonight.

"What do you think Jack?" Jack could not say 'no', so tonight eight o'clock outside the Hotel Negresco on the corner towards the Port. The two boys thanked her again and off they went back into the heat and the sun.

"I'm exhausted," Nick sighed. "Let's have a beer Jack."

"I don't wonder at it, you haven't stopped talking," remarked Jack. "I had promised to see Jacqueline on her own for dinner but I'm sure she won't mind meeting us later as a foursome, hope not. It's great that you have met someone again."

After a couple of beers and a Croque Monsieur, which Jack thought was a bit like cheese on toast, they set off for the gardens along the front by the Palace. These were very exotic with Palms, Banana trees, Bougainvilleas, Pittisporum, Euonymous and even Lantanas with their brightly growing colourful heads. The boys had only seen these growing in the greenhouses at Kew. That was one of the places that Jack had been several times as a child.

The boys were so impressed with the quality of the maintenance. After this they climbed several flights of steps leading up the side of the Casino, which to the front had another amazing garden. They stood at the entrance with the detail of planting, masses of summer bedding, geraniums in red and pink and all set against lawns that were even better than those that they were mowing in the gardens in London. The edging was so good and not a blade of grass out of place. It said to keep off the lawn but Jack nipped over the low rail to inspect the irrigation, which he pointed out to Nick, must be necessary to achieve such green lawns.

There were waterfalls and fountains with no litter and debris in them and perfectly clear water. Old Bert back at the Embankment gardens would be impressed with this. They had now made a complete circle and were back at the Hotel de Paris admiring the flash cars parked outside. Nick was in ecstasy over a Lamborghini and insisted Jack took a picture of him posing against the bonnet. It was now past lunch-time and they could not afford to eat in that area, so back into town, down the hill towards the port. Eventually they found a small bistro and they settled in with glasses of beer waiting for their lunch of risottos. Nick ordered a seafood risotto, full of mussels, crevettes and octopus and Jack had a tomato and mushroom one with added vegetables. They paid their bill finding that here in Monaco food cost twice as many francs.

Off they set down to the port, past the outdoor swimming pool and the road that Nick pointed out was part of the Grand Prix circuit. Nick was very interested in cars and racing and would keep nudging Jack when a Ferrari, Lotus or even a Jaguar went past them. As for the boats in the port harbour, they were just amazing. They thought they had seen money and big boats in Saint Tropez but these were even bigger. There were huge cruisers with all sorts of other little sea craft stacked on the back of them. There were no posers here sitting sipping their glasses of wine but quite a few really tasty girls in bikinis, which were not so common in England and they did make the girls look more sexy. Sadly very untouchable as they lounged on those expensive yachts and most likely had very expensive tastes in young men, which did not fit Jack or Nick.

By the time they had finished the circuit of the port, they sat down and had another beer then wandered back up to the Palace and visited the museum, then it was time to catch the train back to Nice. They had not thought it out very well as the platform was packed with people trying to make their way home. It was no wonder so many commuted to and fro, as the price of property in Monaco was astronomical. They waited with everyone for about twenty minutes before a train came, it was a local suburban train with six units of diesel driven units. The doors opened and everyone pushed on, it was like being back in London on the tube but much more pleasant once inside.

The scenery was a lot more spectacular as Nick now noticed.

"I hadn't seen all this before," Nick commented. Jack explained to him that he was so engrossed in Annette's cleavage, that he had hardly taken his eyes off her all the way up to Monaco.

"Was I really that bad Jack?" asked Nick.

"Well, pretty much," replied Jack.

"She is a cracking girl isn't she and I thought perhaps we could meet up without Colin, I did say about eight o'clock to her tonight, do you think we could manage that?" said Nick.

"I'll phone Jacqueline when we get back to Les Cigalles… I'm sure she can suggest something for Colin to do, it's quite hard for him really isn't it, he clearly is not enjoying himself very much," responded Jack.

The coastline was spectacular as the train passed through tunnels and re-emerged to a small station set quite high with a port or beach below that amazing blue water and sky to match, even this late in the afternoon as the sun began to dip. The boys could not help envying the men and girls working at that radio station.

They arrived back in the bustle of Nice and wandered up to their hotel. Monsieur Christophe greeted them on their way in saying, "The young lady had called to say Colin was out with a friend and she would pick you up at seven o'clock if convenient and left her phone number, if this was not okay. Does that mean you will not be dining with us this evening?"

"Oh no, we will be, we have changed our plans thank you," Jack quickly told him. He smiled at the boys and walked away. Jack was thinking that perhaps he should ring Jacqueline and explain the change in circumstances. Monsieur Christophe showed Jack the phone, he dialled the number and prayed her parents would not pick up the telephone as they spoke very little English. He was saved as Jacqueline answered, he explained about Nick and Annette and although there was a tone of disappointment in her voice, she agreed to pick them up a bit later.

After another superb meal, the boys went back to their room, Jack splashed on his 'Old Spice' aftershave, Nick hated the smell but Jack always had reckoned it turned women on!

"In your case Jack you don't need it, she would be with you night and day if you let her!" laughed Nick. They were then into great discussion about how keen Jacqueline was, Jack had thought her a bit heavy but if it noticed that much, perhaps he should be careful but then they were on holiday, 'so let's enjoy it' thought Jack.

That evening, the boys were driven by Jacqueline to meet up with Nick's new friend Annette. They parked the little Fiat up in a side street and wandered up towards the Hotel Negresco and Annette was there already dressed in a light short dress. Jack had to admit she did look good. They introduced Jacqueline to her and they shook hands and for a moment they chatted in French with a slight grin and looked at the two boys. They had no idea what had been said, Jack then shook hands with Annette and Nick had a kiss on both cheeks. Annette was in charge and suggested straight away that they go off and visit a bar a couple of streets away that she knew then if they wanted to, a club nearby afterwards.

Once settled in the bar, Annette continued to be intrigued in what the boys did as a job. Gardening was not really a serious career in France, so with the help of Jacqueline using some French, the picture was painted. Jack commented that it was not just France, they had trouble convincing people they were gardeners in England too. The evening went well and with a few drinks inside them, Jack now sat with his arm around Jacqueline as she discussed her visit to England. She was due to come over in October to visit one of the English schools she had worked at before. She was still keen to get him to visit her parents before they left for England but they only had a couple of days to go. Jack thought it was a bit heavy and tried to talk his way out of it.

Nick and Annette were deep in conversation and seemed to be getting on really well. They faced each other chatting and Jack could see Nick's face question some of her English in his head looking bemused. Annette's English was good but a bit rusty, although with Jacqueline, Jack had noticed that often some of his words were misinterpreted. So how could he deal with her wanting to come and see him in England, he really liked her but in many ways he preferred the idea of her being in France and he in England. He was thinking that he must not ruin the evening with that worry and just enjoy their time together and with that he kissed her on the cheek.

"What was that for?" she asked.

"A thought that's all!" replied Jack, luckily it was not followed up as he would have had to lie.

It was a super evening, they went on to the club "Le Malibu", which was down beneath a hotel around the corner. The basement was rammed with young people and as they entered, Jack led but struggled to understand what the doorman was saying. Jacqueline stepped in and they had to pay one hundred francs, which also entitled them to a drink. Jack and Nick were a bit shocked at the price but fortunately with Nick's winnings from the Casino, they had enough money. A live band was playing and they turned out to be an English band, which no one realised as several numbers had French lyrics. The rock music thumped away, Jack was amazed how the French jived. He was a rotten dancer, not like Nick, he was great. Jacqueline dragged him to the dance floor, luckily the music changed and they danced close together. Jacqueline tucked her head in close to Jack's shoulder; he ran his hands across her back and ending up on her rather splendid bottom. He could feel her tight in against him and if anything, he lost the beat of the music completely. Soft French ballad type music could send one to sleep but his body definitely was not sleeping; the smell of her mixed with the perfume and the smell of her hair were intoxicating. Luckily the music changed again and he tried desperately to jive with her. He was hopeless and eventually Jack suggested they sit it out. So they went back to their alcove where they had been sitting. There was no sign of Nick and Annette, Jacqueline nuzzled up against Jack as he put his arms around her, their lips touched and again her tongue found its way to interest his every nerve.

Jack tried hard to be sensible, reminding himself of the distance between where they lived, his age and Jacqueline being quite a few years older than he was. Somehow passion always seemed to overrule. Nick eventually returned to the table and Jack bought a round of drinks, they chatted as if they had all been friends for life and Annette was really getting on with Nick. To think they had only just met that day!

The noise in the club increased and Jack suggested they leave as it was quite late. Nick and Annette were not so keen, so Jack and Jacqueline headed for the exit, saying they would catch up later. Once outside in the evening air, unlike the atmosphere they had just emerged from which was still warm even though it was September, but it was fresh air. They headed for the sea and on reaching it, the moon was glinting on the Mediterranean. Walking slowly along the promenade saying very little but enjoying the moment, he suggested they go down to the beach. Sitting themselves down on the stones close to the water's edge, Jack again put his arm around Jacqueline. After kissing for some time, Jack slid the shoulder strap of her dress down and slid his hand inside the dress, where her nipples were protruding through an extremely lacy bra. The light from the moon had become milky as their bodies became closer.

"Come back to our apartment Jack," she suddenly said.
'Why not,' he thought.
"Okay, let's walk back to your car," Jack replied. They found the car and drove a couple of blocks up to some older looking apartments. Coming in past the porter and then up the stairs through the front door. Everywhere was in a dark mahogany wood, the hand rails and panelled doors and inside the tiles were black and white marble. They crept in so as not to disturb her parents as it was now very late. Jacqueline put a saucepan of water on the stove for coffee, funny Jack thought, no kettle?

"Would you prefer a cold drink Jack? Mint is very refreshing," she asked. Jack nodded, so she turned off the gas and went to the fridge to prepare their drinks. She got out two tall glasses from the cupboard and added some mint cordial from Get Freres. This was something Jack had never seen in England. She added ice cubes and chilled water; it was such a refreshing drink on such a warm night.

Opening the door and beckoning him to follow, they went along the corridor to her bedroom. This had English cinema posters on the wall and a bookcase full of books, a large cupboard at the end and her bed was pushed up against a wall in a sort of alcove. Shelves above had model cars and a mix of old dolls, a really funny combination. The floor was carpeted wall to wall, which was unusual even at home in England. 'We don't have fitted carpets at home,' thought Jack. Sitting on Jacqueline's bed sipping their drinks, Jack felt very vulnerable.

"What happens if your parents wake up?" he asked nervously.

"They won't, don't worry Jack," she replied soothingly.

She put her arm around his waist and squeezed him. He leant across and kissed her and suddenly they were all arms, tongues and lips, and clothes coming off. Very soon he was bare-chested and Jack was now admiring her lacy bra which were full of delight he had just felt earlier on the beach. Soon she was down to her tiny, lacy panties to match and Jack in his white 'Mariner' Y front pants. He was struggling to control himself as they lay on her soft bed. The lights were soft in her room, her body seemed to shimmer in the glow. They laid sideways facing each other, her legs gripped one of his holding it close to her warm moist crotch but not allowing his wandering hand to get to her. He ran his fingers down past her gorgeous bottom into the lace and slowly caressed her. She started to move and slowly moved rolling slightly on her back. Jacqueline then started pulling at Jack's pants and raising one of her legs, she tried to push them down with her toes. His mountain of manhood stopped the pants from going any lower but now she changed position and at last he could feel her warmth beneath the lace. She suddenly pulled his hand guiding his fingers into her, arching her back in ecstasy. Jack had not come across a young lady that seemed to get so excited before, he was quite surprised, so he kept caressing her with the risk of exploding in his pants, or should he remove both their pants quickly. The decision was taken out of his hands literally as Jacqueline moved a little and ran her hand up the inside of his leg into his pants. She gently caressed him touching all his genital area, it was too much for him and his moment came urgently. It was difficult in the position to keep caressing that panting girl next to him but as if she knew, she pulled his hand away and moved it to her breasts and pulled him close to her.

Jack must have fallen asleep as when he woke up, a cover was over them both. She kissed him gently on the lips and she murmured, "Follow me and I will take you to the bathroom."

Out of the door they crept along the corridor, past her parent's room and to another door. Turning the light on above the basin, which was sufficient, she passed him a large towelling robe and a small towel. She blew him a kiss and slipped out of the door. He panicked for a moment, what happens if her parents woke up and came in. Jack slid the small brass lock across and set to freshening himself up. The bathroom had a toilet, bidet and basin with soft green paint work everywhere and contrasting wall colour and the same flooring as the hallway. He was fascinated at the lines of pill boxes on top of the bathroom cabinet Jack wondered if the French were all hypochondriacs. Creeping out of the bathroom he panicked as to which room was Jacqueline's, he thought it was the third door, yes there was a soft glow from the crack around the edge. He opened it gingerly to find Jacqueline waiting in bed with the bed sheet slightly turned back. After shutting the door and looking at the clock, which read nearly three in the morning, he sat down on the side of the bed holding her hand…

"I should be going, it's so late!" Jack said softly.

"Not yet, join me and I will sneak you out before the family awakes," Jacqueline replied. That is what was worrying Jack. She ran her hand underneath the thick towelling robe following the top of his leg, she slowly caressed the inside of his leg with her fingers. She was difficult to resist laying there, her bronzed body against the white sheets, a glimpse of two breasts peeking out and the sheet just showing her leg and side of her body. She stopped caressing and pulled the tie loose around his waist moving the towelling off his shoulder. He could not resist her any longer and slid into bed next to her, he tenderly kissed her then with more passion their bodies entwined. She slid down beside him, kissing his nipples and as her body moved down the bed, he could feel himself rising again as her firm breasts rubbed on him. She rose back up the bed and he turned her on her back caressing her firm breasts and kissing with a rising passion. He felt her legs part as he moved on top of her, then her hand fondly guided him into her warm body. Jack was still shocked at the way she moved beneath him as if using him to achieve the maximum enjoyment. He lifted himself up on his elbows with the intention of enjoying the moment more but alas the pleasures became too much and Jacqueline rose up to him with such energy that Jack thought he would burst.

Slowly their bodies softened and relaxed, Jack kissed her gently on the ear as he lay beside her. Some time passed and the next thing he remembered was Jacqueline laying there propped on her elbow just looking at him.

As he opened his eyes she said, "Jack I know you are younger than me, but I do love you."

He was taken aback so he kissed her gently on the cheek.

"Soon you start your journey back to England and I will miss you. You haven't met my parents yet which I wanted and I cannot come to England for at least six weeks and that's only a short course. You will write won't you?" she asked.

"Of course I will," he replied being a little worried about her keenness on him. 'She is tasty,' he thought, 'but she is in France and I am in England.'

"I ought to go," Jack said reluctantly.

"Please wait Jack I will make us some coffee and if you go about six my parents will not be up before seven o'clock."

"Okay, you get the coffee on, while I get dressed."

With that Jacqueline slipped on a soft green dressing gown and disappeared. Jack put his clothes back on, his shirt smelt of the nightclub, Gaulloise cigarettes and drinks with just a touch of perfume. By the time Jacqueline returned with a tray with a pot of coffee, two small cups and some strange bread on a plate he was dressed. She placed the tray on the floor sitting with her back to the bed.

"You will write?" she asked again as she poured the coffee.

"Yes, I said so, didn't I?" replied Jack rather irritably.

"Don't get annoyed with me, Jack!" said Jacqueline getting annoyed. Jack changed the subject and asked her about the bread.

"It's a sweet bread that the maid makes when she is here, it's lovely isn't it?"

He was feeling very hungry and found it very enjoyable and he soon tucked into a second slice. He found the coffee a bit strong but he did not say anything and put lots of sugar in it.

"I know you and Nick have plans for the next few days, but I would like to pick you up and your luggage from the hotel when you have to take the train, if it helps?" she asked rather pointedly. Her English was fantastic, possibly even better than his.

"You had better go Jack before my parents wake up and I am really sorry that they have not met you," she continued, looking at him with her sorrowful eyes. They embraced, her tongue quickly and sexually found his, she moved against him pulling him closer. He was then quietly ushered out down the corridor and with a quick peck on the cheek, he was gone.

He went down the two flights of stairs in a whirl and out through the flowerbeds of Euonymus and Lantanas, through the gate and out onto the streets of an early morning Nice. The streets were amazingly busy and already the sky was bright blue and the sun was out. He nearly skipped the length of the road meeting up with the main road Gambetta, leading up to their hotel. The market-stalls were set up around Place de Gambetta by the old station, Jack, who was very happy, wandered amongst them. The fruit and vegetable stalls had always fascinated him and he still could not get over the size of the peaches even this late in the season, local grapes had started to appear and stall holders were giving him slices of fruit for him to taste. They would not do this in England Jack was thinking. He suddenly spotted the plant and flower stalls, there were boxes of Bougainvilleas, Daturas, Abutilon, Plumbago and a few early Cyclamen. The flowers were all in big buckets to the front of the stall and attractive paper and ribbons on the stall to wrap them, perhaps he should buy some for Jacqueline. But then she might get the wrong idea and he would have to deliver them and then he could get caught up with her parents. No, he will talk to Nick about it and see what he thought, Jack was thinking. He was a long time with the flowers and it took his thoughts back to England and to Penny, with whom he had had a relationship in the Festival Hall. Jack was in a dream, those days together preparing the large baskets full of flowers for events in the Festival Hall, the moments of passion in the flower room, the warmth of her body and her blouses that were not always buttoned up high enough.

"Monsieur, monsieur voulez-vous des fleurs?" the stallholder was asking. He was obviously being asked if he required any flowers.

"Non merci," Jack replied, he was not sure if that was right but it brought him out of his reverie.

He eventually left the market and wandered up the road further to the hotel, he mused how people greeted him at this time of day, even though he did not know them. 'Friendly bunch, the French,' he thought. On entering Jack was greeted by Monsieur Christophe, being impressed at how early Jack was at coming in he presumed from an early walk! He offered him a large coffee, which came in a bowl, like a cereal bowl. He sat outside in the sun not bothering to enter his room, he took out a rather crushed Gauloise from his pocket and mused over the night with Jacqueline and where it would all lead to. It did worry young Jack how keen she was. He was very sleepy and the sun on his face and arms was gorgeous. So far the holiday had been great, such a pity that it had to end but to think how fed up they both were with girls in England and how many they had met so far. Jack wondered whether he would ever get to Holland to meet Helena again, people say it is flat with lots of canals. Then they grow a lot so where were all the glasshouses and if it was such a small country, where did all the people live? His thoughts wandered on, he thought he must get over there one day, it was not that far, just across the North Sea. He had read that you could take one of the ferries from Harwich, perhaps Nick and he could go over there next year. 'Where was he anyway?' he thought, 'I had better go and wake him up.'

Jack finished his coffee and took it to the kitchen and went to their room to find Nick snoring, sound asleep and lying fully dressed on his bed. Jack plumped up his pillows on his bed and leant back against them, planning the rest of their holiday and thought about gifts they should buy and what duty-free he could buy. Then his mind wandered back to Penny again, the days at her flat, lying next to her in her narrow bed, the sun streaming in through the French doors across the bed and the memories of waking with the sweet smell of her next to him. Then he thought about that lovely girl, Jacqueline, he had just been with. She was only three years older than Jack but he had not got that same feeling. His mind drifted from girls to sleep and the next thing he knew was Nick shaking him awake.

"Where were you?" he asked.

"We went out for a walk but how about you?" replied Jack moving the conversation to Nick. He then did not stop talking about Annette, how well they get on, which bar they had gone to and then he had walked her all the way home to her apartment, which was right up the back of Nice. He said he did not go in, as it was a shared flat with two other girls.

"Sure it wasn't her boyfriend?" Jack interjected. Nick ignored him and continued his story. They had been standing outside her apartment for ages and eventually she put him in a taxi for the hotel.

"I'm in love!" he shouted.

"No you're not, just infatuated," Jack retaliated.

"She's really upset at having work on Saturday but she is going to try and get an early train from Monaco to Nice to see me off but we can meet up again before that can't we Jack, we need to plan our last few days." Nick was lost in his thoughts for a moment then he said, "Well let's start with breakfast and you can tell me where you were last night Jack."

In the dining room Monsieur Christophe remarked on how tired the boys looked.

"Have you been out all night boys?" he asked.

"Nearly," Nick replied.

Monsieur Christophe gave them an 'old-fashioned' look and continued serving breakfast.

Chapter XI

Menton onto Ventimiglia

"Come on buddy, let's get a long day in and let's have a good night out tonight," said Nick.

"Who with?" Jack asked gingerly.

"I know you want to see Jacqueline," remarked Nick.

"No..." Jack said doubtfully, "let's wait and see how the day shapes up, we haven't promised anything have we?"

"Okay... if you're sure," Nick was being very amenable this morning, Jack thought to himself.

Today the croissants tasted even better, Jack and Nick tucked into the basket of bread, butter and pot of apricot jam. Jack had more recently got used to coffee from his spell of working in the Royal Festival Hall, where it was nearly obligatory to drink coffee. This French coffee was stronger but with a more creamy sort of milk. It was a delicious drink adding of course dunked bread that they had watched the French visitors doing. With breakfast over so early M. Christophe chatted to them again and this time about the French girls, almost telling them to be nice to them.

"Of course," replied Jack trying to avoid eye contact. Fortunately more guests came into the dining room, so the boys made a quick exit before he could continue. They were finished before nine o'clock for the first time since they had arrived.

They went back to their room to fetch their trunks and towels together, and oil of course for the tan, dropped them into their duffle bag, which they had taken in turns to carry. They decided how many Francs to take and left the rest hidden in the room including Nick's extra winnings.

"Come on let's take a bus and we'll get there quicker and we still have some tickets left in our 'carnet' of tickets," said Nick, Jack thought this was a good idea too.

Down at Place Massena, the bus turned left towards the port, so they got off and strolled through the gardens. There were pine trees, large Catalpas or Indian Beans as they were commonly called, under-planted with Oleandas in bright pink and white. The lawns were generally cut quite long about 2" in length. The regular irrigation kept it all so green, which in this heat was difficult to believe.

Down at Promenade des Anglais, which they joined off Place Massena, where cloistered shops and cafés surrounded the square. Jack and Nick were still amazed at how attractive the French girls were in comparison with those at home, perhaps, it was the olive skins and dark hair, not ignoring the fact that Nice was close to the border of Italy. At one time Jack believed it was part of Italy, perhaps that was why the accent was a bit different, although someone else told the boys that the accent was more from Marseille, but with neither of the boys able to say much or understand, they really did not know. They wandered along the sea front looking at the blue azure sea, totally amazed at how many people were on the beach so early; it was only just ten o'clock.

Arriving at the chosen beach of their Dutch friends, they made their way down the steps to the pebbly beach across to where it dips towards the sea. The pebbles were hard but if you wriggled around and moulded them it gave a headrest with a

127

couple of towels. No sign of their friends so far, so they laid down their towels and changed into their swimming trunks. Nick ran straight into the sea, Jack laid back putting his clothes in the bag and was using it as a pillow. He closed his eyes and thought of Jacqueline with her dark hair and chestnut eyes, it worried him in a way that she kept popping into his head. Perhaps seeing Helena, the lovely blonde Dutch girl would change all that. He dreamed and slept and the next thing he knew, was a few cold drips of water on his face. He jumped out of his reverie with a start, Nick was playing the fool as usual.

"Come on Jack, the sea is warm and out on the raft, there are some gorgeous French girls."

"Okay I'm coming," Jack sighed. He was just enjoying those dreams. He got up and went down to the sea and swam out to the raft to meet Nick's new acquaintances.

After having spent at least an hour out on the raft trying to chat to these French young people, they were getting tired of trying to make themselves understood. So they gave up and swam slowly back to the beach to look for their Dutch friends. Still no sign of them so Nick went off wandering to see whether he could find a snack, even a 'Bounty Bar' that was one of their favourites. Jack dozed, perhaps they had gone to a different beach he was wondering and before Jack had noticed Nick was back again.

"If we walk along the sea edge, we might spot them," Nick suggested.

There was nothing like wandering along the shoreline to check out the girls on the beach. They walked a long way and there were so many beautiful girls but no sign of the Dutch friends. So they returned back to their towels, very disappointed, they lay down to do some serious sunbathing, now becoming a shade of tan rather than lobster pink.

Jack dozed and Nick restless as ever had gone off again. Jack felt a tickle on his nose and awoke to find Helena crouching over him, she gave him a peck on the cheek as he sat up.

"Hello Jack, sorry my friends are waiting for me and we are off to Cannes today. They are saying that they don't want to be with you both, I feel very awkward and I like you Jack, so that is why I come to apologise. I have written my home address and phone number on this card for you or even come and see me in Holland…" With her big blue sad eyes she went to leave but Jack pulled her down and kissed her, this time on the lips, her hands went around his neck and it felt wonderful Jack thought.

"I must go now, my friends are waiting," she said again, tearfully.

"Have you got a pen so that I can give you my details?" said Jack. He quickly wrote his address down, she kissed him on the cheek and ran off up the beach with her beautiful blonde hair flowing behind her.

Jack felt very sad, she was lovely. Perhaps he would catch up with her again one day. Another swim must be the next best thing to calm him down, he suddenly saw Nick back on the beach so he swam in and walked over to him.

"Sorry no girls Nick, well Helena has been here but seemingly we are out of favour," said Jack.

"Never-mind, I have bought some pastries and a couple of beers, shame I thought we were all getting on well with them…" sighed Nick disappointedly.

The beach was filling up and the sun was extremely hot; Nick was visibly getting irritable.

"Let's not waste the day, come on let's go up to a bar and have some lunch." They picked up their things and packed them into the duffle bag and walked back into town. They soon found a small bar offering filled baguettes or Croque-Monsieur, and a couple of beers, they sat down and planned the rest of the day.

"Why don't we take the train down to Menton, we haven't been there have we Jack?" enquired Nick.

"That's a good idea we could have a look around and have a swim from that beach," replied Jack.

So after lunch, Menton it was. They walked up to the station and the train they caught was an Italian main line train going to Turin but stopped at Menton, Monaco and Ventimiglia before turning up through Italy, stopping at a few stops they had never heard of. The train compartments were similar to the French ones but a little more old-fashioned with more wood. They sat down with a couple of ladies who were Italian and did not stop talking. Jack decided they were mother and daughter, although Nick reckoned they were sisters, either way they were pretty tasty and he could shack up with either of them. There was also a young French guy who seemed very nervous and when the boys tried to speak to him, he excused himself and left. Nick now moved to the window opposite these ladies and typically Nick tried to speak English with an Italian accent rather loudly. They smiled having no idea what he was talking about. He tried telling them his name and getting Jack roped in too to say his, Jack moved across to sit a bit nearer to them, which put him nearer the younger lady convinced that she was the daughter. He was fascinated by her dark hair and big brown eyes, which seemed to lure him to her.

She coyly smiled and gave her hand to him to shake saying, "Buon giorno, comé sta?" she said shyly followed by her name, which was Gabriella, she then turned to the other lady who was wearing a wedding ring and said her name was Sophia. Nick followed suit and shook their hands. The conversation, which followed was more than difficult. Sophia moved and sat nearer to Nick, who looked a little stunned and started touching his hand. Jack was amused as Sophia was very good looking, cracking figure and not as old as he first thought. Where as

Gabriella, possibly Jack thought as he studied her a little more, could have been in her mid-twenties not that he would know really. She tried speaking a little English – he was fascinated as no one had ever really tried chatting him up in this way before. He watched her dark chestnut eyes darting about and her full lips that had lipstick of a rich red colour matching her top, which was a light frilly material gathered in around the top and arms. Her skirt was short showing quite a lot of her bronzed thigh and long slender legs.

It turned out that they were sisters and from Ventimiglia and had been down to Nice to try and sort out Sophia's divorce as her ex husband was French. Jack was wondering why she had kept her ring on, may be she did not feel she could not do that yet. Sophia was trying to explain in a bit of French as well as English to Nick what they were doing on their way back to Italy.

Well the boys were so engrossed they never got off the train at Menton in the end and with sheer luck they had carried their passports with them that day, as they had no identity cards as the Europeans had. Although they only had tickets to Menton and not a lot of money, they were persuaded to stay on the train, which did stop at the border. The ladies, Sophia and Gabriella got out their identity cards and the boys with their passports. Soon two men in grey uniforms with green lapels and hats both carrying guns, came to inspect them.

"On holidays?" asked the older of the two men, looking at the boys closely.

"Yes," replied Jack and Nick in unison a little anxiously, why did men in uniform make you feel uncomfortable thought Jack. Their passports were stamped, the ladies chatted to the customs men, who moved on and winked at the boys saying "Enjoy Italy," smiling to them all. The four of them looked at each other's cards and passports, which gave the boys the opportunity to find out how old the ladies were or rather girls. Gabriella was 25 and Sophia was 32. 'How nice,' thought Nick, 'I do like mature women.'

The train trundled on, the large black steam engine belching out smoke as the train went in and out of the tunnels, cut through the coastal rock. The scenery was stunning with little coves and small jetties with yachts moored, the boys wondered how you got down to those great little beaches, possibly a car was the answer.

They arrived at Ventimiglia station and the girls led the way, luckily no-one checked their tickets. They walked out into an incredibly busy street, which appeared to be a sea of taxis and scooters, it was a challenge to cross the road but the girls strode on with Sophia taking Nick's hand and pulling him along with Gabriella following with Jack taking up the rear. It seemed very different to France and the shops were bustling with so many people everywhere, it was a very lively place to live in. After a couple of turnings and then down a narrow street, Avenue Tripoli, Nick had vanished and Jack had lost sight of him. Feeling a bit panicky Jack looked for him as Gabriella took his hand and announced, "This is our apartment." She led the way up two flights of stairs into a large room with a kitchen leading from it and what looked like a bedroom. Nick was standing in the kitchen with a beer in his hand. He always astounded Jack as he always seemed to find a beer. Sophia was nowhere to be seen. Jack wandered through, Gabriella pointed out the beers or wine in the fridge. Beer was safer in the afternoon he thought. She took the cap off and offered the boys some strange looking nuts, they had a hard shell and were half open. She showed them how to open them and then disappeared.

"Nick," whispered Jack, "it's ten past four, what are we going to do, we definitely won't get back in time for dinner." Jack said in a panicky whisper.

"Don't worry, let's just wait and see." Nick replied looking very casual about it all.

The girls re-emerged looking stunning. Gabriella went over to Jack, he was less inclined to hold her, not that she was not very tasty, she looked really lovely with the curves in all the right places. He was very concerned they had promised to meet Jacqueline and Colin that evening, they would not get back in time for dinner at the pension and Monsieur Christophe would wonder where they were, especially if Jacqueline telephoned or turned up. Jack really could not remember if they had arranged anything. All these beautiful girls around had him in a whirl, and all Nick kept saying was, "let's see what happens." He was so infuriating at times, Jack was thinking.

"Jack, don't look so worried, we will take you out to see the town of Ventimiglia," At least, she said something like that, in her bit of English, French and Italian. The boys were mesmerised. With that they were off out of the small apartment and back into the street. Off the main street the areas were paved with terracotta looking bricks and were all for pedestrians. The shops were very expensive and had names that the boys had heard of but rarely seen. Christian Dior, Chanel with all their beautiful clothes in the windows. The people in the shops were beautifully dressed, there were lots of leather shops with coats and jackets, beautiful handbags and shoes. Jack's sister, Katy, would have been in her element, she loved shoes. Nick wandered in and tried on a cowboy jacket, the price was in lire and by the time he had converted it to francs then to pounds, it was about one hundred pounds, he had lost interest and certainly could not afford it at that price. He was only earning about seven pounds a week on his gardening earnings.

The boys were fascinated by the florist shops, which the girls thought was rather strange. They nearly lost sight of them as they had wandered on while the boys discussed the names and merits of the roses, lilies and so many other exotic looking Mediterranean flowers including pot plants of Bougainvilleas, Plumbago and large flowering Hibiscus. Suddenly Sophia appeared at the door beckoning them to come, what they did not realise was that she wanted them to see the town and go down to the beach. She grabbed Nick's hand and walked ahead, Nick could just see that the beach was full of cafés and restaurants.

Jack was really worried now, getting hot and bothered and fortunately Gabriella sensed this. She shouted something to Sophia, and she and Nick stopped to look around. Jack tried to explain that they needed to find a telephone to phone the pension or to phone his friend in Nice, Gabriella was genuinely concerned and knew where they would find a phone. She led him back across the road from the sea to a turning where there was a phone booth. She asked the operator for the number, which fortunately Jack had of the pension, Les Cigalles. She put the money in the phone and waited, finally it was ringing and Jack took the receiver. Monsieur Christophe answered and Jack explained that they were with friends in Ventimiglia and would not be back for dinner and not to worry about them and if Jacqueline, the young lady from Nice or locally known as Niçoise, rang, could he please explain where they are.

He thanked Jack very much for telephoning and added, "Be careful jeune homme, au revoir," then rang off.

Jack came away from the phone booth very relieved and hugged Gabriella, giving her a big kiss.

They now joined Nick and Sophia along by the beach, although they were now a distance away, Jack could see Nick had not a care in the world, sauntering along.

"I know where they go," said Gabriella, conversation was very difficult, Jack wished he knew a bit of Italian, he had never heard it or met anyone Italian before. She tried hard to explain what she did for a living, Jack thought that her job was in a shop, maybe in a ladies' clothes shop, he was not certain. Her sister worked for the Town, so Jack imagined that meant the council or something. He struggled to explain he was a gardener, it looked as though he was playing a game of charades with his actions, they both laughed and nearly fell over. Somehow no one expects two young men to be gardeners. By this time, they had got to the café bar, which was right on the beach overlooking the sea. Nick sat out on the deck with a beer in his hand, he never failed to get a beer in quickly. They sat down and joined them; Sophia had already ordered their drinks.

Nick was getting on very well indeed with Sophia she kept nudging him and putting her hand on his neck, but then the Italians seemed to be very tactile people. They sat watching the sea, many were still bathing, children called out to fathers and mothers, it was funny to hear another language and not French. This was one of the more bizarre things that Nick had got them into: being in Italy in the evening with two strange ladies or girls, although Nick's girl had been married, surely that made her a lady? Gabriella was trying to ask Jack if he had a girlfriend, well not really was the answer. She was pretty but Jack did feel a bit guilty about Jacqueline, especially as they had hinted at being around that night.

"Perhaps one day I come to England, see you… maybe we could write," Gabriella said smiling from under her eyes at Jack. He thought then of the loss of his Dutch friend, Helena, he had missed out on meeting up only that morning, where had they gone he wondered, although she had mentioned Cannes. Perhaps on their return to Nice, they could try their hotel; he thought they were leaving the next day.

They were at the bar a long time and as the light started to diminish, Gabriella suggested they went on to the beach. Taking their shoes off, they walked in the wet sand as the Mediterranean turned its short waves onto their feet, it was so warm. She took hold of Jack's hand and squeezed it, Jack felt like this was a double take as just the other night he had done the same with Jacqueline, the French girl. To the west the bright red huge round sun slowly sank below the horizon giving an orange aura across the sea. Gabriella suddenly turned to Jack giving him a huge hug and kissed him gently on his lips, she was shorter than Jack and stood on tiptoe. What's up with these girls, he was just an ordinary English boy, a gardener and the French, Dutch and now Italian girls were taking a fancy to him. He blushed, he could feel himself going bright red, so he kept on walking. She broke away mumbling something and then splashed him with water. Jack chased her across the sand, she was very quick but Jack was a fit young man and he caught her up. As he grabbed her she tripped and they both fell into the water laughing and splashing each other. Jack was embarrassed as he had tripped her, her pretty white embroidery anglaise dress was soaked through. He could see she was not wearing a bra, just tiny panties

"Come swim, we wet now," she said laughing.

Jack took off his wet shirt, Gabriella took off her dress, and ran into the sea. A bit confused, Jack removed his shorts and then, in just his Y fronts, he laid down their clothes to dry out a bit on the hot sand and then followed Gabriella into the sea. As he swam out to join her, it reminded him again of the feeling of being shunned by Penny, although twice his age, it still hurt and it was not that long ago really. He swam out to Gabriella who was waving her hand at him, Jack wondered whether he took life too seriously? Just enjoy the young lady's company like Nick, however he wasn't really like that. He reached Gabriella, she put

136

her arms around him with her cool breasts against his chest and she kissed him tenderly with great feeling.

"I like you English man…" she purred in his ear.

Jack was not a great swimmer, he nearly drowned as she wrapped her legs around him and they sank below the water. She let go and swam off underwater like a small mermaid leaving him spluttering as he came up to the surface. He swam to the shore and she came up behind him, then under him about a foot below looking at Jack with her hair flowing through the water. It looked very eerie, gradually he could touch the bottom of the sandy shore, it was quite dark being about nine thirty. Being short she could not touch the bottom so hung onto Jack to kiss him again. He could not resist and opened up to enjoy those few romantic moments in the Mediterranean.

Back on the sand her dress was still really wet,

"Come Jack."

She held her dress like a piece of washing between each hand and ran off down the beach.

Jack quickly put his horribly wet shorts back on, held his shirt in one hand and chased after her. She ran in circles as he chased her they passed the odd couple enjoying the last of the dusk on the beach. Gabriella was fun Jack thought as she suddenly turned and ran towards him nearly jumping up at him. He would enjoy explaining the image of chasing a young topless Italian girl around the beach in Italy to his colleagues back in the 'bothy' on the Embankment Gardens.

Eventually, crumpled and wet they walked arm in arm back to the café bar. No sign of his friend or Sophia, Jack wondered what happened to the dinner plan.

"Sophia will be home," said Gabriella interrupting Jack's thoughts.

"We need to go back and get the train."

"No, no stay night, go tomorrow," Gabriella said squeezing his arm.

Back at the apartment where Jack expected Nick to be in bed with Sophia, they were in the tiny kitchen cooking dinner and now drinking Chianti, Italy's finest wine, not that Jack knew much about wines.

"What you two been up to eh?" Nick started winking at Jack, "you are a rogue."

"No just swimming and playing on the beach."

"Oh yeh!?"

"We've been having fun," smiled Jack.

Gabriella disappeared into the bedroom to change and threw Jack a towel.

She emerged in cropped white trousers and white blouse, looking stunning with her beautiful dark features, eyebrows and lashes showing off her chestnut eyes. Nick winked at Jack and mouthed "lovely".

Gabriella noticed and asked what he was saying.

"It was a compliment, you are pretty."

She turned away giggling and asked Sophia if she could help he gathered, they laughed together and chattered away. Most likely about them but who cares. Nick came over and the boys sat chatting at the table.

"We're in here, you seem to be getting on well with Gabriella," nudged Nick.

"Come on we are just having fun,"

"We are staying the night Jack, Sophia has suggested it," smiled Nick like a Cheshire cat.

They all sat down around the small table, it was nearly ten o'clock, red checked tablecloth and a couple of candles in bottles. In front of them was something Jack had never seen before, like wafer thin raw bacon rashers with squares of melon and some long red pointed things they called pimentos. 'So here goes,' thought Jack, his dad had always told him it was rude not to eat what was put in front of you. He watched how Gabriella

138

began to eat it, she cut a bit of the bacon, then a cube of melon, bit of bread, some of the red thing, then a sip of wine. So Jack followed.

Nick not being as polite, ate some of the bacon, tried chewing it and commented, "Hey what's this Jack, uncooked bacon?"

"Be quiet and eat it, it must be some sort of ham" retorted Jack.

With that, Nick cut what they discovered to be a strong pepper in half and popped it into his mouth. He started chewing it – well, hot was an understatement! He spat it out, and rushed to the kitchen for a drink of water.

Sophia rushed after him, "No, no Nick, no water," and grabbed bottled water out of the fridge for him. "Water no good in Italy." He guzzled it down and gasped for breath. "Poor Nick I should tell you pimento very hot." Sophia could not help laughing.

The dinner continued after the outburst and both boys finished that course with the exception of the red pimento. The wine was good and flowed freely, the conversation got better. They were told it was bolognaise. When it was served Jack was waiting for Nick to say 'where's the meat' but apparently in Italy the spaghetti is often served with just a heavy tomato and herb sauce and bread to push the sauce around the plate.

What a fantastic meal, Jack was feeling very woozy when it came to the dessert. Nick did not stop talking about girls and even got on to talking about Jack and his different girlfriends. Fortunately they did not understand a word he was chatting about. The dessert arrived which was a sort of tart of peaches with a thin milky custard in the base, very strange but very tasty. They were fit to collapse, fancy two nice girls keeping them fed and watered and boarded, just by a chance meeting on the train.

Nick reckoned that Sophia having now been divorced just wanted to get to bed with him having looked around at the little furniture in this small apartment. There was only one armchair and a sofa. Jack had already slumped on the sofa and Nick had helped clear the dishes.

"Don't exert yourself Jack," grumbled Nick.

"I won't," replied Jack.

Gabriella came and sat next to him, it was hot and after this big meal he was not feeling too good. She cuddled next to him and laid her head on his chest. Nick disappeared into the bedroom with Sophia. Jack just laid there, Gabriella sensed he was not feeling too good and fetched him some bottled water. He sipped it slowly and was feeling a lot better, she held his hand for a while until his colour came back, 'she seemed such a caring girl' he thought.

As the evening passed by, Gabriella caressed his chest and neck and turned towards him. Her soft lips touched his neck, he in turn ran his fingers across the top of her blouse and he could feel her nipples lifting towards the soft material of her blouse. That was not all that was lifting, Jack thought, and turned on the sofa to make it less obvious.

"It must be late and we should sleep, you here and me in there," she said in some sort of jumbled English with a really sensuous kiss, her tongue touching his, she pulled away blowing him a kiss. She knocked at the bedroom door and waited, Nick appeared shirtless but not undressed as Jack had expected.

"Sorry Nick, I was here first, you've got the armchair," laughed Jack.

Sophia appeared in a black silky looking dressing-gown, some sleeping bags and pillows, kissed Jack and disappeared into the bathroom. When both the girls had finished, the boys quickly washed and settled down to try and sleep.

"Nick what happened? Are you alright?" asked Jack surprised to see him sleeping in the sitting room with him.

"I'm tired, go to sleep, I will tell you on the train going back," and with that he curled up in the armchair and fell asleep.

The boys were woken by the girls, who were hurriedly showering as it was eight thirty, they were running backwards and forwards, from nightwear, to bras and knickers to being dressed. The boys had quite a parade, they were two very special ladies or girls Nick and Jack decided. They explained they had left fruit juice and coffee, their names and address. Gabriella went over and kissed Jack tenderly, "Please write, we would love to see you again..." they tried to say. The boys laid there in stunned silence as the girls banged the door shut. They crawled out of their sleeping bags to enjoy a great breakfast, tidied up and wrote a thank you note with their addresses and they too left the little apartment.

Nick and Jack hardly spoke on their way to the station. Nick suddenly stopped at another leather shop, "I must buy something, at least a belt, they are so cheap," Nick said. There was a long rack outside which tempted them. Nick eventually chose one with a huge western style buckle. They stood outside looking longingly at the jackets, when suddenly someone from behind Jack dug him in the ribs. It was Gabriella, she worked in the lingerie shop opposite, no wonder her briefs were especially saucy Jack thought. Another kiss and one on the cheek Nick and she was gone again laughing and blowing kisses to them.

"She's crazy," Nick commented jibing at Jack.

They had a bit of trouble at the railway station but eventually the ticket man took their French money and accepted their return tickets. The boys checked they had their passports and sat and waited for the train to go in the Nice direction.

Nick then started to talk of his time with Sophia, Jack asked him to spare him the details of the very heavy petting that went on, he had obviously had a good time. Apparently Sophia did not approve of love making before people got to know each other. He was amused to find how keen she was to see him again and had even suggested she should come to England! They enjoyed their journey back in amiable silence broken only by the usual border control check, they soon arrived back in Nice.

"Shall we go straight to the beach or take the bus up to Cimiez to look at some gardens, which Jacqueline had suggested. We could always try and fit in a swim this evening before dinner or afterwards?" suggested Jack, "I am getting used to these evening swims," he smiled cheekily at Nick.

Chapter XII

Cimiez, old town Nice

Straight from the station they went off to Cimiez on the bus, the old part of Nice, which lay behind the port on the hill. This was an area much frequented by Queen Victoria, hence the statue, it was said that she stayed there with a Frenchman. Those Royals travelled all over the place, 'randy weren't they,' thought Jack. The bus dropped them at the bottom of a wide road leading up hill with huge villa type houses on them. The road was shaded by large London Plane trees, which helped in the hot sun. They followed Jacqueline's scribbled instructions on Jack's piece of paper. They turned several corners, rising all the time and suddenly in a narrow quiet road with even larger modern villas, they found the one they were looking for. It had railings all around it with a kind of turret built on each corner and painted in a light terracotta colour. These turrets gave it a palatial look, almost toy-like in its pastel colour.

To Nick's delight a Trans Am American sports car was parked in the driveway, he went into raptures. It was red with a blue strip down the middle from the bonnet to the boot.

"These people must be worth a few bob," he exclaimed, a little too loudly. They rang the bell and were ushered into the hall announcing that Jacqueline Thiery had said that they could call and visit the garden of Monsieur and Madame Ricard to the young French girl, who the boys presumed to be their maid. She looked at them enquiringly as they tried their best French to make her understand.

"Un moment s'il vous plaît, je vais chercher Madame Ricard..." she disappeared upstairs.

"Madame," she called "il y a des jeunes hommes qui disent ils veulent regarder votre jardin?"

"Ah oui, Jacqueline Thiery m'a rappellé l'autre jour, ils sont jeunes paysagistes," replied Madame Ricard. The young maid went back to the boys feeling very relieved as by their appearance, they did not look very smart.

"Madame Ricard viendra dans un moment, allez y au jardin," said the pretty maid showing them through the house to the garden.

Madame Ricard appeared at the top of the elegant staircase before they left the hallway. She was a very elegant lady with curly blonde hair caught back with hair combs, she wore cream trousers with neat creases and a white blouse. She glided down the wide stairs, which had cream painted wrought iron ballustrading. They were standing on what looked like marble flooring and there were Greek statues set into the walls. She greeted the boys in perfect English and said how pleased she was that the boys had made the effort to come and visit her garden. She led them through her long dining room, which had an amazingly long dark wooden table and elegant chairs set around it. At the other end were French doors opening onto the terrace, Nick was wondering if that was where the term "French" doors had come from. On the terrace there was a large canopy shading a beautiful glass-topped table and chairs, keeping the sun away.

"Would you like a mint drink or Coca Cola?" Madame asked, inviting the boys to sit down at the table. The boys were mesmerised looking around them trying not to gape at everything. Jack was stunned, he had never seen garden furniture like it, each chair had an attractive cushion to sit on, which added a splash of colour to the whole set. Madame Ricard called the maid and asked her to fetch them all drinks.

"We are not good at gardening but have a man who comes to maintain it," she said feeling a little awkward having two young experts looking at the garden. From where they were sitting, the lawns led down to the formal part, box hedges framed each side of the lawn neatly cut to about fifteen inches high and nine inches wide and in really good condition. The lawns were so green considering how hot and dry it was. Madame Ricard explained that the whole garden was irrigated and she showed the boys the little pop up jets that came out of the lawn.

"Do you think that we could do something like this in England. We do get the odd dry summer and even normally it would save having to use hoses and sprayers wouldn't it Nick?" Jack asked Nick.

"In the future perhaps when we work together in our big gardening company, we'll have to look into it won't we?" Nick commented.

To the end of the garden there was a swimming pool but this was very different, the boys had never seen anything like it before. It was built like a pond with stone edges and the water was nearly at the top and then on the far side it was lapping over the edge. Where did the water go? The boys were fascinated. They were so high up that Nice just stretched out below and the house below them could only be seen by its rooftop. They climbed through the plants to the side to check what happened to the pool water, so instead of having the skimmer inside the pool like a gutter all the way around, this had one on the outside. It was just the same principle but the pool appeared to join up with the sea, when you sat on the terrace, which intrigued the boys.

"Boys," called Madame Ricard, "if you would like a swim, we have some swimming shorts."

"Thank you," they called in unison and wandered back to have their drinks, which were cold Coca Cola with ice cubes and slices of lemon. The maid returned with a large plate of little rounds of toast with bits on. Jack struggled with some of them, they were very fishy and ever so salty. His face obviously showed his distaste as Madam Ricard explained they were anchovies, which were also found on pizzas. She went on to say how Jacqueline had told her so much about the boys and if she could help in anyway to make their stay even more pleasant they had just to ask.

"How about starting your visit here by staying to lunch...?" Jack and Nick looked at each other dumbfounded. She continued, "My husband Gerard, will be home for lunch soon and he would love to meet you, so why not have a swim, there are swimming shorts in the changing room and I will get Lucille, our young maid, to fetch you some clean towels. Then we can relax with a glass of wine until Gerard comes home," she added. The boys thanked her very much and wandered off through the garden to the changing room.

"Wow, this is a surprise," commented Nick a little too loudly.

"Shsh... she'll hear you Nick," Jack replied. They found the shorts in very garish colours with ties around the waist, so they fitted them both and as they emerged, the maid gave them two large fluffy beach towels. Jack felt rather self-conscious as Lucille eyed them up and down. The water was so warm, they soon jumped in and they were fascinated watching the water lap over the far edge. After a couple of lengths, they stood against the edge of the pool looking at the water from below, the pool appeared to join the Mediterranean sea. The water was salty and not chlorinated as expected.

Madame Ricard came down to the pool-side checking out if they were okay.

"We are fine thank you, it is just glorious..." responded Jack.

"What a couple of handsome young men I have in my pool today," she said slightly flirtatiously as she brushed her long slim fingers across Nick's shoulders.

"White, red or rosé wine with your lunch mes jeunes hommes?" she said smiling.

"We have no preference Madame Ricard," replied Nick, enjoying each moment.

"Please call me Arlette," said Madame Ricard.

"We have enjoyed the rosé, the wine of the south, sounds good to us," responded Jack as she walked back up the garden.

"She's a bit cheeky isn't she Jack, still for a married woman she looks pretty good to me..." Nick watched her walk up the garden, "I reckon I should call again on my own for a drink and a swim, maybe a bit of skinny dipping!" Nick was getting carried away with all sorts of possibilities.

"Stop it Nick, behave, she's a friend of Jacqueline's mother," retorted Jack

"So...? Who said anything about age, she's flirting with me Jack," Nick was getting a bit irritated by Jack's pompous attitude. "What about you and Penny eh...?" What could Jack say. They soon dried off and dressed back into their shorts and shirts, they hung the towels and trunks up to dry and sauntered back to the terrace area.

The table looked fabulous with a large bright yellow and blue cloth on it, wine in a cooler jar and bowls of cashew nuts and some other green looking nuts. They tasted good but they had no idea what they were. Arlette returned and Nick could swear that another button was undone on her blouse showing a very lacy looking bra and tanned flesh, Jack noticed too and they

147

nudged each other. The cool wine was poured and they sat back with Arlette asking them questions about their work and aspirations. They told her about their ideas of running a garden company together as they got on so well. She asked about their parents, their gardening work, girlfriends, in fact quite a lot of searching questions.

By the second glass of rosé wine, Jack commented quietly to Nick while Arlette had gone to check the lunch, "Wow this is strong stuff, don't drink too much Nick," he knew how Nick enjoyed his drinks and got carried away. Arlette returned with her husband, Gerard. He was a bit older than Arlette, tall and very distinguished with his black hair greying at the temples and a bit bald at the front. He greeted them in French and had a really strong grip as he shook hands with them.

"Sit down, relax..." he reverted to English, a little broken, not as good as Arlette's. He had a light linen jacket on that he slid off and put on his chair. Underneath was a leather strap and shoulder holster with a gun in it. The boys' mouths dropped open, which Gerard noticed immediately. He apologised for scaring them and explained he usually left it in the house. He continued to explain that he worked for the French Government in connection with the drugs coming into France through the airport and particularly the harbours and marinas all along the coast. The boys had never seen a real gun close up, Nick being Nick asked to see it. Gerard obliged removing the clip of shells before passing it to him. Nick turned it over and over in his hands, asked Jack if he wanted to look at it, 'no' was his quick response. Nick gave the gun back and wanted to ask lots of questions.

"Have you shot anyone Monsieur Ricard?" asked Nick.

Jack jumped on him quickly, "You don't ask questions like that Nick."

"No I don't mind really, my work is quite dangerous but I am not in the front line, my men work undercover acting as drug buyers and other such unsavoury people, which is very dangerous. This area of France still has many members of the Mafia living and working here. Some of them are professional people as accountants, lawyers and even hold positions on city councils. However they then help the agents and shippers that we are trying to catch. Huge amounts of cocaine are coming in from Africa as well as heroine…" Gerard continued with many stories about his work, the boys just sat there with their mouths and eyes wide open.

Nick and Jack had never seen cocaine. 'What was it?' Jack wondered. The only drugs they had seen were purple hearts being handed around at some of the South London parties they go to, but this stuff… 'What was it?' Jack was wondering. Nick luckily left it alone and Arlette offered them another glass of wine to have with their lunch. Lucille came out with a big bowl of salad. The boys were getting used to all this unusual food and loved it but was this it, just salad or were there some surprises?

"Enough Gerard, if you are not careful he will tell you his life story! So what should these boys see around Nice that they might not have seen already?" she asked Gerard.

"Have you been up behind the War Memorial?" Arlette asked.

"Yes," replied Nick

"To St. Tropez?"

"Yes, with Jacqueline," replied Jack.

"The Casino?" asked Arlette.

"Yes and No," replied Jack, Arlette looked confused, so Jack explained he was too young to go in, she looked amused.

"How about Eze to see the village and cactus garden?" asked Arlette.

149

"Well no, we had planned to go to Menton but we never got there!" Nick explained how they had met some Italians and they were invited to see where they lived.

"How about after lunch I drive you up to this charming village of Eze, you must see it before you go back to England," offered Arlette. Gerard suggested taking them to the gardens and showing them the exotic cacti area first then the village.

"Is the afternoon long enough Gerard for them to see it all?" Arlette asked him.

"Well you could go tomorrow," Gerard replied.

Jack quickly responded and said, "The trouble is, we said we would see Jacqueline tomorrow," and hoped he didn't sound rude.

"Well we will go after lunch, now where has Lucille disappeared to, I'm hungry," said Gerard. Having brought out the salad with dressing on, Lucille brought out a large bowl of what they called 'couscous' with chopped peppers. Jack thought they must be as they did not taste like tomatoes, also a strange pastry a bit like pizza but with a very strong hot cheese on top and French bread all chopped up, a feast indeed.

"So Jack, I hear that you and Jacqueline are very good friends?" Arlette asked Jack, who was looking rather embarrassed, 'oh dear I wonder what she has been saying,' Jack thought to himself.

"She hopes to come to England, is that right, and see you?" Arlette was grinning at him looking very amused.

"Yes she does," Jack was beginning to feel uncomfortable.

"Leave the boy alone!" Gerard chimed in and they carried on eating and discussing Nice. The boys explained how one day they hoped to come back and run a garden maintenance business from Nice.

"What a good idea," Gerard commented and he offered to help if he could. Arlette disappeared and returned with a platter of small fish, which after enquiring, turned out to be sardines.

They showed the boys how to pick them up and chew from the bone, leaving the head and tail. Lunch continued on with cheese to follow. The boys were getting used to different types and Nick was getting used to a great deal of wine, which was making him more and more talkative. Jack was dreading him starting on about the Dutch girls but sure as anything he did, luckily describing them as a crowd of friends and how they had caught up with them in a bar in the 'Red light' district.

Arlette was amazed to think that the boys had even found this unsavoury area, Gerard agreed and he then pointed out again the drugs and the girls went together with men running them from complete houses full of young women. The discussion followed with Arlette going back indoors in disgust. Gerard described the way it worked and how in theory it was not legal but the police ignored prostitution unless it caused major problems. The boys asked him questions, had he ever raided these houses, to which he nodded and yes his teams had and on occasions they had found some amazing bundles of drugs and even guns. Arlette returned with the most amazing sweet, looking like a bowl of creamy custard with large spoonfuls of meringues floating in it. Jack tucked in, he loved his puddings, Nick just had more wine. After some coffee, Gerard left for work with Nick asking him who he was going to arrest that afternoon. Jack dug him in the ribs telling him to shut up. They thanked Gerard for his kind hospitality, shook hands and he kindly said that they were very welcome anytime.

Arlette returned sitting in between the boys putting her arm on the back of Nick's chair and occasionally brushing his neck. Nick was trying hard to resist and in the end he got up and suggested they should get off to see Eze before it became too late. They all left the table and after a few minutes Arlette returned looking refreshed and very chic with her smart bag and car keys in her hand. Lucille cleared the table and they all set off for the afternoon. Arlette pressed a button on the garage doors and they opened automatically exposing a beautifully shiny black Peugeot car. She reversed the car out and Jack climbed into the back, it had cream leather upholstery, a stereo radio, which was tuned into Radio Riviera. Jack was amused as that was where they had visited with Annette in Monte Carlo and she had taken them around the radio station.

Chapter XIII

Eze Village

The Peugeot floated through the back streets of Nice coming out just above the harbour. As the road climbed out of the area of St. Roch, starting to go higher, it curved around a large mountain now a sparsely wooded area with less houses. The road curved and twisted, it suddenly entered a harsher, rocky area and then there were some superb houses perched on the hillside. This was the Grande Corniche, the highest coastal route and the way towards Italy. The road was cut hard into the rock passing through tunnels and hanging on the edge of the cliffs. The views were stunning looking all the way across the Mediterranean. Jack sat back totally mesmerised by it all.

Nick was in deep discussion with Arlette as the automatic car with its big engine purred along. She had her hand on his knee and Jack was there just for the ride. The road they took went on with houses that seemed perched on the cliff side, funnily enough to the right closest to the coast, some had car parking spaces on their roofs, others had swimming pools! Walls covered in purples of Bougainvillea and blue of Plumbago not forgetting the orange trailing trumpets of Campsis, window boxes full of trailing Geraniums nearly all red with a few Petunias but not many. Jack was fascinated with the gardens as they passed by Moint Leuse and on towards Eze. They pulled off right and down a twisty narrow hill leading down and round, ending up on a small strange flat plain area. This had another main road running through it, there were a couple of restaurants, a car park and a hotel and that was about it. Arlette drove the Peugeot into a parking slot beneath the trees and as she put the handbreak on, she leant across and kissed Nick! Jack couldn't believe his eyes, she was at least twenty years older, although Jack's previous girl friend was eighteen years older, but twenty plus was just too much, he thought.

Out of the car and into the dazzling heat, they left the car park to walk up to the village of Eze. It was a good way up to the medieval village keeping the cars well away from it. Arlette looked stunning in a calf length cream skirt and a turquoise silk blouse with a large stone in a blackish colour hanging from a silver chain around her long neck. As Nick and Arlette walked ahead of Jack, he watched as her bottom and hips swayed from side to side. She had a very good figure for her age and her blonde hair bounced as she went up the steps towards the village. She must have felt Jack's eyes looking at her, as she turned around and asked him to catch up and then putting her arm through Jack's on one side and Nick on the other, they marched on up the steep steps. A few other people were on the climb up to the village but not that many considering it was a busy time on the coast.

"What a stunning dramatic village Eze is," Jack commented to Arlette, inland from the coast it looked precariously perched on the mountain side. The little streets were a maze of vaulted passageways, crooked steps and secret corners and full of restaurants, shops and galleries. The view at the top was breathtaking and they still had not reached the exotic gardens. Jack was amazed Nick had not asked to stop for a drink, they stopped and looked at the little shops and the views all around towards the Maritime Alps. Arlette, Jack noticed, could not resist touching Nick, on his shoulder or his hair, or even pat his bottom, Jack hoped her husband did not suddenly appear brandishing his gun! They continued up climbing the steps and found the ancient medieval church dating back to the fourteenth century.

They got to the Exotic gardens at the top, there was a fantastic range of succulents and cacti from around the world with an amazing range of Agaves throughout the area. 'Wow,' thought Nick and Jack, this was well worth the long climb up. They all stood together looking across at the views, it was breathtaking, Jack and Nick were totally awe-struck. To think that all those centuries ago, this little village was fortified and a stronghold and the original castle would have been where the gardens were planted.

They all made their way back down to the car park and Arlette suggested she drove them towards La Turbie for an aperitif. Back in the car, with the windows open to let the hot air out, the Peugeot purred out of the car park. Arlette drove along the coast road, going through smaller villages and again beautiful coloured gardens and walls with the sea on the other side and the sun shining reflecting its turquoise blue. Arlette drove this way so they could come back to Beaulieu sur Mer, she pulled over to a small block of shops with the railway running behind them. Jack imagined how they must vibrate when the main line engines pulling the coastal trains up to Italy went by. He sat bemused in the back as Nick got out with her to pop into the shop, she was really playing up to him, where would this go Jack wondered. On their return to the car with a couple of small bottles of orange drink with straws to cool them off, Arlette definitely needed cooling off Jack was thinking.

Arlette suggested having dinner out too and why not meet up with Jacqueline.

"What about Colin, he is Jacqueline's guest?" Jack asked.

"Oh I will ask Jacqueline what plans they have tonight, I had forgotten about her English penfriend. First we need to find a telephone box." Arlette started looking around. Jack was thinking they really ought to phone M. Christophe at Les Cigalles too, as he would be expecting them for dinner. They found a phone box and arranged to meet Jacqueline, Colin wanted to stay in and catch up with writing postcards. Then they rang M. Christophe. He was very polite as usual and thanked them for letting him know. They arranged to meet Jacqueline by the port in Beaulieu. Arlette got Jack to get out of the car and pointed towards the hill above the railway and he could see the road they had driven down and in front of it, the Plateau St. Michel visited by many a keen walker when staying in Beaulieu. The boys were glad they had driven down and not walked, it looked a very long way. Nick had started to put his arm around Arlette as she leant towards him by the car, then they all got back in the car.

As they entered the town, huge works were being carried out to build a new marina or port, the boys remarked how it would house even more expensive yachts. It was quite an impressive sight as large trucks were dumping huge rocks into the sea, cranes and diggers worked to get them in the right place. Perhaps one day when and if the boys could return, it would be finished with its chic shops and restaurants overlooking the new area on the coast. Driving along the boys were impressed with the villas, many with columns and balustrades, many of them were huge with very green lawns and areas of what Jack believed were Corsican Pines, but he was not sure. Arlette kept up the description of the various points of interest as this was one of the most sheltered areas on the Riviera. The Palm lined promenade overlooking the Baie des Anges was known as "La Petite Afrique" or Little Africa for that reason. They journeyed on around past the Hotel de Ville and into the port where small fishing boats with blue and red numbers on the sides, gently bobbed at their moorings, then up a road by the Casino to a square where Arlette decided to park.

Time was getting on but they still had time to have the aperitif Arlette promised before meeting Jacqueline. Arlette decided to go along to her favourite restaurant near the port to book a table for later and then they could have a stroll and a few drinks beforehand. The restaurant was called 'Poisson Bleu', which looked out over a promenade type of walkway and beyond the sea. The headwaiter obviously knew Arlette and promised to keep a good table on the front terrace area but Arlette changed her mind and decided they would have their drinks straight away. So he kindly moved the tables around to accommodate her and asked them what they would like to have. Nick needed no encouragement but Jack really needed to go for a walk and have a bit of space. So he excused himself, saying he would look out for Jacqueline.

He wandered off, he felt quite relieved to be on his own for a change, up through narrow streets with interesting houses, bars and restaurants. There were a few tourists but generally the streets were quiet. He found he had back-tracked and ended up on the other side of the port and there in front of him was a splendid Greek looking building. Being a curious person, he wandered on to find it was a museum of precious metals and archaeological documents, not Jack's 'cup of tea' but the gardens made up for his lack of interest in the museum,. It had loads of Oleanders in different colours, olives and Palm trees, was it supposed to be a Greek garden or just French, he was not sure. He would ask Arlette, the guide lady for the day. What a shame Nick wasn't there to share this garden with him, he was great on plants. This was called Villa Kerylos with wonderful views of what Jack thought was Cap Ferrat. 'I wonder what the time is?' he was thinking, 'my stomach tells me it is late.'

Considering it was early evening, it was very hot and Jack's shirt was beginning to stick to his chest as he hurried back around the port to the restaurant, where Jacqueline had already arrived.

On seeing him, she scowled a little, "Where have you been? We've had to order already," scolded Jacqueline but on him greeting her with a hug and a kiss, not on each cheek as tradition, but on the lips.

She whispered is his ear "You're forgiven," she smiled cheekily at him. He sat down all hot and bothered. The first course had just been served and white wine was already in a glass in front of him. Jacqueline moved her seat closer to him and touched his knee and his body jumped.

Nick was engrossed with Arlette, a bit public Jack thought especially as she was known to the restaurant but then perhaps she has done it before and the French are perhaps discreet, who knows. Jacqueline winked at Jack and frowned, obviously not really approving. They asked Jack where he had been and he described the gardens around the Villa Kerylos and Arlette explained all about how they were modelled on traditional Greek gardens after the building, which again followed the same style. She was a mine of information chatting about how some American had tried to build a new port and marina there years ago. He was refused permission and now at last the work had started, by the French of course.

The first course of their dinner was an 'assiette', which turned out to be all different cold meats and sausisson or sausage, some of which he did not really like and on the edge were green and black olives. Arlette was holding one to Nick's lips trying to get him to eat it, he was enjoying the attention, just when she had pushed it to his lips, she leant across and with her lips she took it back. He thought this was hilarious and laughed. Jack was so embarrassed he drank more wine and told Jacqueline all about Eze and the fantastic gardens with the Cacti and Agaves. The main course came which was lobster and a large bowl of green salad, which was covered in a sort of oil dressing. Jack was not over the moon with all the fishy dishes he had been trying, Jacqueline came to his rescue and showed him how to eat it and get all the meat out of the different shells. They all chatted away, more and more wine flowed so freely, surely Arlette was not going to drive after this. Jacqueline, Jack noticed was mainly drinking water. As Jacqueline served Jack with salad, she explained it was 'to cleanse the palate' ready for the cheese course. 'Not like England,' Jack thought, although he was beginning to like the way they ate here and life generally as he dreamed looking across the old port. 'Could he perhaps run a company on the coast, looking after and building gardens but his French was terrible and France did not really welcome young Englishmen coming and taking jobs that the French could do. Perhaps it was too complicated, their gardening skills he felt were better than the French, let's face it, gardening was an English tradition.' Jack was lost in his thoughts until Jacqueline nudged him asking him which cheese he would like. He came back to Earth and thought the brie looked nice, so he tried that, there was another one which looked good too called 'Rablachon' a creamy cheese.

"Go on try some," said Jacqueline insistently. It was quite strong but nice with some bread, which Jacqueline popped into his mouth touching his lips gently with her fingers at the same time. 'This girl was a tease,' he thought. 'Perhaps with her help I could learn French and work down here in this part along the coast. Okay it was cooler in the winter but not all that rain, snow and fog that we have in England. Could I cope with working in ninety degrees in the summer, perhaps not. I would get a good tan though!' Jack's thoughts went on.

"Where are you Jack?" Jacqueline asked him again as coffee was served in little cups and glasses of cold water too.

"Oh, work," Jack replied.

"Work?" Nick picked up, "Why work?" he asked.

"I was wondering if we could work down here, lots of advantages, we did talk about it before Nick, but I don't think it is feasible," Jack concluded. He filled his coffee cup with lots of sugar, he did struggle with these strong coffees.

Arlette suddenly excused herself and on returning, she suggested that they should go as she wanted to be back home before Gerard returned. Jacqueline suggested she took the boys back to their hotel. Arlette settled the bill, the waiters fussed over her as they left, 'she must be a regular,' Nick thought. They thanked her for the delicious dinner and watched her drive off in her posh Peugeot, Jacqueline collected her bag and keys and set off with a boy on each arm to her little Fiat parked nearby.

The little Fiat awaited them and they were soon off down the road driving through Beaulieu sur Mer town. Jacqueline pointed out all the places of interest like the Conference Centre, which was used as a hospital in the Second World War and in fact was a very large hotel in Victorian times. The road ran around the coast. Jack and Nick with wine and good food inside them, sat back and enjoyed listening to Jacqueline's running commentary of the coast she loved so much. Nick was soon fast asleep, which Jacqueline noticed so she put her hand on Jack's knee and started caressing him. Jack was beginning to feel very aroused. 'Oh God I want this girl,' his thoughts were away again.

"My parents are out this evening, why don't we go back to my place and leave Nick asleep in the car," suggested Jacqueline.

"No not tonight, let's get together tomorrow night," Jack was feeling very uncomfortable as her hand was getting more and more intimate. 'How is she able to concentrate on driving?' he thought.

"Oh come on Jack, Nick won't even notice, he is so drunk," she whined. 'She really did like having her own way' Jack was thinking.

"No not tonight Jacqueline, it has been a very long day," he replied. 'To think they were in Italy last night, all these adventures were exhausting,' Jack thought, Jacqueline had no idea what they had been up to.

Back to Les Cigalles pension it was, much to Jacqueline's disappointment. Jack gave her a long lingering kiss and then tore himself away. He dug Nick in the ribs to wake him up and they climbed out of the little car.

"I will pick you up early tomorrow Jack about ten o'clock, okay?" she said pouting.

"That'll be great, see you then," and waved to her.

"Phew these French ladies they know how to turn a man on don't they Jack?" Nick remarked. "Did you see how Arlette was teasing me through dinner, cheeky woman, I can't believe the way she has been coming on to me all day. Do you remember that film we saw a while back, what was it called? I know the "The Graduate" with Dustin Hoffman and Anne Bancroft, she played Mrs. Robinson, do you remember Jack, Dustin Hoffman was Ben and she seduced him. Wasn't it Simon and Garfunkel music in the film?"

"Yes that's right, definitely some similarities there Nick, good experience," he said nudging Nick as they climbed up the steps.

"Good evening mes jeunes hommes," greeted Monsieur Christophe, sitting on the terrace, "you are back early from your dinner, would you like anything to drink, some coffee may be?" seeing Nick swaying.

"Coffee would be great, thank you. We had bit of a heavy lunch in Cimiez and then dinner in Beaulieu sur Mer," said Jack feeling a bit embarrassed.

"I will arrange for some to be brought to your room right away. You have some wealthy friends, boys," Monsieur Christophe commented and then disappeared inside.

Nick flopped onto his bed straight away, Jack started to undress when there was a knock at the door. A tray of coffee, a jug of cold water and some packets of dry-looking biscuits were brought in. Jack took off his shirt and his sandals, he stood looking out of the window, what a muddle he had created with a French girl, a Dutch girl and not forgetting the Italian girl too. He was fond of Jacqueline but she seemed frighteningly keen, then Helena, who he felt he had offended sadly without meaning too. She was rather nice, he had felt a bond with her, which he had not felt for a number of years, well that wasn't true. Then Gabriella, well she was gorgeous but it was unlikely he would see her again.

"Come on Nick drink your coffee and some water, or you will feel terrible in the morning, why on earth do you drink so much?" scolded Jack.

Chapter XIV

Madame Moisan's Garden

Jacqueline was determined that Nick and Jack would see a great garden while they were in the South of France, she had organised to pick them up the next day about ten o'clock. This was bit of a strain for them considering they had done so much yesterday. Rolls and coffee were brought into their room with that delicious apricot conserve and croissants.

Jacqueline was her usual prompt self without Colin as he refused to go looking at gardens. The garden belonged to a friend of her friends and apparently they were fanatical gardeners.

They drove towards the harbour area and then off up the hill past some huge mansions, turning into a narrow road with many houses with railings and huge gates. The area she explained was Cimiez, where many English including Queen Victoria had come to stay in the past, which Jack and Nick had already been told. At that moment, they drew up to some huge gates and Jacqueline nipped out to ring the bell. A young girl dressed in black, who must have been a maid, came to the gates, unlocked them and pulled the gate back to allow the little Fiat into the drive. Nick was saying how he could see the mosaics of many little stones set into the cement driveway, which led to a double garage, which had a tiled area to the front of it. This had one of those large funny shaped Citroens parked on it, which to Jack, had a bonnet that looked like a duck-billed platypus! They were indeed a very modern car.

Jack remarked, "Bit posh isn't it?" as Jacqueline led them to the side of the house. Nick dug him in the ribs. They were introduced at the door to Madame Moisan, who was a close friend of Jacqueline's mother, she greeted them with a shake of the hand and she kissed Jacqueline on each cheek. She was a very smartly dressed lady in a beige linen skirt and blouse in lemon. Her bronzed skin set it off with short grey blonde hair. Nick whispered to Jacqueline asking her if she had any daughters, which she ignored.

With Jacqueline as interpreter, they were taken around the garden, which was large having hedges of Mimosa trees to two sides. Madame Moisan explained how they were cut in April after they had finished flowering. Many small edgings divided the garden all in a warm golden brown rock, much dry set, paths leading through lawns that although being told were watered, were quite dry to feel. Many Cistus with their bright single rose type flowers in soft pinks and whites, Viburnum tinus, Oleander and Pittisporum rambled amongst a Rosa banksiae "Alba plena". This had lovely double white flowers and through this with its azure flowers, Convolvusus mauritanious weaved its way from this area down a gravel path opening out to a wall, built in the same stone. She explained her husband's enthusiasm for stoned fruits, so on this beautiful old wall, he grew apricots, peaches, nectarines and cherry trees, all neatly fanned and tied to wires along the wall. Through an old looking pale blue door, Madame took them to the swimming pool, up one end was a terracotta-tiled summer-house, which was used as changing rooms. In front of that was a terrace with chairs and a table in metal. There were towels placed on the backs of the chairs, Nick stood there with

164

his mouth open, Jack quickly admired the palms, Daturas in gentle shades of apricot, massive bushes, which the boys had only ever seen in plant books. Bougainvilleas rambled up this side of the wall still in full colour and also they spotted Jasmine, the tender variety with sweet smelling flowers, normally only grown as a houseplant. Against the wall, there were tall terracotta pots of a light shade, not like the ones the boys hand washed at Kenwood Nurseries back in Hampstead. These were rammed full of red trailing geraniums, these flowers fascinated Jack, so he wandered off to look closer at the flower head. It was a sort of single petal formation, bright red in colour but did not create a dead head so seed did not seem to show. Although the old flower heads were still there, they did not show.

They were moved on, Jacqueline grabbing Jack's hand, pulled him across the bottom paving by the pool.

"I wish I had brought my camera," said Jack.

"She wouldn't like that, they are very private people," said Jacqueline.

Around to a shaded area of gravel in a grey crushed stone, Madame Moisan pointed out a huge old tree. This was a very large craggy lime tree and beneath this in dappled shade in what looked like old wine barrels, was a range of citrus trees with oranges and lemons growing from them. She offered them all a cold drink and told Jacqueline to take Nick and Jack to the outlook from the garden.

Back into the bright sunshine, they turned right around the house, across another paved area to a terrace overlooking Nice town. As this house was the last but one house in this curving road, the Moisan's had a cliff on this corner of the garden. There were Thymes all different varieties planted in the paving and a stone wall about three feet high stopped one from falling over. Large rocks were in this part of the garden with a soft light gritty sand. Agaves in several varieties and many of them, some really large and Cistus, the little alpine variety, were growing up in the crevices with groups of scented Pelargoniums in a strong cerise colour. The perfume that wafted up from these was beautiful. More chairs in metal with wooden slats, the fold up ones and a round metal table, like you saw in cafés were placed here. Soon Madame Moisan arrived with a tray of glasses and an opaque liquid in a huge glass jug.

"Quelques chose à boire mes jeunes hommes?" asked Madame. The boys nodded not really knowing what she had asked but guessed it must be the drink. It was incredibly lemon flavoured with a touch of sweetness and turned out to be made from their own lemons. Jack and Nick stood at the wall looking right across Nice with the Baie des Anges lying to the left with its blue, blue sea, the roof tops in all their multi terracottas, the flower market with its long roofs and the patches of green where the gardens were. They could have stayed for hours but Jacqueline moved them on, the boys shook hands with Madame Moisan, Jack could have hugged her. What a fantastic garden and the view was out of this world.

Chapter XV

Villefranche

They eventually left after the large gate had been opened and it was getting towards lunchtime. "How about going to Villefranche?" asked Jacqueline. The boys looked at each other, they were getting short of money and it sounded a bit expensive. Jack remembered the restaurants the other night and they were right on the little harbour.

"Well..." He started to say.

Jacqueline interrupted and said, "The treat is on me."

"No, no," they argued, "you have been so good to us and the garden we've just been to was absolutely fantastic, come on you can't."

"I insist," she said and took off in the Fiat smiling at Jack. "So it's Villefranche for lunch. I love going there," she said with a twinkle in her eyes.

From Cimiez, the road wound around the back of the port in Nice and down to the bottom road, which wound around the cliffs with the blue sea to the right. Eventually at the traffic lights the road forked slightly to the right, dropping down to the harbour. As before she parked by the harbour wall and Nick who had not been there before leapt out and straight to the harbour wall, calling to Jack to come and see all the little fishing boats bobbing on their ropes. It really was gorgeous, Jacqueline explained that if you walked the length of this narrow road there was a small roundabout and beyond a narrow beach, which goes quickly to deep clear water.

"If we had more days we could come here again," Nick commented.

"Another time, perhaps," Jacqueline said squeezing Jack's arm and with Nick on the other arm, she led them down to one of the smaller restaurants on the other side of the road. After being greeted and sat close to the front to get a view of the sea, Jacqueline wanted to make it her day and asked if she could order a light lunch. She ordered rosé wine, no beers for the boys, Moules mariniere and frites to start with.

"So what have you ordered?" Nick enquired when the wine turned up.

"Wait and see," she replied.

It was very hot and Nick drank the rosé wine very quickly.

"Doucement," Jacqueline said.

"What's that mean," replied Nick, looking a bit put out.

"It means gently does it, our wine is very strong here in the South and so is the sun," said Jacqueline looking a little concerned. Nick slowed down but had another glass anyway. They chatted about the garden they had just been to and some of the plants the boys had seen growing up at the Kenwood Nursery near Hampstead, London.

"Where's that?" asked Jacqueline.

The boys explained how in north London there was a massive open space with trees, rough grass and paths where people from London could go to exercise and walk, relax and take their dogs. There was a nursery, which Jacqueline thought was for children, so no wonder she was confused. Anyway they explained how plants were grown there for London Parks, the Festival Hall and County Hall.

"Ah," Jacqueline commented. She had been to a concert at the Festival Hall, so the connection was slowly coming together, even though she could not understand totally why they had chosen to take up the career of gardening.

"You boys will have to show me these gardens when I visit England again," she looked at Jack with a longing look, which made him feel rather anxious.

A large terrine arrived with soup bowls to each of them, side bowls and one with water and lemon in. Then a large dish of very thin chips, Jacqueline opened the terrine announcing, "Voila Moules Mariniere!" and started serving the two of them, explaining that they must not eat any that have not opened. With a little bread eaten in between and dunked into the white wine sauce and extracting the mussel with a fork from the shell, they all tucked in. The heap of empty shells grew and Jack watched Jacqueline as she pulled the fork away from her lips when she ate a mussel. They were lovely lips or was it the wine, sun and sea getting to him again? He was suddenly shocked out of his dream by Nick suddenly excusing himself and rushing out of the restaurant to a group in the harbour car park. Jack's gaze must have been spotted as Jacqueline moved towards him kissing him on the lips, then asking how he liked the lunch.

"A perfect day with perfect company and I still cannot get over the garden we have just seen," Jack commented. Nick reappeared saying that he had spotted the Dutch girls, they had met with a crowd and he wanted their addresses in Holland.

"So Jack what have you been up to with these Dutch girls?" asked Jacqueline. Poor Jack went very red. "So are you going to tell me?" Jacqueline went on, riding his guilt. Nick butted in that they were a crowd they had met on the beach and gone to a bar and had had good fun but no attachments. She left it alone and kissed a rather red faced Jack on the cheek. They soon devoured the huge amount of mussels, dipped their fingers in the finger bowl copying Jacqueline and Nick had ordered another bottle of wine, possibly a mistake. No one wanted cheese so after a break, she ordered crêpes for them, all with Grande Marnier liqueur then coffee in little cups. Jack was struggling with his eyelids nearly closing. Time to go, Jacqueline paid the bill, with Nick on one side with Jacqueline and Jack the other, they staggered back to the car. Nick slumped in the back and fell asleep. Jack and Jacqueline sat on the harbour wall close to the car, he put his arm around her and thanked her for a wonderful day.

"It's not over yet Jack," said Jacqueline smiling, he wrapped his arm around her body pulling her to him. He could feel her flesh through the thin material, Jack turned sitting along the wall with his legs out but slightly apart and she snuggled in between. His hands went around her but the wine and sun made Jack feel randy and he found it very difficult to resist running his fingers inside her top. There were people coming and going past them, so she nudged him in the ribs to behave, so sliding her hair across and kissed her on the neck.

"Come on we better go before you get too amorous!" The trip back to the hotel was uneventful except for the snoring of Nick in the back of the Fiat. They soon turned into the gateway of the hotel.

"What about tonight?" she asked.

"I feel guilty saying 'no' but Nick gets a bit fed up, even though we are very good and don't miss him out. So sorry," he repeated. She leant across and kissed him with great passion on the lips and what lips they were. Nick snored on like a baby as the two of them became more entangled. Her tongue found sensitive spots in his mouth and he felt himself getting aroused, so he slowly pulled away kissing her gently on the neck then on the cheek. Finally leaning over to his sleeping friend in the back.

"Time to go," called Jack. Nick always seemed to wake quickly, with Jack out of the car, Nick extracted himself from the little Fiat, thanking Jacqueline on his way past. Jack returned to the left of the car and kissed her through the window. "Je t'aime," she whispered and backed out of the drive and drove away.

Chapter XVI

Digne

The boys had got used to catching up with someone each day, particularly Jack, who suddenly felt Jacqueline should be meeting them. He did not say anything as Nick was still a little tense about how much they had seen of her. Annette seemed very keen on Nick and she was going to try and catch up with them if she could return from Monte Carlo in time. Working for a radio station seemed to incur very long unsociable hours. Who would have dreamt that they would have had a trip round a real radio station. They discussed their escapades over another coffee sitting on the terrace. They had not succeeded very well with the Dutch girls and they had missed their actual departure. What would Helena do, write to Jack, who knows?

"As for that young tasty lady staying here she's wasted on Serge," Nick said suddenly, "She's really tasty…!" As they sipped their coffees in the sun, Jack pondered where they should go.

"Antibes sounds good, we haven't been there, apparently there are lots of yachts there…" Not that either of them were really interested in boats, good restaurants and bars interested the boys and a good beach.

"Or we could take the old train up to Digne in the mountains behind Nice," responded Nick. Monsieur Christophe thought the railway would be very different and might be a change from the beach, bars and particularly the girls. Nick laughed.

"Have we been that bad?" he asked.

"Well you have achieved a great deal in a two week holiday, some very fine girls from some very smart areas of Nice, like Cimiez, you have been picked up and dropped off and taken to some of the best places on the coast, mes jeunes hommes. I hope you will not break their hearts! I sound as if I am lecturing you, I do not mean to, you have been good to 'ave as our guests and I hope you will return," Monsieur replied smiling.

"We will, you can guarantee that. So with your sound advice, it's the little train to Digne," Nick said very positively. "Okay, let's go, no swimmers just us that will be nice not to carry any bags, come on Jack."

"Would you like a picnic?" Monsieur Christophe asked.

"Yes please," responded the boys in unison.

With a small bag for their picnic, sunglasses and wallets, they strode off down to the road. The station was just by Place Gambetta, a grand building, large pillars to the front with steps up to it, the boys nipped up them and into the grand booking hall. The stone floor was like polished marble and even the counters to the booking kiosks were stone. They bought their two return tickets for Digne and hurried onto the platform. A train soon arrived, Nick was fascinated with it, he loved trains. Although Nick had been a friend for sometime, Jack had not realised he was so keen on them. He left Jack to take a closer look at the train, Jack had not realised it was a narrow gauge railway, he became excited too. There was not really a platform and the carriages had a type of running board along the side, so you could climb in, all very different. There were lots of people getting on this funny little train, some were visitors like the boys but many had shopping bags filled to the top with vegetables,

French baguette bread sticks and many other good things. They took two seats by the doorway each side so as to enable them to look out. The guard walked the length of the train, blew his whistle and waved his baton, which looked like an extended table tennis bat. With rumbling and general commotion they set off. They went under a small tunnel and then across a road, past houses that were tight up against the railway and across more roads. The boys had not realised that this funny little train literally crossed Nice. "Perhaps it was here before the houses," Nick remarked as he hung out of the window to have a better look. Jack was amused at Nick's enthusiasm for trains.

The train stopped in what was a station, a little urban stop at Gambetta but appeared to be at the back of someone's house. The train continued its stop and start journey through tunnels to little La Madeleine and St. Isodore stations, until suddenly they came out alongside a dual carriageway, past houses, factories, freight yards and even schools. The train rumbled on, then suddenly slowed down, lots of clanging of bells and the little train crossed the roadways whilst cars waited alongside a very wide river.

"Do you think that's the Var River Nick?" asked Jack.

"We'll look at a map when we get back, Monsieur Christophe is bound to have one." replied Nick. He chatted on about the train in his brief time at the station, he was amazed to think that originally narrow gauge steam trains went up these tracks, a bit like the trains used in the slate mines in Wales. It was not until about 1935 that these Renault railcars were used, they had a carriage being pulled but often small box vans were used to carry freight into the Alps. To think that this railway served all those little stations, people literally stood on a small platform, which was often nearly in their back garden and the train stopped for them. It was like putting your hand out for a bus at a request stop.

Jack was pleased to point out the deep crevice with waterfalls and torrents of water as they crossed a metal bridge causing the railcar to reverberate on the metal. Well, thought Jack, it stopped Nick talking about railways and diesel railcars at least for a little while. The terrain became more rugged and rocky as they ducked in and out of tunnels and along the very edges of cliffs running down to the river. Nick was off again, "To think they cut these tunnels by hand pretty well in the late eighteen hundreds. I bet lots of men got killed and it must have taken years…" They suddenly spotted a man with a huge herd of goats high up on a ridge.

"Do you reckon they milk them?" Jack asked Nick.

"How should I know!" responded Nick. The countryside soon changed to Alpine meadows and areas of cows grazing. They were a lovely soft beige colour nothing like the black and white ones the boys saw at home.

They had been travelling for a couple of hours and many people laid what looked like small cloths on their laps, broke off pieces of bread from the long baguettes and with knives spread cheese on to it. The men were even taking swigs of red wine to wash it down. It made the boys feel hungry as it was nearly lunchtime. The railcars slowed and the driver seemed to collect a baton from a pole as he entered a section of two lines of railway next to each other. This information was all relayed to Jack as Nick hung out of a window.

"Jack look there's a station and another train!" Nick was so excited as they pulled past the other railcar, which to Nick's delight had a boxcar on the back.

"I told you that's how they moved freight didn't I?" The baton was passed from one driver to the other; a method he explained was that not more than one train at a time was on the line. People got off the train and wandered about buying food and drink. It had that kind of familiar feeling.

"Do you remember in Paris, lots of people did the same thing?" asked Jack.

"It must be a French thing," he said to himself as Nick had disappeared. Jack was getting worried when Nick suddenly re-appeared and the guard was blowing his whistle for everyone to get back on board. Nick was beaming as the driver had let him climb up into the cab to have a look around and showed him the controls. "Did you know these cars were first brought back into service in 1946, after the Second World War? On the line to Digne many of the bridges were washed away in storms and in winter up at Digne, it is covered in snow for most of the time. Earlier this century, it was one of the few ways of getting food and goods up there." Nick and Jack settled down again and decided to get out their picnic and tuck into their lunch too.

The train rattled on higher and higher and eventually entered an area of very green countryside, full of cows and sheep, which was not something that they saw very often in that part of France, then Jack spotted another herd of goats. They were very dark brown with a dark stripe almost black running down their backs. Eventually the train slowed as if breaking, drifting down through a valley with conifer covered mountains in the distance all around. It was beautiful but rather remote, many of the houses were timber-clad, Jack thought they were like the chalets in Switzerland that he had seen in magazines. Then Digne appeared and that was strange as the houses were made of stone and in fact, reminded Nick of a trip he made to Yorkshire up to Keithley to see the trains there. Those houses were made of York stone, the boys wondered if it was the same type of rock that had been used here. The train pulled into the station as a man got on, again dressed like a guard but his hat had gold braid around it, perhaps he was in charge of the station, Nick suggested.

175

Jack suggested they went off to the town to have a look around.

"No," said Nick, "I am just going down to the siding to have a look at the water tower and any of the old coaches that are parked."

"Nick, come on, we haven't got that long, so let's see the town and have some more lunch," Jack was getting irritable. Nick relented and they strode off into Digne. The buildings were similar to those they had already seen, built in that harsh looking York stone and had weathered to blackened stone over the years. Some of the side streets were cobbled and looked really old. There was a very large church they had passed and then there was a central area with bars and shops.

"I'm really starving again, are you Jack?"

"Yes I am, it was a lovely picnic but I could eat it all again," laughed Jack. So they strode off to find a café to have a 'Croque Monsieur', becoming their favourite, or was it the only thing they could say in French and 'pression' beers to drink! They sat outside enjoying the warmth of the sun and total peace after the rickety train.

They sat and enjoyed their lunch in the long boulevard shaded by plane trees. After this they decided to go for a long walk. The town is nestled beside the fast-flowing Bleone river with forested mountains all around. Jack had read somewhere that Digne was known for its hot springs not far out of the town in a river called Eaux-Chaudes.

"Nick can you smell bad eggs in the air?" asked Jack

"Yes it must be sulphur; didn't you read it out to me from a book in our room?"

"Yes that's where I had read it, Digne Les Bains is known for these springs, which are supposed to help people with rheumatism. I think Harrogate in Yorkshire has similar waters. I seem to remember mum telling me about her grandma going up there, as she had suffered so much with aches and pains. So I imagine this is the same. Shall we climb down and find them?"

"Yes why not, but we must watch our time as the last train goes back at half past five," replied Nick rather responsibly for him.

They set off on their walk, the views were incredible with vast lavender fields in the distance, orchards of olive trees and oak trees, unlike the English oak, all protected by the high mountains all around. The path they took was very steep with wild flowers growing all over the meadows, this was something Jack knew little about, they had not studied wild flowers at college yet, so he was intrigued to see them growing. In the distance were different types of pine trees, some looking very different with a strange appearance like an open umbrella. They could see the river and smell the sulphur.

"Do you really want to climb all that way down Jack?" asked Nick not so sure of this idea.

"Yes why not, it will be a new experience for us!" They continued down the mountainous slope and reached the river's edge.

"Look Jack, they are up there, can you see the steam pouring out the side of the hill?" asked Nick.

"Oh yes, come on Nick we can climb into the river and make our way around the rocks, we can leave our clothes here and get in with our pants on."

"No there's no-one about I'm taking mine off."

With that they climbed into the river and walked around the boulders in the icy cold fast flowing river.

"Wow, this is fantastic," exclaimed Jack, the scolding hot water was gushing out of the hillside into the river like a torrent. The river currents were strong so they had to hang on tight to the tufts of grass at the side.

Feeling totally exhilarated, Jack and Nick climbed out, with the hot sun they soon dried and dressed again. They laid back on the riverbank and soaked up the sunshine and dozed off.

"Nick wake up we have only got an hour to get back up the mountain to the station," exclaimed an alarmed Jack.

"Don't panic Jack, it won't take long, I could do with a drink though, perhaps we will have time to grab a couple of beers before we get on the train."

"I doubt if we will have time, still let's get a move on."

"Ssh, look over there Jack, just behind those bushes, can you see them?" Nick whispered.

"What, where, oh yes a herd of deer, are they Roe deer Nick?"

"How should I know, although I should living near Epping Forest, don't move Jack, can you see in the long grass, it looks like a big dog, oh my God, let's get out of here quick." With that the boys scurried up the hillside back into Digne and down the road to catch the little train back.

Jack and Nick just managed to catch the train, having rapidly bought some bottles of Evian water. They sat back and talked about their exhilarating time by the river and all that they had seen.

"We must ask Monsieur Christophe what that strange large dog was, it looked like a wolf. I was really scared for a moment, weren't you Jack?" asked Nick

"Yes, I am sure he will know, it was really only interested in snatching one of those young deer, perhaps they were Ibex and not deer, still I'm sure Monsieur Christophe will have all the answers. Talking of which, we are going to be rather late for dinner again, let's hope he saves us some. He's such a nice guy isn't he Nick?"

"Yes we are lucky he is so understanding."

"Nick didn't we promise to meet Colin before we go back home for a night out in Nice?" asked Jack.

"Oh yes so we did. Still he is bit of a bore so we won't miss much," remarked Nick.

"That's not the point if we hadn't met him we would not have got to go to so many great places."

"True, let's see what time we get back, then we can phone him," Nick added. With that he suddenly got up and as the train had started up its engine, he wandered off down to the siding where one of the very old steam trains were. Two cars long and a little box wagon on the back. Jack slumped back in the corner by the window, he put his jumper on the seat opposite so that Nick could have a window seat going back as well. The cars soon filled up and in one of them many tourists had sat down up the other end, they were very noisy, which annoyed Jack. He decided they must have been German, as their language was a bit like Dutch but more a throaty type sound, as he did not know any German he had no idea really. Nick eventually re-appeared just before the whistle blew and off they went rattling through the mountainous countryside.

Nick suddenly remarked loudly, "Aren't they Germans down there, what a noisy bunch?"

Jack cringed and hoped that not too many of them spoke English. Nick had also noticed that one row down on the other side of the carriage, were two very nice looking girls. They both had dark hair, one with beautiful long silky hair to the shoulders, dark eyebrows with stunning hazel eyes. Next to her the other girl had short dark curly hair, an olive skin and was very petite. Jack had not even noticed as he had his back to them, mind you Nick teased him saying he was probably dreaming about Jacqueline again. Jack punched him in the arm to shut him up, they both laughed at themselves.

The boys had had a wonderful day, they arrived back in Nice around nine in the evening after three hours or more on the train. They were very hungry and rather tired. Monsieur Christophe had kept some supper for them and ushered them into the dining room.

"You had a good day I think mes jeunes hommes, it is a long journey but well worth the time. You have had a phone call from your friend Colin, perhaps you would like to telephone him back when you have eaten?" said Monsieur Christophe.

"Oh yes thank you," replied Nick. "Monsieur Christophe, perhaps you could answer some of our questions about our trip?"

"Why of course, I will try."

"We saw some deer up on the mountainside, we had already seen some herds of goats, but these were different, what were they and also there was a huge big dog stalking them?" asked Nick.

"Well I am very glad you were not 'urt, it would 'ave been a female wolf I would imagine, there are a few about. She was probably hunting for her family and the deer were probably Ibex, which look rather like deer but they are a mountain goat. So you 'ave 'ad some adventures too!" said Monsieur Christophe smiling.

"Oh yes it was great. We also climbed down to the hot springs in the river, that was so exhilarating, all in the rapids too, we didn't like the awful smell though," laughed Nick.

"Really you went there too, you did make the most of your time. Yes the 'ot springs are quite well known but sadly as they are not easily accessible very few people go there. Perhaps one day the government could make a proper building with an access, the waters are supposed to really 'elp with rheumatism. Excuse me, I will leave you to eat your dinner now." Monsieur Christophe slipped away back to the kitchen.

After their dinner, Jack and Nick telephoned Colin at Jacqueline's home, Nick spoke to him, as Jack really did not want to talk to Jacqueline at that moment. She was sure to ask him to see her parents before they left for England. Nick agreed to meet Colin for a drink, Colin was so pleased, he was beginning to think the boys did not like him. He had not really enjoyed his holiday and decided to stay in England next year, he really preferred English girls, he could understand what they were saying! They arranged to meet Colin at the main line station.

"If we meet him there Jack, we can take him on a cruise of the bars, how about the one where the prostitutes go, that will give him something to think about," Nick said laughing. 'Mmm, might not do my reputation a lot of good,' thought Jack. So it was all planned. Still rather scruffy from their rail trip to Digne, the boys hurriedly changed and set off down to the station, rather a late start to the evening.

They arrived at the front of the station and there was no sign of Colin, they walked inside to find him engrossed in car magazines in the paper shop or 'Tabac' as they called it in France. Nick was really funny, as he had ended up shaking hands in greeting Colin, just like a Frenchman, so Jack copied him.

"Just look at this Trans Am car in the magazine here," Colin said enviously.

"Well we got to see one up in one of the gardens in Cimiez Colin," Nick said proudly.

Colin was enraptured, "Was it red, the traditional colour?" he asked.

"Yes."

"Which engine and how old was it?" asked Colin excitedly.

"Come on we're gardeners not mechanics and I know we are keen on cars and Nick is on trains, especially narrow gauge trains," Jack said laughing, "but car engines and sizes, I don't think so!"

"Whose was it?" Colin was so intrigued.

"A friend of Jacqueline's, you should get her to take you up there but watch the lady of the house, she's a man-eater," Nick was egging Colin on.

"No, I don't believe it," Colin replied.

"Yes," Nick carried on…"I thought I was in with a chance there, she had even suggested taking me to the harbour to see their boat, yes a mere fifty foot one. I don't think it was the lines of the boat she was going to show me either!"

"Why didn't you take her up on it," Colin asked.

"Her husband was due home and he carried a gun," Nick really was having fun.

"No come on you're kidding me," Colin was looking quite shocked.

"He really does Colin," Nick replied. The boys left it at that, teasing Colin leaving him not really knowing if it was true. On to the bars they strolled.

Down through the town, working their way across to one of the more business areas to the corner bar they had found in the first week of their holiday. Jack and Nick had planned to say nothing to Colin about the working girls and see whether he caught on. He chatted on about different cars he had seen and that he was thinking of next year coming down to watch the Formula One race in Monte Carlo, but it is difficult to get a good position to see the race. Apparently there are some good public areas with tickets at reasonable prices Colin was telling them. Eventually they arrived at the bar and the boys went to the end of the bar and sat at the corner table.

Nick's favourite blonde was in with her short tartan skirt and thin white blouse. She smiled at Nick as if she knew him.

They sat down with Nick ordering a round of beer without even asking Colin what he would like. Colin started to grumble about being stuck with Jacqueline, who was keener on seeing them and particularly Jack.

"Come on, you've always been included, it's not as if you fancy her or anything," Nick retorted.

"No of course not, she's a family friend not my type anyway! That blonde at the bar is more my scene," Colin sipped his beer and eyed her over. Jack and Nick ignored the comment for now as more girls arrived and stood at the bar.

"I like it here, how did you find this bar?" he asked innocently.

"By chance," Jack replied quickly.

"I am trying to get the same train back, the sleeper one, the same as you guys. I have had enough of the formal evening meals with Jacqueline's parents, they are very nice but we have to politely chat through all the courses and they speak very little English. As bad as my French, which is dreadful."

'Oh dear,' thought Jack.

"It can't be as bad as mine," Nick interjected.

"Jacqueline works a lot and I really don't like Nice that much, it's just like any other big city with the sea at the end of the road," Colin said complaining.

"No, come on we don't agree, it's a fantastic place, beach, bars, restaurants, the port, access by rail all up the coast and some cracking women." Nick sounded like a travel reporter but he was quite right Jack was thinking, 'I just love it here'.

Another round of beers was already on the table and Colin was becoming quite chatty the boys discovered, so when he had drunk his third glass, he announced he was going to chat up the blonde girl at the bar. The boys not wanting to say to Colin that she was a professional lady, Colin went on about how few blondes there were down in Nice. He loved her little tartan skirt and white blouse, which made her look very attractive. They had to agree smiling to each other.

"But Colin, you just said your French is terrible, how on earth are you going to chat to her?" asked Nick.

"Perhaps she'll speak some English," he replied hopefully.

"Possibly, she may have to use it in her work," Nick smiled cheekily. With that Colin was off leaning against the bar, she turned and smiled, he bought her a drink. Jack told Nick off for leading Colin on.

"Well surely just by looking around at all these girls and women in here it's obvious something is strange," Nick replied pointedly.

"Not obviously to Colin. I wonder if it is true that the girls just drink a made-up type of drink as a deal with the barman, who keeps hold of the money. I bet that round was expensive," Jack commented as he watched Colin get out his wallet.

More girls came and went, men old and young joined them in the bar having a drink and then off they went together and the girls returned alone some time later. Jack remembered the first time they had come into this bar and how one of the girls came over to them to ask if they would like to join her and quoted a price. This time they had been left alone.

"So where to tomorrow then?" Jack asked Nick.

"Well Annette said she would ring Jacqueline if she could get the day off, so we could drive down the coast, leaving the decision to us, as it was a last chance to see anywhere we fancied," Nick replied a little sadly.

"There's Cannes, Juan but we've been there, what about Antibes? Monsieur Christophe said it used to be a walled city with a fort and huge harbour full of yachts. But is there a beach, we've got to go swimming? I'm sure he said there is sand if I remember him correctly," Jack said.

"Okay, Antibes it is, let's hope Annette can get the time off," replied Nick.

"You rather like her don't you? Considering we've only met her a couple of times. 'Media Lady' not mediocre, she stacked up well in both our eyes with her long legs and pretty dark eyes and... good figure," Jack teased Nick.

'Her figure, Jack was musing, which had fascinated Jack with Jacqueline and the way they both spoke English with their sexy French accent, so sexy,' thought Jack.

Colin suddenly came over and said, "I am off to see her apartment, she's a real cracker." Nick started to say, "But Colin..." but he had gone out of the door hand in hand with the young blonde.

"Do you think you should run after him?" Jack said starting to get up.

"No let him get on with it, he's an adult, well old enough even though not acting as one much!" commented Nick. He hoped Colin did not get the same rail sleeper home as them, he would be whingeing all the way across France to home.

"Come on Jack, while we are waiting for him, let's have another beer." Nick made his way to the bar. They started chatting again about when they will have finished their apprenticeship and whether they could go down to that area and work.

"What about that for an idea?" Nick asked Jack.

"But you can't just start as we are English and the French don't allow you to just set up a company here," Jack replied despondently.

"Well Jack you could always marry a French girl!" Nick said laughing.

"Not bloomin' likely, I'm not marrying until I am at least thirty!" Jack retorted.

"Oh I've seen the way you look at Jacqueline, you're nearly there...!" Nick continued to jibe.

"No seriously it does worry me how keen she is, I hope she doesn't keep trying to work in England as a teacher. I reckon she'd never leave me alone." Jack said looking anxious.

"But hey…you've had a great time, you can't tell me that you have just been sitting chatting the evening away when you've been together," Nick replied.

"No we have had some great times together I must say but I also have a bit of a hankering for Helena, the Dutch girl," Jack said drifting off to thoughts of Helena.

"Too young for you Jack after your experience at home with Penny, let's face it she was nearly twice your age, you can't go back to young girls again, Jacqueline has a bit of age on her side for you Jack…" Nick commented.

"Come on Nick, you're no saint, fancy you lecturing me on women. Well let's face it last year must have taught you lots in the bedroom and beyond. Do you remember Tammy and that strange party she had? Didn't you come to that with Penny and me? I'm sure it was you. Anyway I bet Colin is learning a thing or two right now! They both laughed noisily and the girls at the bar turned around and all smiled at them. Jack wished he had not as two of the girls came over to sit with them at their table.

"Non merci," Jack said nervously to which the one next to him ignored him and carried on chattering in French.

"Je ne comprends pas," Nick said getting up and went to the toilet. Eventually the girls gave up with these funny English boys and returned to the bar. It must have been getting late, they had left their watches up at the hotel and there was not a clock in the bar. It seemed ages before Colin returned, he arrived first and about ten minutes later the young blonde returned beaming at them all.

Colin started to get angry, "You never warned me to start with did you?"

"Well we sort of tried to but you weren't listening anyway." Nick said trying to smooth his feathers.

"What an experience, you've never been with a working girl before have you?!" Colin exclaimed smiling.

"Well no," Jack and Nick said in unison. "Well tell us about it!"

"She says she is twenty two with a baby and that's why she does it, to support her child for a better life than she has." Colin explained to them.

"I thought your French was terrible Colin?" Jack jibed.

"No she spoke broken English and me my pigeon French, anyway I'm not telling you here, she will know you will be asking about her. I tell you though she is lovely and the best twelve francs I've ever spent," Colin told them dreamily.

They thought it rude to leave straight away particularly as Amelie, Colin's new girl was watching them and smiling, perhaps she thought they were all up for it, Nick commented. "Oh shut up Nick, leave it alone will you. Now tomorrow Colin we are going hopefully with Jacqueline to Antibes even though we haven't told her yet or even asked her," said Jack. "Do you want to come?"

"No thanks, I have been there with Jacqueline, there was a museum and lots of yachts," replied Colin.

"You sound really thrilled with the place, is it worth us going?" Nick asked.

"Well if you haven't been there, why not, there's a great restaurant by the wall, it's mainly painted yellow, can't think of its name but the seafood was great, get Jacqueline to take you there," Colin finished. Jack had been having a coffee while the others had knocked back another beer, Colin was getting noisier…

"I think it's time to go," Jack said as he took Colin's elbow to steer him out.

He blew Amelie a kiss, who responded by saying, "A tout a l'heure!" which Jack thought meant, 'see you later'. So was Colin going back Jack thought to himself. They had just turned the corner and Nick was straight onto Colin.

187

"Well come on Colin, tell us what did she do?" Nick asked, Jack laughed saying, "Give him a break Nick."

"Yes Nick and you can buy me another beer down at the beach," Colin retorted.

"Okay then Colin," so they walked the rest of the way with Nick leading the way. They ended up just along from the flower market where there were a couple of very ordinary bars that seemed to be open day and night as Jacqueline had said before that traders go to them in the early hours of the morning. Jack stayed on coffees and let them tease him as they drank their beers at a small table on the pavement facing the sea. The clock in the bar had reminded them how late it was as it was now a quarter to one. To get up for a nine o'clock start would not be easy but as Nick pointed out, they only had one holiday a year.

Colin waited for Nick to stop asking him questions about what was Amelie wearing underneath, where was her apartment, on and on he went. Jack told Nick again to leave Colin alone and let him tell his story if he wanted to. Jack thought to himself, 'I wouldn't tell my mate if I'd done what he's done but then they were with him at the time. It would give Colin something to talk about back home and he hoped Jacqueline never found out, as she'd blame Nick and him for egging him on, well not letting on at least,' Jack mused to himself.

Colin suddenly spoke out, "She is a lovely looking girl you have to admit don't you?"

"Well she's got blue eyes and soft looking lips…" Nick was off again, "Did you kiss her?"

"Listen I'll tell you, so shut up, if not I'm off home," Colin was getting very annoyed with Nick. He continued, "Well after having bought her a drink, which reminds me, I didn't pay towards the bill up at the 'Pleasure bar'."

"Don't worry you can buy these, come on Colin get on with it," Nick commented, Jack was amused at Nick, all he wanted to hear was the story.

"So I bought an expensive drink, she talked about Nice and how she had moved from Marseilles as her step father, well I think that's what she meant, was a cruel man and she had her little girl of three. Then she said to come back to her apartment. I thought her a bit forward but agreed and on the way out she said something about money, but I didn't understand what she said. When I got to the apartment, it was in a very large old house and after going up two flights of stairs, she opened the door and held my hand leading me in. I could smell food and there were lots of people there and much chatter. We went past the kitchen where an old lady seemed to be working, past lots of other doors and then she turned to me and said, "My room," and let me in. It was a cool room with a big fan in the ceiling, chairs, wardrobe and a big 'tallboy' closet. She sat me on the bed, at this time I realized Amelie was not just an ordinary girl. She unbuttoned my shirt and caressed my chest, again she said "Ordinaire, twelve francs, speciale eighteen." Well I only had twenty francs on me in my wallet, so she said 'ordinaire' not knowing what I was in for. She nibbled my ears briefly and then said 'come' and took me back down the corridor to the bathroom."

Nick interrupted, "Hang on, let's have a sip of beer," his eyes were nearly popping out of his head.

Colin continued, "You clean she said, I had no idea what she meant... so she undid my trousers, pulled my pants down and washed my old 'fella' with a carbolic type of soap!"

"How did you not explode there and then?" Jack interjected, "I would have done!"

"No come on, it was like being at the doctor's. She gently dried me off and I pulled my trousers back up and then she passed me some soap to wash my hands and a towel. We went back down to her room, she pulled off the coloured blanket to reveal a sheeted bed. Amelie said for me to undress and she took her blouse off to reveal two lovely shaped breasts and she hadn't been wearing a bra at all. I was down to my underpants having

189

put my shirt and trousers tidily on the chair, she took off her tartan skirt revealing a very scanty pair of white knickers, only about an inch and a bit anywhere."

"You're getting me all excited," Nick said, "Who'll lend me twelve francs? No seriously get some drinks, I'm on sodas, how about you guys?"

"I'll have a brandy please Nick," Colin asked, Jack had a soda like Nick.

"At this rate Colin we will be carrying you home old chap," Jack commented.

"No just drop me at Amelie's door," Colin laughed.

"No you can't afford it," Nick remarked quickly.

Colin continued his story with a brandy in his hand he explained how Amelie had laid on her bed beckoning him to do the same. "She ran her fingers down my chest down to my pants feeling me there taking my hand to fondle her very firm breasts and nipples. She lay back appearing to enjoy this and I leant across to kiss her lips, she did have her eyes shut. Suddenly she stopped dead, sat up saying 'Non, non' pointing at her lips, touching mine and gesturing anywhere on her body but 'Ne pas la bouche'. It quite put me off, my old fellow sagged. Amelie funnily looked guilty and so she caressed me more and slid off her tiny briefs to reveal a line of hair but not a triangle as I expected. She took my hand gently and from her now taut nipples, she ran my hand down to her hairy strip between her legs. My fingers felt the warmth of her as she pulled me to her. I was now back on form and she slid me into her. It was strange as she held her head to the side so I couldn't kiss her lips, so I kissed her neck instead. She arched up and suddenly it was all over and we laid together side by side, then she offered me a Gitane cigarette but I refused. I was feeling shattered, so she caressed my arms then got up. She offered me a drink of water, which was cool and fresh. She disappeared out of the room in a sort of dressing gown and on returning she gestured for me to go to the bathroom and gave me a towel. I was scared stiff who I'd meet but everywhere was quiet and so I slipped along to the bathroom to wash and returned to her room. She was already dressed as if nothing had happened, she re-made her bed and I got dressed and then she asked for the twelve francs, which she put in her purse. Once outside, she suggested that I walk ahead and then there I was back with you guys, poorer but perhaps more experienced," Colin concluded his story.

"I just can't believe you did that Colin...!" Jack said totally amazed. "I wouldn't dare would you Nick?" Jack asked.

He thought for a while and then said, "No you're a braver man than me! Are you going back again Colin?" Nick asked with tongue in cheek.

"Might!" Colin replied, he had definitely drunk too much and the large brandy was taking its toll. Jack guided him around the tables and back up Avenue Jean Malecin towards Jacqueline's apartment. When they had got to Boulevard Dubouchage, where normally the boys would go straight up to the hotel and Colin would turn left, he was trying to wee through somebody's railings.

"Colin for goodness sake not here," Jack was horrified. "Come on, Nick we had better take him to the door." It took them a long time as Colin wandered from side to side of the pavement. He was getting abusive towards them, finally they reached the apartment door. Getting the key in the lock was proving difficult as Colin kept slumping against the door but luckily Jacqueline heard the commotion and came to the door.

"What have you been up to, it's half past two, don't worry Jack, just go and leave Colin with me." She told them sternly. Jack and Nick did not need telling twice, they were off down the stairs and out of the apartment, they still had another half hour's walk back to the pension.

Chapter XVII

Antibes, the holiday
is nearly over

Jack and Nick were awoken by a banging on the door. Nick opened it to be confronted by Monsieur Christophe.

"Mes jeunes hommes, two pretty filles await you!" he said amused. "Should I bring you two bowls of coffee to help you and perhaps leave the young ladies on the terrace with a coffee?"

"Oh could you Monsieur Christophe, that would be great," Nick said nursing his head as Jack came to asking what was going on. It was ten o'clock and Jacqueline and Annette had arrived to take them out, fortunately Jacqueline had come later than arranged.

"Well if it hadn't been for Colin we wouldn't have been so late would we?" Jack complained. "Oh... just get down to the bathroom while I wake up." With hurried washing, shaving and teeth cleaning, Monsieur Christophe arrived with a tray of fresh bowls of coffee with lots of warm milk and two croissants. All spruced up, Old Spice splashed on his cheeks and under the arms, Nick and Jack went to see the two lovely girls.

"Apologies, apologies," Nick started.

"No don't worry Jacqueline has explained me," Annette replied.

"Colin also apologises to you and hopes you enjoy Antibes, so is that where we are going today?" Jacqueline asked. The girls rose from the tables now and properly greeted the two shocked English boys as they were convinced they would be in trouble. Monsieur Christophe wished them all a good day and they all went down the steps to the little Fiat. Annette and Nick squeezed into the back, Jack did offer but he could see that Annette wanted to be close to his mate, Nick. It was great that Annette had got this last day of their holiday off but she would have to work the next day, Saturday up at the Radio Station to get the late summer promotions started.

Jack was amused to hear her chatting away to Nick as if they had known each other for ages. What a pity they had not bumped into Annette earlier, Jack was thinking to himself. They drove past the airport, which was at the far end of Nice on what looked like a man-made peninsula and the planes came in over the sea to land. As they drove past two large planes landed and they could see the logos on the tail, one was Air France and the other looked like K.L.M. which the boys did not know until Jacqueline explained. Onward down a straight road with a very scruffy beach to one side and equally scruffy old shops and houses on the other.

"Not the best end of Nice," Jacqueline commented.

"You're not being a snob are you, just because where you live is more posh?" jibed Nick.

"No not at all," she replied wishing she had not said anything, the boys both joined in teasing her until Annette asked them to stop. What was strange was that this road, that went through a very seedy part of town, with small warehouses and workshops, then all of a sudden arrived at the racecourse. Around this were some very wealthy looking villas.

"Let's face it, race horses are a wealthy man's hobby," Nick pointed out from the rear.

"Are you two okay squeezed in the back there?" Jacqueline asked.

"Yes it's very friendly thank you," Nick replied, "but I like it." They suddenly swung off to a more minor road under the railway and on to the beach road, at Villeneuve-Loubet plage, which was not one of Jacqueline's favourites. It was just like Nice with pebbles and she always ended up at Juan-Les-Pins for the sand and young people she was telling them all.

'I wonder what she got up to,' Jack thought, he hadn't really met any of her friends, only the girl whose family owned some hairdressing salons, she was a nice blonde but she never mentioned any boys, he will have to ask but perhaps not in the car. They travelled on until the road rose up around a small point and they could see the fort in front of them. The flag was flying on it.

"Is it still used by the Forces?" Nick asked.

"I don't know," Jacqueline replied, "but we fly our flags with pride everywhere don't we?!"

"We are not very good at that in England are we Nick, even in London. They only seem to put them up for State visits and Royal Family occasions, I think our Union Jack goes up when the Queen is in her palace, to let everyone know she is home, or something like that. Perhaps we should fly our flag more often," Jack mused.

Annette, who had been very quiet suddenly came into her own explaining all about the fort with Jacqueline's help interpreting all about its eight star pointed bastions and then as they came down towards the port, where the old walls remain, she showed them where the former cathedral had been. Jacqueline was directed this way and that for them to take in the sights. It was another one of those towns that in medieval times had been squabbled over. The boys admitted to know nothing about history to Annette but showed interest in all she was showing them.

"Perhaps plus tard Jacqueline we could show them 'Le Jardin Thuret,' I have never been there either, so that should be good." Annette was getting very enthusiastic with their sightseeing trip.

"But first let's park up and have a look at the harbour," Jacqueline said swinging into a car park, she found a parking space below the trees. Nick and Annette 'shoehorned' themselves out of the back of the car. Jacqueline suggested they wander around the harbour then meet back at the gateway through the old wall, which she pointed to. "How about meeting at one o'clock and then lunch?" asked Jacqueline.

"Great," Nick replied and strode off hand in hand with Annette. You would think they had known each other for years.

"I'm glad Nick has found someone he really likes, he fancied a Dutch girl he met but she just didn't like his ways," Jack commented wishing he had not.

"So what Dutch girls were those?" Jacqueline asked.

'Oh dear,' thought Jack, 'why did I say that!'

"Oh some we met on the beach on the first day we were here," he said casually.

"So did you meet anyone Jack?" she asked quizzingly.

"No, they were just a big group of guys and girls, nearly all paired off," he lied. "You're not jealous are you Jacqueline?"

"No not at all," she said through clenched teeth. Jack continued, now was his chance to start asking questions.

"I've heard nothing of your friends, boys or girls."

"Nothing to tell with my spells in England teaching, relationships don't last," Jacqueline commented.

"Why not? I'm going to write to you," Jack promised.

"Yes but when a pretty English girl appears at a party, you will not be thinking of Jacqueline sitting in Nice will you Jack?"

"Yes but come on Jacqueline, it would be no different for you!"

"Ah but I like English boys just like you Jack, so it's different," she said pointedly and with that she threw herself at him, giving him a fantastic kiss, even though it nearly knocked Jack over.

"Come on let's look at the yachts," said Jacqueline.

They wandered down the rows of huge boats, sailing and powered ones alike. Many were tied up stern to the harbour with wooden gangways leading on board. These boats were equally expensive as those at St. Tropez. They then walked up the old sea wall past one of the sandy beaches, ladies were sunbathing topless and some swimming. Jack had his lovely lady on his arm, so he did not stop and let his eyes wander as they normally did. The sea wall was of grey stone and at the end built into it, was a little type of lighthouse sending out a bright beam. The walkway they were on was on the outside of this defending sea wall but this wall was not necessary against the gentle sea breeze, sun over head and the blue lapping Mediterranean. They sat on the edge of the walkway, legs hanging over the edge dangling, Jack put his arm around her pulling her into him and kissing her gently on the side of her face.

"I'll miss you when you have gone," Jacqueline said sadly.

"No you won't, someone else will turn up," said Jack.

"No I've fallen for you Jack in a way possibly that I hadn't intended."

"Don't get all serious on me Jacqueline, we're in Antibes with friends, just look out to the sea and we realise how lucky we are for just this moment in time," Jack replied philosophically.

"You are right," and she leaned towards him kissing him passionately on the lips, her tongue finding his. Jack struggled to cope with this passion so early in the day!

They noticed a rather large boat, well, ship; nearly the size of the cross-channel ferry, it was approaching Antibes very slowly, it must have been quite a distance away, when a huge commotion appeared on the decks.

Jack got up very excited, "Look Jacqueline, it's going to anchor out there."

"Yes they do sometimes, the size of the yacht is too big to come in," Jacqueline replied straining her eyes to see it.

"That's not a yacht, that's a ship. Can you see the name on it, I wonder who owns it?" he continued.

"Well lots of wealthy people use our lovely Mediterranean coast for summers before the weather changes and then they go south to catch the sun again. The President of Fiat has a huge boat but that is a grey-blue colour, so it cannot be his, perhaps we will later be able to borrow some binoculars and check out its name and see if anyone knows whose it is."

"Look Jacqueline, there's a couple of guys with binoculars, will you ask them if we could have a look through them?" Jack asked.

"Oh I suppose so, is it really that important?" Jacqueline whined.

"Yes I am curious, I have never seen boats like these." So she strolled over to the two men and politely asked them if they could have a look through them.

"Look Jacqueline, it says 'Christina'. Hasn't Aristotle Onassis got a daughter called Christina?" he asked.

"Yes Jack you're right, he's marrying Jacqueline Kennedy soon. Wasn't it so tragic President Kennedy being assassinated, she's such a lovely young woman. I wonder why she wants to marry Onassis, he looks too old for her. The boat looks magnificent, I'd love to be a fly on the wall and see who goes on board," Jacqueline said whimsically and handed back the binoculars.

They wandered up to the gate in the old wall at about one o'clock, the more Jack was with Jacqueline, the more he worried about the seriousness of her intentions. He was young and she was a thousand miles away, so why worry he thought to himself. They met up with Nick and Annette, Nick smiled to Jack the

'I'm doing okay' sort of smile. The boys had got used to each other's facial expressions meaning something. They all wandered along a street with lots of restaurants and cafés just inside the old wall. They checked the menus as they went along, not as if they understood what they read. The boys were now walking together, it was surprising how well the girls got on considering that they did not know each other at all before.

"Have we got enough money to treat them to lunch, we seriously ought to Jack," Nick asked.

"I've still got some traveller's cheques we could use those to buy presents to take home and if we get really stuck, our new found friend, Monsieur Christophe, I'm sure will help out," Jack replied.

"Okay let's do that then. I like the look of this one Jack, let's ask the girls what they think," Nick said suddenly. The girls were still in deep conversation, most likely comparing notes. When they caught up Annette thought it looked fine, they were ushered to a table and passed the menus.

"Beers, Nick?" Jack asked.

"No come on, our treat, let's be Mediterranean and have some of your pink wine," Nick replied.

"Rosé," Jacqueline corrected him. Looking at the list it meant nothing to Jack,

"You choose Jacqueline."

"Voulez-vous du vin Rosé Annette," she nodded.

"Okay Jack it looks like we're all having rosé then?" he beckoned a waiter and Jacqueline ordered the wine and a carafe of water. The wine arrived cold as it should have been served. Jack served the girls first and then Nick, who sadly nearly drank his before Jack had filled own glass. He discretely topped it up and gave Nick a glaring look, which confused him. Jack sat down, lifted his glass and made a toast.

"A toast from the two of us to you two great girls and the South of France," he said smiling.

"I'll drink to that," Nick responded and they all chinked their glasses together.

"Now let's choose what to eat, all that walking has given me an appetite," Jacqueline commented. Annette decided just to have a Salade Niçoise,

"What's that?" Nick asked her.

"Well, it starts with salad, then has tuna added, hard boiled eggs and anchovies on the top," Annette told him.

"Is it filling?" he asked.

"Very, especially when you have eaten bread and wine with it."

"Oh… I think I'll join you, sounds really good," Nick responded.

Jacqueline decided to have Mediterranean prawns in a garlic sauce and Jack would have decided to have the same as her, but the mention of garlic in the sauce always put him off, so he ordered veal and french fries, he knew that would be safe.

"You like your veal don't you?" Jacqueline asked.

"Well in England it is very expensive and not many butchers sell it and anyway my mum wouldn't buy it, she'd most likely think it was cruel," Jack replied.

The lunch went on with another bottle of wine, much chatter and superb desserts, ranging from ice cream filled crêpes, apple tart with loads of cream on, glacés or ice creams in some great flavours and chocolate mousse. Generally the boys had not eaten many desserts and with the wine inside the four of them, they had such a laugh trying all the different ones, the more they swapped, the more they laughed. Blobs of mousse on Jacqueline's nose, ice cubes down the back of the neck from the ice bucket, they had great fun and a real laugh.

When they had quietened and asked for the bill, Jack said, "Do you think we will all do this again?"

Nick replied, "Why not?" and to his surprise, Annette said how she thought it would be great if they could.

With the bill paid and a suitable tip, there were big hugs and kisses from the girls to the boys, that made it really worthwhile.

After an enjoyable lunch, Annette suggested that they went to the Jardin Thuret. It was rather a long walk, and it was getting late in the afternoon, so she suggested they drove there. They all piled into the Fiat again and off to the gardens.

"I've been to a garden already today," Nick whispered to Jack. "I'll tell you more later."

They were soon there, it was just a little way away situated in the centre of the Cap or peninsula.

"How fantastic to keep all this park for the people to just wander in, considering how much land must be worth for housing down here," Jack commented.

Annette told them that the garden was established in the nineteenth century by a famous botanist, who was keen to try and grow different plants here and watching to see if they could adapt. The main body of the park had loads of pines but interesting varieties that they had not seen before. All the plants were labelled in Latin, which amused the girls as the boys knew what the plants were and the girls did not. The park was full of shrubs and trees, many from England and many they had never seen other than at Kew Gardens and the Royal Horticultural Gardens at Wisley. One that fascinated Nick was called Photinia, a bit like a Laurel with green based leaves but the new leaf was bright red. Yes really bright red.

"I wonder whether that would grow in England, Jack?" Nick asked.

"I don't know but this is a fascinating garden, tell me Nick, what was the comment about gardens earlier?" Jack asked him curiously.

"Ssh… I'll tell you in a minute," Nick nudged him. They walked on ahead looking at the shrub areas out of earshot from the girls.

"Well?" he asked.

"Well Annette took me around the harbour and then into the little old town behind where we had eaten, to a lovely square with a neat hedge around it in Laurel."

"Come on Nick, I don't want to know each and every plant that is in the park! What's the story?" said Jack getting exasperated.

"It has big trees," Nick said.

"And come on get on with it!"

"Well it was so cool in the shade and the garden was divided into segments, each small area had a group of seats and an area of lawn. There was no-one about, so peaceful, then Annette intimated to me with a smile that she had brought me there to show me the park and plants. No such thing, when we sat down on the grass, she announced that she just wanted some time with me to find out more about me. I told her about you and me being such good mates, where we worked, where I lived and all about my family! She leant into me and kissed me gently, so hang on, I thought to myself, I know nothing about her other than where she worked. So we chatted and then she pushed me down to the ground. I couldn't relax, seriously though, but she was so passionate and worryingly keen on me." Nick concluded scratching his head.

"Not just a holiday romance?" Jack commented.

"Oh yes! Well I think she'd have made passionate love there and then given the chance, I just couldn't there in a garden in public!"

"I should hope not Nick, not like you to be shy though."

"Anyway..." he continued, "her English is good because she was schooled in London as her father worked in a London office for 'Le Monde' covering politics and city business. At about the time she was just finishing college, he wanted an easier life with less politics so he came to the 'Nice Matin' as editor. They have now lived here for five years."

"So how old is she then?" Jack asked.

"Twenty-five, twenty-six in November," Nick replied.

"All these older girls we find…!"

"Yes but they're tasty aren't they?" he said laughing.

"Seriously Nick she really is a cracker. So why do you think she's really keen?"

"Well the story goes that Annette has been trying to get an attachment in a position in the BBC in London, which may come off in the spring. As she said, she'll be able to see more of me then perhaps come back with you next summer. Not a bad idea eh Jack?" They had not realised the girls had caught up while they were discussing Annette.

"What's not a bad idea Jack," asked Jacqueline.

"Coming back next summer," Jack replied.

"I hope I will see you before then," and Annette agreed, as they carried on hand in hand around the park. Nick as mad as ever, starting skipping along with Annette.

"I think he's seen enough of the park! Come on let's catch them up," he said laughing with Jacqueline.

When they were back at the car, although it was now getting late, the boys really wanted to have a swim. Jacqueline and Annette had not brought their costumes but the boys had. Annette again suggested the most secluded beach with great sand, which was the Plage de la Garoupe just five minutes away. As soon as they parked, they clambered out of the car, and the boys found a shady spot under the pines with the sand and blue sea in front of them.

"Why aren't there any private beaches or hotels here?" Jack asked.

"The land was preserved before the developers moved in," Annette replied.

"Oh… so why Annette do you know so much about Antibes?" Jack asked curiously.

"Well, this was where my parents rented a place when they first moved down here and I had got a job here on the paper, so it was best to study the town and find my way around. My parents then moved back inland behind Nice and eventually, when I got the job in Monaco, I could afford a small studio apartment in Nice. I'll show it to you Nick later on."

"Hold on, we've got to have a quick swim and we must get back, even if we're a bit late to have dinner at Les Cigalles. Monsieur Christophe has nearly adopted us and will not be happy if we miss our dinner," Jack commented.

"Come on then boys, get your trunks on and get in that water!" Jacqueline jibed at them. Quite funny, they all sat in a line, girls together in the middle and a boy each side. Nick and Jack trying to be discrete with a towel across them as they removed their shorts and pants, Jacqueline started it pulling the towel off Jack, then Annette from Nick. The boys became really embarrassed, especially Nick. Eventually amongst more laughter, they were off down into the sea. The girls sat chatting, there were very few people on the beach, they launched themselves into the coolness of the water after the hot sand.

"We're lucky we are," Nick commented. "Come on I'll beat you to the raft." Nick always did, as Jack couldn't do front crawl and breast stroke and was always slower. Out at the bobbing raft they sat for a little while, silently soaking up the late sunshine. The season was nearly finished here, the paint on the side of the raft had faded, some of the ropes to the side connected to the ladders were broken. It was also the end of the holidays for the boys and they really needed to get back for dinner. They both dived back into the beautiful azure sea and swam back to shore and up the beach.

"So what have you girls been talking about?" Jack asked.

"You!!" Annette replied.

"Boring," Nick retorted.

"Just comparing notes," Jacqueline said whimsically, "so what were you up to on the raft?"

"Ahh… that would be telling!" Jack said laughing. The boys sat down to change looking for the towels.

"Where are the towels?" Nick asked.

"I don't know," the girls answered in unison.

Jack then said, "I don't know who is worse out of you two, do you Nick?"

"I think Annette. Come on then time for a swim." With that the boys grabbed hold of her and went off towards the water with a screaming girl! Jacqueline was now up and attacking Jack, trying to pull him away. They reached the water's edge and all fell in a heap. Jacqueline missed the water, Annette was not quite as lucky but only just had a wet skirt and she could not stop laughing.

"I told you Jacqueline about these English boys, they are terrible aren't they?!" Back up the beach, reluctantly the girls dug up the towels they had buried in the sand and with no more interference, the boys dressed.

Back in the Fiat, Annette and Nick were cuddling although it was still hot.

"I'll get you back as soon as I can," Jacqueline said to Jack reluctantly.

"But what about tonight, will Colin come out?"

"I shouldn't think so after last night and today he was trying to change his ticket to get on the same sleeper as you. I can let you know later, why not come over and meet my parents for a drink Jack, they would like that as they have heard so much about you."

"No, I'd rather not, I know it sounds rude but it's our last evening. Let's just meet up at that bar near the Hotel Negresco and go from there. What time, nine o'clock? What do you think Nick?" Mumbles of agreement came from the back seat as he came up for air. "I think that was a yes!" Jack said trying not to look around.

204

"Do you want picking up Jack?" she asked.

"No let us gather at the bar, then we can give time to Monsieur Christophe tonight," Jack replied.

Back in Nice Jacqueline asked Annette if she wanted dropping off.

"No after the boys is just fine," she answered.

Up at the hotel, a very hot and red-looking Nick extracted himself, Annette grabbed him before getting back in the car.

Jack came around to the driver's side and said, "What a great day," and kissed Jacqueline firmly on the lips.

"A toute à l'heure," she said, Jack looked puzzled. "See you later," she said in English.

"Oh right, must remember that one!" With that, he and Nick leapt up the steps, falling through the door. Before they reached their room, which was only just inside the door, the old lady made hurrying signs to them. They dropped their swimming gear and went straight to their table to sit down. It was all cold meats that evening including spicy sausage, seeing them at their table, Monsieur Christophe came over to greet them.

"Out with those lovely French ladies and be'aving yourselves I 'ope?" he asked smiling. The boys nodded as they tucked into the bread and meat delights, he then returned with a carafe of rosé wine.

"For you both as a 'thank you' for making the end of our busy season such an enjoyable one. We 'ave enjoyed very much your company and all your little escapades, anyway the ones you 'ave told us about!" he said chuckling. The other guests could not quite understand what was going on but when Monsieur Christophe raised his glass, "À votre santé mes jeunes hommes," he said, the other guests joined in.

'How embarrassing,' Jack thought to himself, going bright red. He then left the boys in peace to enjoy their first course. Salad and a fantastic steak followed with a bowl of the best

205

Hôtel Les Cigalles french fries, finishing off with crème caramel, which neither of the boys liked when they first arrived. Now they really had begun to enjoy it.

Monsieur Christophe asked if they were dashing out or would they like a coffee on the terrace this evening, they both agreed to one. They sat quietly waiting with the sun now quite low in the sky enjoying the stillness while it was so peaceful. Monsieur Christophe first came out carrying a tray followed by his wife, Grace and their little girl, who the boys had not met. Her name was Isabelle, she was only about nine years old and she was so intrigued by the two strange English boys. They joined the boys and sat down altogether, Isabelle sat on her father's knee. Jack looked at her and thought one day she will be a beautiful young lady. They chatted about the different places they had been to, so many of the coastal resorts, medieval villages and how lucky they were to meet those lovely French girls. They all chuckled together and as there was not a lot more to say, Madame Grace took Isabelle off to bed.

"Where to on your last night, mes jeunes hommes?" Monsieur Christophe asked.

"We don't know yet, we are all meeting at a bar first of all," Jack replied.

"Enjoy your evening, Bonsoir," with that he left the boys to finish their coffee.

Chapter XVIII

Last evening

After a quick wash to get off some of the Mediterranean sea salt, a shave to tidy up their few whiskers, Jack and Nick strode out feeling good.

"How nice to feel so welcome at this little hotel or pension as they say, my father had stayed here before and had nothing bad to say. He again found Monsieur Christophe absolutely charming as he is," Nick said seriously.

They decided to get a bus down to Place Massena, which would save them over ten minutes of walking and they still had some tickets left on the little book they had bought when they first arrived. Jack was pleased to remember it was called 'un carnet'. From Place Massena it was a short walk across the gardens and then to the bar. It was situated just behind the Hotel Negresco. So they walked parallel to the Promenade Des Anglais and ten minutes later they found it and the girls sitting chatting at a table. Jacqueline was wearing a lime green dress of a soft material buttoned through the front, with her tan and dark hair she looked stunning. As the boys turned the corner they could see two young men chatting to the girls, seeing Nick and Jack approach they soon disappeared.

Nick said nudging Jack as they walked up, "What a lovely pair…!"

Jack took it he meant the girls and not what he could see with Annette's low cut top all in pale yellow and a short white skirt. They were too close for Jack to pick up on the remark but he thought smiling to himself, Nick always was a man with a keen interest in ladies' bosoms! Annette was smoking and there was a packet of Gitanes on the table, which had become one of Nick and Jack's favourite type of cigarette. Jacqueline did not seem to smoke much if at all, and Jack had realised he didn't smoke as much either when he was with her.

"What are you smiling at Jack?" Jacqueline asked as they greeted each other 'French' style kisses on both cheeks.

"Nothing, just thinking how lovely you both looked as we came down the street towards you…" Jack replied still smiling.

"I'm glad you chased your other admirers away before we got here," Nick chipped in.

"Oh…we are catching up with them when you've gone home," Annette added and laughed. She was a real tease.

"Sorry we're late," Jack started to say

"Yes it is half past nine already," Jacqueline complained.

"Monsieur Christophe wanted to spend a little time with us," Jack added quickly. He and Nick ordered their beers and Baby Cham for the girls.

"What is this drink?" Annette asked Jack.

"It is a new drink back home in London, I had wondered if the barman had heard of it and he had, so I would like you to try it. My sister always has this now and she thinks she is very with it!" Jack carried on with telling Jacqueline about their dinner and coffee time with Monsieur Christophe and his family.

Annette explained how again she had tried phoning her boss at work trying to get Saturday off but there was no one to cover her, so it could be "Farewell my lovely Nick tonight". As it got dark they still sat outside chatting continuously. Realising it was nearly ten o'clock, Annette moved much closer to Nick and suddenly said, "I'd like to show Nick whereabouts I live, so when I write to him he will visualise where I'm talking about."

"Nick write back, you'll be lucky," Jack piped up.

"I might you know for someone special in France!" Nick retorted.

"Well, let's say goodnight now. Goodnight Jack, if I cannot get to the station in time. It was lucky that we met on the train, it's been fun..." said Annette putting her arms around Jack, giving him a big hug and kiss. She said a formal 'goodbye' to Jacqueline and whispered something in French to her. Off she and Nick went hand in hand, suddenly he stopped and ran back, leaving Annette standing on the pavement. He had the remains of the 'kitty' and had not paid the bar bill.

"Thanks Nick, see you outside the hotel later..." Jack called after him.

"Where to my lover?" Jacqueline asked him. "It is too late to meet my parents now, you are a devil Jack, you were determined not to meet them. I don't blame you but on your next visit you must. Oh there will be a next time won't there Jack?"

"Of course!" he replied thinking, 'what am I getting into here?'

"You can stay at the apartment with us Jack. So when are you coming over again?"

"We'll see let's just enjoy every moment tonight Jacqueline. Don't keep worrying about next time or next year. I like Villefranche don't you Jacqueline?" he said quickly to change the subject.

"Mmm, memories of the sandy beach," she reminded him. She had parked around the corner and they made their way up around the harbour and dropped down to the small port. He ran his hand up her leg gently stroking the inside of the soft smooth skin.

"You nearly put me off driving Jack," so he moved back towards the knees. "Oh but don't stop, I love your caresses..." She drove the car past the bars and followed it along the length of the beach to the far end where a couple of cars were parked facing the sea. He leant across and pulled her gently towards her.

"Thank you for being you, I've had the best holiday ever," and kissed her.

"Don't get all soppy on me you saucy man, let's go for a walk..." Jacqueline said pulling away. They went down the short flight of steps through the trees that looked like some sort of Poplars. Jacqueline kicked off her smart sandals, they had little pearls up to the thong between the toes and held them in her hand.

"Ooh, the sand is still warm from the day's hot sun. Jack take your shoes off! Oh you are so English, I'm amazed you're not wearing socks as well!" she commented. They walked down to the sea, it was warm to the touch.

"Shall we go skinny dipping again Jack tonight?" she asked cheekily.

"No, I was just remembering the moment we had doing that, it was fun wasn't it!"

They strolled on, his arm around her narrow waist, there was a gentle breeze and wisps of her hair blew behind her.

Jack pulled away saying, "Just stand there for a moment!"

The moon was up higher not full but still gave some light on the water.

"I feel silly just standing here," Jacqueline whined again.

"But there's no one here Jacqueline, if I had my camera I'd have taken a picture."

"You're mad Jack because you haven't...!" and with that she ran towards him, nearly jumping on him putting her arms around his neck and they fell back in a heap. With her on top of him, she kissed him, firmly on the lips, their mouths met sending a tingle through Jack's body.

He was so emotionally mixed up that half of him felt like making love to her there and then and the other half wanted their relationship to be one of tenderness, today had really thrown him.

"What's wrong Jack?" she asked.

"Nothing!" he replied.

"Yes there is!" she argued and as she replied she rolled off him and lay by his side. They both laid there silently looking at the stars, listening to the Mediterranean lapping gently on the sand. Jacqueline eventually broke the silence saying, "This memory will stay with me for a long time and may never be repeated."

She leaned gently across Jack and kissed his forehead down to his straight roman nose to his lips.

He felt her full moist lips gently and slowly brushing across his, his mouth opened slightly as he shared her kisses. Her hand ran to the back of his neck, first caressing with a touch of damp sand on her fingers but as it dried off amongst the hair on the nape of his neck, her fingers started to have an effect on Jack. She was leaning on her side on her elbow as she continued to kiss him, he with one hand started to pop the buttons on the front of her lime green dress.

'Was it lust or was it love,' he wondered to himself as he finished undoing the buttons to her waist.

He turned towards her running his hand around her back, feeling her soft flesh. Their kisses became more urgent and Jacqueline undid his shirt pulling it from him, revealing his tanned body. With his free hand he slipped the catch to the back of her bra and slipped her sleeves from her arms revealing her beautiful breasts. Partially sitting they clenched each other's naked torso, Jack could feel her breasts squeezing against his chest as he nuzzled against her neck beneath her hair, kissing it gently. It was as if Jack was somewhere else, the lust that had got him to that position had partially gone but a feeling that he

211

had not known before had come over him. She kissed his ears, neck and shoulders and he could feel her hand moving to his belt on his slacks. Slipping the buckle and top button, she moved down and as he became more aroused he pulled away momentarily.

"What's wrong?" she asked.

"Nothing really but again we are on a beach!" Jack replied.

"Yes, but this time there aren't any lights," she smiled as she said the words.

Jack leant across finishing undoing the buttons and Jacqueline stepped from her dress. The sand was still warm, Jack had taken off his slacks and was now in his underpants. He took her now in his arms sliding her lace knickers down her legs for her to kick off then urgently removed his. Jacqueline opened up to him and their passion came together with sweat and sand all mixed together. He laid on her for some time gently kissing her then with his tongue working around her nipples, they started to rise forming hard mounds. He slithered down her working his way to her stomach and the inside of her legs, running his fingers through the dark mound, she moved against the sand. Sliding back up, laying against her side, he played his fingers across her soft skin.

"Jack I will miss you!" she said.

He did not answer and continued with his fingers like teasing tendrils across her body. He could feel himself becoming aroused against her, who suddenly pushed him to the ground and sat on top of him guiding him into herself. His hands caressed her breasts, the sensation suddenly became too much for him and again they were united. Jack sat up pulling her to him as she pushed his hair back and kissed him on his forehead. Suddenly she jumped off him and ran towards the sea.

'She's mad,' he thought, 'again we have no towels!'

This time he did not want to swim so slipped on his underpants and wandered to the water's edge just as a couple appeared from the left with no shoes on wandering through the edge of the water. Jack being totally embarrassed, pretended to look the other way and not notice them. The couple of lovers most likely did not notice him either. Jacqueline called to him standing up to her waist in water.

"No, not tonight Jacqueline," Jack called back. She walked towards him grabbing his hands.

"Come on, don't be a 'spoil sport'," she said pouting.

"No," he said again, so she brought her moist body against him, kissing him gently on the lips.

"Come walk with me then!" They strolled up the beach away from the car park and hopefully with no people around as they were just in their pants hand in hand. Jack was relieved they did not see anyone, the night air was warm and the moon was shining, it was a glorious moment. As they returned Jacqueline had dried enough to dress.

Fully dressed they returned to the little Fiat, it was now very late but it was their last night together for some time as Jacqueline kept reminding Jack. The little car that had possibly brought them together, well may be it was Colin, but that little grey Fiat 500 with its cramped rear seats was a much more romantic idea. They sat half on the bonnet, or boot as it was on the Fiat, looking out at the sea. Jack in his own thoughts wondering if Nick and he would ever be bold enough to come and work down here or perhaps another holiday. Could it ever be the same again. Jacqueline was in her thoughts and Jack reckoned it best not to ask about her thoughts. He nudged her in the ribs saying they ought to go.

"Come on then lover," she replied.

Jacqueline drove slowly back around the Corniche to Nice harbour and back up to the Hotel Les Cigalles.

Outside the gate, they sat in silence, suddenly she said, "I love you, Jack."

213

He replied, "You're gorgeous," kissing her firmly on the lips, running his hand through her hair.

"Stay with me tonight, Jack."

"No, I must go in," he said firmly kissing her again and opening the car door. She tried hanging onto his hand, he kissed it and released it, then ran into the hotel.

Jack had no idea of the time as he entered the hotel quietly and crept into their room.

'No Nick' Jack noticed, he looked at his watch he had left behind, it was two in the morning. He washed himself and quickly got into bed and fell asleep. Suddenly Jack was woken up by Nick, who had clumsily fallen over Jack's bed.

"Woah..." Nick said, "these French girls, I can see why you like them Jack."

"Come on then, what happened?" Jack asked wearily.

Nick sat on his bed explaining how Annette had taken him back to her studio apartment. It was small but lovely with two rooms. They had sat drinking and chatting and then she seduced him taking him to her bed.

"Then?" said Jack.

"Well you never tell me the details of your love life so why should I start? But Jack, we must return to Nice..." Nick got off his bed and went to clean his teeth and finally fell into bed. Within minutes he was sound asleep snoring leaving Jack wide-awake and wondering.

Jack woke early and as the sun shone through the shutters, he could hear the sound of Nice waking up. The mopeds coming up the hill and passing the entrance, the occasional siren of a police car and just outside Madame was washing down the front step with a hard brush. Everything here at the pension was so clean and tidy, the paths of tiled terracotta all washed off daily, the areas of gravel by the terrace were raked daily. He crept out of bed and dressed in his pyjama trousers only, slid out of the door and out into the entrance hall. The tiles were cold under his feet as he tiptoed towards the front door to be confronted by Monsieur Christophe, who had just finished raking the gravel.

"Monsieur Jack, what you doing up so early?" looking amazed to see him and in his pyjamas.

"I've come to see the morning. Isn't it a beautiful day?" he replied.

Monsieur Christophe, a little shocked at the young man's reply being so philosophical said, "I'll get you a bowl of café." Jack sat down in a chair on the terrace; the sun beaming down was warm and soothing. He stared up at the sky, which was crystal clear and blue, just as it had been every day since they had arrived. Fancy waking up to that every day, it must be wonderful to live here but it must rain sometime. Monsieur Christophe returned with a large bowl of coffee, a bit like a cereal bowl, bigger than the large cups they were served with at breakfast and sugar, which Jack needed to drink the French strong coffee.

"What is the weather like in winter?" Jack asked.

"Some cloud and rain but many bright sunny days, cooler but we rarely get any snow down 'ere, although it 'as been recorded. I 'ave only seen it once in my life," Monsieur Christophe replied. "Why? Are you thinking of moving 'ere? A girl you 'ave met maybe, that very pretty petite girl who has been collecting you perhaps? The French ladies are the loveliest in the world you know, jeune homme!" With that he left Jack to enjoy sipping his hot coffee.

He thought how he could perhaps get used to working down here but did they have gardeners like he and Nick. Jack leaned back in the chair and dreamed, letting the sun warm his chest and face.

Suddenly the shutters were thrust open and Nick shouted, "What the hell are you doing Jack?"

"Sshhh, quiet! It is only seven-thirty and I am just enjoying the sun and peace until you woke up, go back to sleep!" replied Jack quietly.

"You're not even dressed, fancy sitting out there in your pyjamas!" retorted Nick.

Nick was quite a prude really. Jack had been brought up with a sister and was if anything, quite liberal and after his experience last year with that lady, Penny, who was nearly twice his age, he had become more brazen in some ways.

Thinking back to the other night with Jacqueline and how she was so gentle and wholly loving, more than most of his previous experiences. With his eyes shut, he could still see her naked body lying there on the warm sand, thinking about how the sand had not interfered with their love-making as he would have expected. Was he in love? 'No, get a hold of yourself, Jack', he thought to himself. With all those delicious thoughts running through his head, Jack thought he had better go back to his room and get dressed. They would have an early breakfast and walk down to the beach and have their last swim. Nick, to Jack's surprise, was half dressed, having already washed and had the same idea as Jack.

After breakfast Jack and Nick decided to have one last look at the sea, the women on the beach and then get a couple of presents for home. Jack had already bought a wooden cheese board in what he thought was polished walnut, perhaps some brandy for his dad to keep him sweet as he did lend him his car, then there was his sister Katie and boyfriend, Richard, what on earth could he buy them?

The sea was again azure blue, the sky bright blue with no clouds and they were soon stripped off and in the sea. They swam out to the pontoon, climbing up on to it where a couple of girls were lying enjoying the sun and an older lady, who was English, greeted them. They sat on the edge with their feet dangling in the water.

Nick suddenly said, "I wonder when the Dutch girls went home, they were fun!" For the next half an hour they sat there reminiscing about the girls they had met here in France.

"Jacqueline and Annette are very keen on us aren't they? Not ideal when we live in England!" Nick said chattily. Jack was tired of hearing that and so he dived into the sea but more of a belly flop on his stomach. They swam ashore and settled on the pebbles to make the towels comfortable and fell asleep.

Nick woke suddenly realising it was lunch-time, they really must get a move on and do that shopping. They strolled up to the shopping area and were approaching one of their favourite bars.

"Come on Jack we must have one last drink in here and let's have some lunch too." Nick exclaimed.

It was a small friendly bar called 'Jacques' that they had been to several times on their way up to the hotel. They did not know whether the owner was 'Jacque' but he was a very friendly man. One beer led to another and they decided to have a 'croque monsieur' for a snack one last time. Eventually Jack and Nick left the bar saying their farewells and promised to return and so they might.

Before the shops closed for their long lunch break, Jack found some typical Provence style pottery pieces for his mum and he decided to buy some perfume for his sister in the duty free shop on the ferry. Nick eventually got into the swing of things and bought a few presents to take home, including some disgusting smelling cheese called 'Camembert' for his father.

"Surely you're not travelling on the train with that smell Nick?" said a horrified Jack.

217

"Yes Jack I'll wrap it well and put it in my suitcase," Nick replied.

"Rather your clothes than mine!" Jack commented.

The day was passing quickly and they had not even packed yet. So they walked back towards the station with Nick leading the way, Jack was wondering why they were going that way. So to his horror, they had arrived in the 'red light' district again and Nick went straight into the bar to order beers again. Jack was getting really annoyed, he refused a beer and was getting worried about not packing and leaving their room as promised, ready for the newcomers. Up in the corner three girls sat the table, Nick stood staring at them, Jack nudged him to behave, then Amelia walked in that Nick had chatted to before and Colin had gone off with. She was wearing the same little tartan skirt and white blouse that he had noticed before, she smiled at Nick as she walked past him to join her friends.

Suddenly she stopped and returned and said in a low sexy voice, "How about a treat this afternoon?" as she looked into Nick's eyes.

He choked on his beer and Jack stood there with his mouth open. She stroked Nick's hand and smiled, running her tongue around her lips, if Nick had had enough money on him, Jack was sure he would have gone off with her. She left them and strolled over to her friends wiggling her hips as she went again, and with a wink as she passed Nick she went out to a waiting car. Jack was horrified, how could they do this for a living he was wondering.

"Come on Nick we must get going. We have lots to do and Jacqueline is picking us up to take us to the station at half past seven," Jack was getting exasperated with Nick.

Neither of the boys really wanted to hurry, they kept looking in the shops and delaying what they had to do, as they really did not want to leave. They both had girlfriends, Nick was being a bit secretive about Annette and what he had got up to last night. They left the area of shops and started chatting about the English gardens they had left behind, wondering who had been looking after their patch. Being September the summer bedding would probably have been stripped out by the time they had returned, Jack was wondering what had been planted in its place.

Suddenly Nick said, "Funny how you always pick older girls, Jacqueline is a few years older than you."

"Only five years Nick."

"Well better than Penny who was nearly eighteen years older wasn't she?" Nick was niggling Jack.

"Leave her out of it will you!" Jack retorted.

"Bit touchy still? Still you've got a nice French girl now." said Nick laughing. Jack went very silent for a while as they walked along.

"So have you or haven't you with Annette?" Jack retorted back. Nick laughed and Jack did too eventually.

"Well that would be telling wouldn't it Jack, let's call it a truce, sorry if I upset you." That settled they ambled up the road to the hotel.

"Ah mes jeunes hommes," Monsieur Christophe greeted them. "You are back early good as we have our new guests arriving for dinner."

"We will get packed and ready to leave before dinner Monsieur Christophe," Jack replied.

"That would be excellent, normally my guests leave their rooms before lunch time but as you are young travellers, I 'ave made an exception for you, we have enjoyed your stay with us," he responded as charmingly as ever.

The boys thanked him and hurried to their room to pack. Why was it always more difficult to pack going home, although neither of them had packed their cases coming over, their mothers had done that. Trying to fit in the presents amongst the clothes to prevent them breaking was a challenge. The beers Nick had drunk were starting to have an effect and he tried to lie down to sleep but Jack dragged him off his bed to get finished. They showered and put on their long trousers and smart shirts and prepared an overnight bag for the train journey. Jack reminded Nick to have his toothbrush handy just in case they met some nice girls.

All scrubbed up, bags packed they checked their room and went to reception to let them know they had vacated their room. The old lady who helped out thanked them and started to prepare the room for the next visitors. The boys sat outside for a last taste of the Mediterranean sunshine. It was soon time for an early dinner and they again savoured the French food that Jack and Nick had grown accustomed to. Monsieur Christophe gave them wine with their dinner again and an aperitif called 'Noilly Prat', that they had had fun joking about the pronunciation.

Chapter XVIX

Time to go

Jacqueline arrived, as promised, at seven-thirty and Monsieur Christophe and his charming wife, Grace gave them a big hug and kisses on both cheeks.

"Come back and see us again, won't you?" he called.

Down through the orange and lemon trees they put their bags in the Fiat and climbed in, a bit squashed and off to the station.

"Colin wouldn't have fitted in would he," said Jacqueline.

They found their train easily and on the platform to the side was a paper chart showing where each carriage was, so the boys soon located their compartment. With some luggage on the platform, Nick and Jack were moving their bags into their couchette when Jacqueline started throwing her arms around Jack's neck so tightly.

"I'll miss you Jack, you will write won't you, will you please?" she was pleading with him and tears were falling down her cheeks.

"Of course I will, you silly sausage," he said trying to cheer her up, he really was not a letter writer.

"Silly sausage, I am not a sausage Jack," as she stamped her foot. Oh dear thought Jack, our language is so different.

"I don't mean it Jacqueline, it's an endearment," he said hugging her. Nick appeared in the nick of time and he gave Jacqueline a big hug and a kiss on each cheek, he liked this style of greeting.

Suddenly out of the crowd came a panting Annette, she had managed to get away from work earlier.

"I couldn't let you go without a 'goodbye'," she cried.

She and Nick embraced.

'Some girl, this Annette' Jack thought, 'they had only recently met and she was seeing him off!'

The boys broke away for a moment to check that they had put all their luggage safely stowed away then back for a final kiss. Jack was given a little bag from Jacqueline, he started to fumble to open it, but she put her hand on his and asked him to open it later on the train. Meanwhile Nick was heavily involved and seemed to be thoroughly enjoying his send off. Jacqueline held his hand tightly…

"I am so lucky to have met you Jack, please come back to Nice as soon as you can, I won't be over to England for several weeks yet," she pleaded.

"I will try but I have to work most weekends at a local nursery and it is expensive to come for just a few days," he replied.

"Well try won't you, you can stay at the apartment with my parents," she continued.

The conductor moved his way down the platform closing all the doors and as he came to where they were, he muttered something in French and went on to the next carriage. Jacqueline said he was telling them to get on the train and close the doors, she turned to Jack, their bodies met, lips closing together, her sexy tongue moved into his mouth. Jack's body was aroused by her passionate embrace as he struggled to deal with it and had to pull away as the train started to move.

"Come on mate, time to go," said Nick standing on the steps of the train. Jack jumped on as he pulled the door shut and opened the window.

"Write to me Jack," she called out after him as the train started to move. They moved down into their compartment and waved from the window blowing the occasional kiss to the girls as they walked beside the train. The engine wheels span with the weight of the carriages and smoke from the engine now drifted back down the train as it pulled out passing the apartment blocks that backed onto the railway. No one else was in their compartment but there were reserved tickets on the seats.

"Perhaps they will get on later, so what's in the bag Jack?" said a curious Nick.

They sat down next to each other, Nick continued with his banter, "She's keen, that Jacqueline, isn't she? Older than you, you will have to watch it Jack!"

"Shut up Nick," Jack opened the little bag and inside was a wrapped box with a card attached saying 'I love you'.

"So come on, open it," Nick was bullying him to get on with it. "I think she has bought you a ring!"

"Don't be bloody silly, she wouldn't do that," retorted Jack. He pulled the lid off after removing all the paper all neatly stuck down with cellotape and ribbon. Inside was a bracelet, heavy silver chain with a panel to inscribe a name on, they had seen lots of the French guys wearing them.

"Let's see, there is something written on it," said Nick grasping it. "'L'amour' or something, that's 'love' isn't it Jack? Good job she's in France and you're in England, if not she'd be getting you really collared," Nick jibed at him.

Jack said nothing, he was a bit embarrassed and worried that this girl had got so attached to him, 'why me' he thought, 'we're just a couple of gardeners with not very special prospects.'

"Well her family seem wealthy," Nick dropped in as if reading his thoughts.

"Come on, that's nothing to do with it. I am young and we have both got some serious good times to have. Anyway, what about you and Annette, you've known her three days and she sees you off at the station? She's keen isn't she?"

"Yes, and she's threatening to come to England too! Let's enjoy the journey while it is still light," Nick replied.

The train passed along the coast with the beautiful beaches that they probably would not see again for years. It pulled into Frejus station and stopped. A couple arrived in their compartment and took up the reserved seats. They were about thirty and were going on holiday to England to see friends for the first time. After greeting in their best French, the boys decided to stroll down to the buffet car to have a drink. They watched the sun set over the Maritime Alps, they were both a bit sad as they sat at the bar and neither of them said much. Jack was still worried about Jacqueline, it was such a beautiful place, perhaps he would return to this area again before long, he mused.

Feeling shattered and tired, the boys wandered back to their compartment, the conductor had already pulled the couchettes down and the French couple were asleep on the top already. The boys took off their shirts and trousers and slid into their beds under the sheets and they too were soon asleep.

Suddenly Jack woke up, the train was pulling into Paris, with a lot of shunting and banging. Nick slept on and eventually they were on their way again for Calais. Jack woke up with a start, Nick, who was already dressed was shaking him to get up and go down to breakfast. He felt rotten, he got dressed and put on his shoes and then followed Nick to the restaurant car. The smell of fresh French coffee wafted through the carriages, they sat down at a table and were served warm croissants and pots of apricot jam and large cups of coffee too, just what they both needed. The train soon went across the flat areas of Pas de Calais full of fields of vegetables being grown. There were crops of salad, spring onions and as the train passed by, Jack could see greenhouses with what looked like tomatoes still on their vines.

"I wouldn't like living here, bit flat isn't it?" Nick remarked, as Jack thought the same.

"We are good mates aren't we, thanks for this holiday Nick, I'm a new man!" said Jack laughing.

Unloading the luggage in Calais the customs men hardly looked at their passports and very soon Nick had got them in a corner of the lounge bar at the front of the ferry. The bar was still closed, as the rules were to wait until the ship set sail, Jack fell asleep again, he felt shattered. When he awoke the table next to him had a pint of beer already and was surrounded with all their luggage and no sign of his friend. He sipped at the warm beer ugh! Not so nice and definitely not the best drink to wake up to. Nick eventually returned with a couple of plates of sandwiches.

"You've been asleep for ages, we're nearly at Dover," Nick remarked. They ate their sandwiches washed down by the beer and enjoyed the ferry trip.

"I must go down to the duty free shop and buy some perfume or something for my sister. Coming with me?" Jack asked.

"No I had better stay here with the bags, otherwise we would have to cart them about with us. Jack ambled off down to the shop, there were lines and lines of bottles of drink, a huge area of perfumes and jewellery. He managed to find the perfumes and bought Katie, his sister, a bottle of Chanel No.5. She should be very pleased with that he thought. He paid with the last of his French francs and went back to join Nick.

It must be time for tea, thought Jack, that beer was horrible. He queued at the café and joined Nick.

He still felt in a dream, he tried to snap out of it as Nick said, "No word about the girls we met," Nick suggested.

Jack thought that it had been hard for Nick having just met Annette and he was obviously keener than he had let on, so Jack felt he was in for less teasing now, which would be nice.

Chapter XX

Dover

The ferry soon docked but ages before they had even got through the harbour walls, people had started to queue ready to get off. The English do love to queue; even the boys did spot a few French pushing to the front. After the ordeal of dragging their bags from the boat down through customs, past the passport control and luckily they did not get stopped. Some poor man about their age, had the contents of his case laid out all over a table. He had quite a job getting it all back in again. Everyone as a foot passenger walked up towards the waiting train, it was soon full and pulled out back across the piers to the land.

Jack's mind was alive again as he dreamed imagining the wooden struts giving way and the train falling into the water. He always ended up have tragic thoughts when he was tired, he wondered why that was, very strange. Nick nudged him to look up the corridor, his eyes opened wide. Girls, very tanned girls with flowing blonde hair, just how Nick liked them, English too. They glanced at the boys but did not seem interested, Jack thought that would not stop Nick.

"Come on Jack, you're a man, dump your bag on your seat and we'll go and chat them up," Nick was getting excited.

"Leave it Nick, they are not interested, they are just on their way home," replied Jack wearily. Nick got up anyway and pushed past some people and got himself to one side of the girls. Jack watched with amusement wondering how he had the nerve. It was funny to watch, they were not that interested as he had predicted. It took Nick about twenty minutes to give up and return to his seat.

"Well?" Jack asked.

"They are from Sussex somewhere near Brighton, they have been to Nice on holiday to some friends of their parents…" Nick replied feeling rejected.

"But don't tell me you don't know their telephone numbers and they did not take yours!" Jack laughed. Nick dug him in the ribs.

"I told you didn't I?" jibed Jack.

Soon the train pulled into Victoria Station and the same scramble started again. The boat trains were very predictable and at the barriers both fathers were waiting patiently for their boys. Jack was thrilled to see his dad and gave him a big hug. They all went down the stairs to the underground to get on the District line. The boys did not stop talking about how they had met this girl who had taken them to all the different places to see, like St. Tropez and Monte Carlo.

"I hope you boys behaved yourselves! You have both got a great tan!" Jack's father asked smiling.

"Of course," replied the boys in unison winking at each other. Parting company at Embankment station, Jack and his father got off to catch a train on the Northern Line to Waterloo.

"Shall we stay here until Monday for work?" Nick asked jokingly and with that he was gone with his father to Essex. Once Jack and his father were on their way to Woodmanstern, he chatted about all the gardens they had seen and the plants that were so different from England.

"Perhaps one day I could work in the South of France," said Jack dreamily.

"Maybe," his father mused.

Back at home Jack's mother gave him the third degree as she made him a big mug of tea, not quite the reception his father had given him. Rummaging through his bag, Jack located the walnut cheese-board and knife for his parents and he had bought a few cigars for his dad in the duty-free shop and perfume for his sister, Katie.

Jack dragged his bag upstairs leaving it on the landing and then slumped onto his bed. He remembered the gift from Jacqueline, he just got to it in time before his mother was getting ready to sort the dirty washing out for the wash. She might not have liked her son being given jewellery from a French girl, best left out of sight at the moment.

"Where's my big sister then?" asked Jack

"Oh out with Richard somewhere. So you had a really good time?" Jack's mother asked. "Yes, you would love it Mum, the sun shines most days and the food is good, not forgetting wine!" said Jack enthusiastically.

"Hope you didn't drink too much!"

"No all I've brought back is a bottle of rosé for Richard, thought he ought to get a taste of France."

"Hope you didn't get up to any mischief Jack with those French girls."

"No, but I did meet a very nice girl called Jacqueline, who says she will write to me."

"Tell me more," asked his mother curiously.

"She's a teacher, teaching English in France but comes here a lot to work in our schools." Jack went to explain about Colin and how he had introduced them and how she was in her early twenties, he crossed his fingers as he lied a little. "We'll see, she most likely won't write anyway."

"Well as long as she was a nice girl, I'll leave you to have a little rest, I expect you're tired after your long journey although you look very well!" his mother said closing the door.

Jack was relieved to be left alone for a while, he dreamed of the beautiful sea, blue sky and the lovely hot sunshine with all those beautiful girls he saw and met.

Chapter XXI

Back to work

Jack rang Nick that night to thank him very much for a great holiday, as without him and his parents doing the organising, he would definitely never have gone to France. Nick then went into great long discussions of the times they had enjoyed, the girls, the booze and not forgetting the magnificent gardens.

"See you tomorrow and let's see what Bert and Frank have got in for us, eh?" said Nick laughing.

Jack was glad to be back in bed and soon fell asleep feeling worn out but full of delightful memories. His mind drifted back to the beach and the late afternoon sun still full of warmth on his face and of course Jacqueline… and Helena too, she was such a lovely girl.

Up early, dressed and sitting in the kitchen talking to Lady, the golden retriever, mug of tea in one hand and two slices of bread quickly popped out of the toaster, with butter and Mum's home-made marmalade, Jack tucked into his breakfast with Lady drooling waiting for his crusts. Jack dragged his bag from under the stairs, took his sandwich box from the fridge for his lunch, which his mother had prepared the night before. He took the little bottle of perfume he had bought for Penny, which he had put in a bag with some pebbles from Nice beach, so no-one asked about it.

Chapter XXII

The Air Ministry

It was now September and he had enjoyed the sun for two weeks and having a good suntan. He still put on a good woolly jumper before dragging his combat jumper from the cupboard under the stairs, where his mother always put it. Off down to the station over the bridge, he looked at his watch. There was a bit of a queue at the booking office and his father had given him the money to buy his season ticket. The queue moved slowly and Jack kept looking up the line, just as he got to the booth he could see the train coming.

"You look well Lad… been on holiday have 'yer?" asked the clerk.

"Yes, but can I have a weekly to Waterloo please," Jack asked getting very anxious.

"Got it already for you, saw you in the queue, have a good day back at work," said the clerk.

Jack pushed past a couple of people as he needed to be at the front of the train, if not he would be late by the time he had crossed Hungerford footbridge to the yard at the Embankment gardens.

He sat in the compartment feeling rather overdressed as the men were still only in suits and not many coats and the girls were still wearing thin dresses, skirts and blouses. Sitting dreaming, thinking of Jacqueline, bit heavy going wasn't she, he thought, maybe she won't bother to write to me, I'm only young and she is twenty something...' Jack pondered. The girls here were not too bad as he looked at a lovely blonde in the corner, she looked all embarrassed as he looked at her and she turned her head to look out of the window. Penny, well she was really nice but twice his age, was he still in love with her, there was no-one really he could talk to about her. His mates all thought it was great for him to have slept with an older woman, his parents were definitely a 'no no' and his sister, perhaps he could talk to her or maybe not. Was it just the sex or that she fancied him, infatuation? He dreamed on and then suddenly, the train arrived at Waterloo Station. He was one of the first up and noticed the blonde girl still sitting in the corner, she smiled as he passed. That made Jack feel good. Out of the compartment and onto the platform, he walked very quickly along through the station and down the steps. He always came this way and sometimes he passed some of the South Bank crew, past the Arches and Shell building and down the side of the Festival Hall and quickly up onto the iron bridge and across the Thames. Amazing how busy it was and he could see the big clock on Shell Mex house on North Bank and he had his usual few minutes to spare. Down the stairs around the underground station, past those dreadful public toilets, where the tramps always hung around, into the gardens and right through the wooden gate just as Bert was coming out of his office and down the yard.

"Just made it Jack," Bert said as Jack slipped into the bothy and dumped his bag.

"No time for tea," Harry shouted.

"I'll get the earlier train tomorrow," Jack replied as Nick came bursting in and everyone else was going down to the front of the tool shed to await instructions. Usually Paddy was going to Temple Gardens with the girls. Nick and Jack waited as they have always been separated in the past but they were last, just left there.

When everyone had gone off to collect barrows and tools, Bert said, "Now can we trust you together, you have both done good work, so I am going to give you the Air Ministry."

The Air Ministry was an extension of Whitehall Gardens and in front of the Ministry there were not many flowerbeds but lots of grass and a wide path both sides which lots of young secretaries used, to go to the Ministry to work. There was an ancient wall, which was a bit of a ruin one end with return walls each side and rhododendrons growing at the top and side. This had a steep grass bank leading down into it, which was always dreadful to mow.

Nick and Jack did a convincing job on Bert and went to pick up their brooms, rakes and besom brooms and dropped them into the barrows. Maurice was not there, so they had nicked his two-wheel low flat barrow instead of the coffin type. They went off and on the way deciding a strategy for sweeping everywhere quickly letting Bert walk round then nipping off to the Lyons on the corner at Westminster opposite Parliament. Nick had learnt that although besom brooms were meant for lawns, it was possible to sweep nearly a two and a half yard wide path with one. So Nick rushed off down the path one side, flicking from one side to the other and Jack was on the other path. It took nearly forty minutes and was quite exhausting, they met at the far end towards Scotland Yard and strolled up the lawns picking up the odd piece of litter. Once at the top again, with long handled brooms, they swept each side of the path, pushing the broom along the edge by the edging board.

"Needs some of these edges having the grass cut back," Jack commented.

"Perhaps later if Bert will allow it," Nick replied.

As they were sweeping half way down, Bert appeared in his brown jacket. They could see him a long way away and he was pretty predictable with time.

"Well done Lads," as they got up to talk to him.

234

"After break, shall we do the edges? They've been left for ages?" said Nick, as he smiled to himself, 'Brownie points all around!'

Bert agreed, 'so a nice cushy one for the rest of the morning,' Jack thought to himself too.

Soon as Bert was gone, the boys put down their brooms and disappeared off up to Lyons. They went past Scotland Yard, around the corner and upstairs into the café. They both ordered poached eggs on toast and Jack got extra teas and they both suddenly realised they would be late for the break at the bothy.

"Let's get the train," Nick said. So they ran down the stairs to Westminster station, an underground train soon arrived and they were on the train. They got out at Embankment and ran through the gardens to the bothy just in time. Harry was already there and commented on how flushed they were looking.

"You both look very suntanned and very red, you must have been working hard."

They smiled and agreed, it was possibly hurrying up the stairs from the train, so they did not miss more mugs of tea, which they suddenly realised how they had missed not having any for two weeks.

Chapter XXIII

Life back home again

Jack was at home feeling sorry for himself as Penny was now going out with an electrician, she had met while he was on holiday in France. Jack had a great time in France and had even responded twice to the regular flow of letters from Nice but he still had an eye for Penny. Just seeing her in her tight trousers and duffle coat as she came in to work or came over to the yard some days still made his heart jump. He knew she was too old but 'no come on Jack', he thought to himself idly as he watched the television. His dad did like 'Rising Damp' he thought Rossiter was a great actor. A bang on the door brought his mum from the kitchen, it was David from down the road. His mum ushered him in and Jack asked him through to the dining room.

"Fancy a tea, David?" Jack asked so surprised to see him.

"No thanks I thought we could go for a beer?" David replied.

"What in?" Jack asked.

"I've got myself an Austin 10," said David smugly.

"Not doing badly for a university boy are we?" said Jack taunting him.

"No Dad helped me and it saves me going up and down to Leeds on the train."

"Okay fair enough I'm with you, how about the Retreat over towards Barstead, popular with young girls I hear!" Jack commented.

"That's what I like to hear," replied David. Jack pulled on a jumper, put his shoes on, borrowed a couple of pounds from his mum and they went off down the road to David's. In his driveway was a two-tone Austin 10 with smart running boards and it started without the handle to crank it. They had to push it out of the driveway, as the reverse gear in the gearbox was broken. Away off down to the main road across the bridge and they were soon turning off towards Barstead. It was not an old pub but it had a big paved area to the front and a few benches. Jack got the first couple of pints in and David got chatting about university life and the times they had there. At Christmas he hoped to help out with some girls' school trip to Switzerland, so he chatted on to Jack about his plans. Jack then told him all about his holiday with his friend Nick, who he knew from work and lived in Essex. David was amused at their antics and the girls they had met.

They were just sitting by a pillar at the bar and on the other side there were a short brunette and a taller blonde, they seemed to be chatting with strange accents. A cockney boy was trying to 'chat' them up but from the look on the blonde's face, he was not getting far. Jack lit up one of his Gauloise cigarettes he had taken to smoking and David began rolling his own of Golden Virginia.

The blonde girl that Jack had been watching, leant across saying, "That's not a French cigarette is it, I haven't had one for ages," the girl remarked.

Quick as a flash, Jack offered her one. Her friendly round smiling face with blue eyes, curtained by straight blonde hair to her chin. The young man who had been trying to 'chat them up' soon gave up and the brunette turned to face them. They introduced themselves, the brunette was called Plum.

'What a funny name,' thought Jack.

The blonde was called Carol. Now Jack was not keen to make an instant decision but David spotted how he switched from chatting up the blonde to the brunette in a flash. Jack thought Plum was tasty, with her dark brown hair with a touch of red in it, full lips, dark eyes and strong features, short enough to tuck under his chin.

David and Jack bought another round of drinks and Jack shared round his cigarettes. They found out that they were two schoolteachers, who had just finished teachers' training college in the summer and had just begun teaching in a school near Croydon. At the moment they were staying in a flat just behind the Fairfield Hall with another teacher friend, who had now gone off with a young girl he had just met.

Closing time soon came and they were surprised, as most people were, to find out that Jack was a gardener and David claimed to be a tour operator, he hated admitting he was a student really. The boys were amused how the girls believed David's cock and bull story but did not believe that Jack was a gardener. He went through the same routine showing his hands and nails, which always amused him. Last orders rang and it was time to go. "Do you want a lift?" David asked.

"Yes that would be great, thank you," they replied in unison.

"Or would you like to come back to Woodmanstern on the way for coffee and toast?" asked Jack, quick as a flash.

"Why not," replied Plum with her beautiful Welsh accent from South Wales, Jack discovered. They climbed into David's car, which they loved, the girls climbed in the back and they trundled off down the road.

Back at Jack's, in through the dining room and no sign of Jack's mum and dad thank goodness, David put the kettle on the gas and Jack cut some bread for toast.

"Mum's home-made marmalade and mugs of coffee?" he called out.

"Yes please!" the girls cried out in unison. They chatted on about their home town of Abbervan in South Wales and how bad it had become since the mines had been closed one by one. Still they had some great friends down there and often went back home to stay. Jack put on a Beatles' record 'A Hard Day's Night,' which he had recently bought. He put it on quietly so as not to wake his dad or he would be banging on the floor upstairs.

Jack had really been quite taken by this 'Plum' girl and sat down on a stool next to her.

"So what do you girls get up to?" Jack asked nonchalantly.

"We like going to folk clubs, have you been to any?" asked Plum.

"Well no not really, only locally, but not in London" replied Jack.

"Okay, next time we go to one over in Hammersmith, which could be next Friday, we'll give you a ring. You provide the transport and we'll take you then, deal?" Plum asked.

"Sounds good to me," Jack replied.

"But come on Carol we must go it's late," Plum stated.

"We'll give you a lift," David said.

So they all piled back into the Austin and drove down to Croydon to drop the girls off at their flat. It wasn't a very smart area of Croydon but the girls made up for it. David was very put out as he will be back up in Leeds at university before next Friday.

"She won't ring," Jack said doubtfully.

"I bet she will," David replied, "especially that Plum with her dark eyes looking at you Jack. He parked the car and Jack promised to see him later in the week and went off home to bed.

Chapter XXIV

Back at college

Work was good, college was good; some of the lads had left the course, which was a shame, in fact more for Royal Parks than anyone else. There was nobody that Jack was close to at the college other than his good friend, Nick, who was still talking about their holiday together. Jack had to trundle by train, across to New Cross and walk up, whereas Nick just popped on the tube. These Essex boys had it easy in some ways. Little Marilyn was still there, Jack remembered her from his first day and she sat right next to him again. She commented on how sun-tanned he was and asked him how he had spent his summer, had he met anyone special, the questions kept coming. Jack recalled his trip to France and not embellishing the affair that he had got into with Jacqueline. Stories of how they had got up to tricks down at the Embankment gardens, teasing the boys.

"So what about the girl you seemed really in love with?" Marilyn asked.

Jack was stunned; he had never talked about Penny to her, 'how had she picked up on that one?' Jack wondered.

"Well," Jack started feeling a bit uncomfortable, "where do I begin? Firstly she was a lot older than me and in the end she thought it best that we parted company." said Jack feeling a lump in his throat, would he ever get over her he wondered...

"That must have been difficult as you worked with her didn't you?" Marilyn said sympathetically.

"Yes it was but in the end I was moved back to the Embankment Gardens to help out." Jack sighed.

"You must have been so upset."

"Yes I was but I have tried to go back to see her even after my holiday. She's so friendly but I'm kept at arm's length, which I really can't deal with. My heart jumps a few beats and then I have to walk away. So I have taken to avoiding being anywhere that Penny might be working. I shouldn't have burdened you with all that Marilyn," Jack finished, "thanks for listening." She squeezed his arm and pulled him forward to get a cup of tea.

"So I wonder where we'll all end up after our apprenticeships." Marilyn continued.

"I've thought of going to the South of France and starting a little business down there," Jack commented.

"Have you really? That could be good," she said sipping her tea.

"But Marilyn all I have talked about is me, me and me! What about you?" Jack asked munching his sticky bun.

"Well, if you go to France, count me in! I got good marks at GCE French and I had a French pen-friend exchange in Avignon when I was at school. So I'm pretty good at the lingo!" she exclaimed much to Jack's surprise.

"You really mean that don't you?" he replied.

With the tea break over, it was time for their first tutorial of the day, as they got up and left the canteen. Jack was deep in thought about his idea of a new French business.

He nudged Marilyn and whispered, "Well partner, France here we come!"